# CRIBBINS

## R. H. DIXON

CORVUS CORONE  PRESS

Front cover by Carrion Crow Design.

A CIP catalogue record for this title is available from
the British Library.

ISBN: 978-1-9997180-4-6

Corvus Corone Press.

To all the autoimmune people, this one's for you!

## Other books by R. H. Dixon:

# EMERGENCE
# A STORYTELLING OF RAVENS

'I am terrified by this dark thing that sleeps in me.'
**Sylvia Plath**

R. H. DIXON

# 1

# Diagnosis Day

'Relapsing remitting multiple sclerosis.'

The consultation room was small, but suddenly vast. The space between Sophie Harrington, Dr Conroy and the blonde nurse grew. One minute the two medical professionals were sitting on chairs about eight feet away from Sophie, then they were a whole hospital's length away. Or at least, that's how it seemed. The room was filled with a blurring of time upended, as well as grey-blue carpet squares, white scuffed walls, office furniture and stationery; all normal things which upon receipt of this new information suddenly appeared overly and unreasonably harsh to Sophie. Every single item and piece of fabric had taken on a hostile edge because of some heightened sense of reality as life's latest sucker punch rang through her head.

Within milliseconds of Dr Conroy having spoken those four awful words, a fly began to zap about like it was an embodiment of the diagnosis itself. An unseasonal omen, it became the focal point for everyone in the room. On some perverse level Sophie was amused, but also offended by its audacity to strive for attention at such a time as this. Mostly, however, she was pleased for the temporary distraction, otherwise the weight of those four awful words might have pulled her under, like anchors too gargantuan for her mind-set.

*Bzzz. Bzzzp. Bzzz.*

The fly cruised over Dr Conroy's head with seeming purpose then swung round in a wide arc, veering too close to Sophie's face. The blonde nurse shuffled in her seat and looked to the window, perhaps wondering if it would be inappropriate, given the timing of what had just been disclosed, to go and open it. Apparently it was; she stayed put and her dark, alert eyes were back on Sophie, as were Dr Conroy's, creating mounting pressure for Sophie to say something. To do something. To react.

This was only the third time she'd met Dr Conroy.

Third time unlucky.

Diagnosis time.

D-Day.

*Relapsing remitting multiple sclerosis.*

What did that even mean?

Sophie suspected the blonde nurse, who she'd never seen before and who seemed more embarrassed than irritated about the gate-crashing fly, was there in case she flipped out. In case the news was more than Sophie could handle in a publicly respectable manner. Dr Conroy was a neurologist, not a counsellor. Clearly he was all for the personal approach when it came to delivery method – face to face with no formal, formidable desk in the space between them – but if Sophie was to get highly charged and emotional, he'd undoubtedly (and perhaps understandably) prefer back up.

There was no need for any such precaution though. Sophie was holding it together. The fly's maddening buzz and the balminess of heat from the radiator in the huge, cramped space of the unventilated room helped to encourage a growing numbness of emotion as she tried to process the information he'd given her. His serious face, a mile away at least, yet right there before her, was very much in focus and she imagined she could make out each pore on his nose and every individual grey whisker on his jawline. His blue eyes, behind gold rimmed glasses, waited for a response, any response, while Sophie was worried by a sudden thought that she might not have put enough money in the parking meter. How long had she been at the hospital already? Longer than two hours? Surely people ran over on their parking all the time. Surely she could top up the fee if need be. Did it even matter? Probably not as much as she'd have liked.

At last Sophie nodded, in acceptance. Because that was all she could do.

*Relapsing remitting multiple sclerosis.*

So, her immune system had turned on her. Mistaking the myelin sheath around her nerve endings for a foreign body, deliberately and savagely attacking it. Stripping it away. Exposing the nerves. Seven months of exacerbating, soul destroying, shit-luck symptoms had led to this point. Three days before Christmas too.

*Relapsing remitting multiple sclerosis.*

But at least now she knew.

For weeks she'd felt as though life's variable carpet had been pulled from under her feet. She'd gone from healthy and out-going to sensorially defective. And scared. Downright scared. But now it was as though her rogue B and T cells, having worked their way through her entire dermatome, were no longer content to mess solely with the myelin sheath that covered the nerves affecting her limbs, extremities and torso, and so had found a way into her actual psyche to numb her mind.

Sophie had suspected MS for a while. Everyone had, she reckoned, even Dr Google. But it was never mentioned in conversation. No one ever brought it up, maybe in case to do so would automatically make it real. Now it had been confirmed though, it would need to be talked about.

Sophie felt like she should feel something emotionally. Maybe even relief, just to know why it was that she'd spent all those months unable to feel various body parts.

Why she'd spent all those months with excruciating neuralgia and stabbing sensations in her hands and feet. Unable to drive. Unable to cook. Unable to walk far. Unable to get dressed without feeling like her body belonged to a mannequin. Why she'd spent three months with the muscles around her ribcage contracted so tightly that it felt like she was wearing a corset. All of the time. No let up. Barely any sleep. All of it hideous. So exhausting. Why she was now heat sensitive and perhaps always would be. Why her hands and feet tingled each day like the onset of pins and needles. But she didn't, Sophie didn't feel any emotion whatsoever. That would come later. For now, it was too epic. And at the same time, it simply was what it was.

Finally, Sophie knew what she was dealing with after so many months, weeks, days, hours, minutes, seconds of uncertainty, helplessness and frustration – yet she absolutely *didn't* know what she was dealing with. She had no idea what the future held. It stretched out before her in a fug of goodness knew how many relapses and varying degrees of debilitation and numbness, sleeplessness and pain. Terrible unrelenting symptoms that would last for months at a time before the mangled myelin sheath and exposed nerves were left alone to heal. And of course the terror. For the first time in her life she didn't feel in the least bit in control of her own destiny, which was terrifying. Mostly because there was nothing she could do to regain control. Relapsing remitting multiple sclerosis wasn't something she could work out and overcome with a healthier regime or altered lifestyle. Hell, till a few weeks ago she didn't even know what it was, aside from something that other people probably got. It wasn't something a loved one could make disappear. It wasn't like getting a bank loan from Mam and Dad. Or calling in a favour from a friend. Nobody was going to make *this* problem disappear.

Nobody. Because nobody could. Disease modifying treatment was her best chance, but with no cure for MS, she'd be left in psychological limbo not knowing how long treatment would delay the next relapse. She would always wonder how long she'd be able to cling to her mobility and, till lately undervalued and very much taken for granted, her sense of touch. If she was lucky the treatment would halt the disease in its tracks and she may never have another relapse, but the 'what if' would always weigh heavy. It would lurk in the peripheral part of her mind, no matter what. She knew that.

The fly landed on the window sill and all was quiet.

'What now?' Sophie thought to ask, not entirely sure whether she was asking Dr Conroy or herself, because as well as the diagnosis, there was other stuff going on in her life. Scary stuff that coincided too well with the timings of her first MS symptoms and therefore made her wonder if it was all related.

What if she knew what had caused the initial inflammation of her brain? What if she knew that it was much more than a genetic anomaly or a viral infection that had triggered her immune system to go rogue? What then? Because deep down she knew this to be true. Deep down she knew there was something other than her own immune system that sought to destroy her. Something terribly dark and predatory. Something she could feel inside her, like clawed fingers violating the dermis all over her body and plucking already-damaged nerves. Cold, slithery hands smothering the cortex of her brain to suffocate old memories so she might not know the truth. These hands and fingers, they belonged to the spirit of a man she'd once known. Her old neighbour, Ronnie Cribbins.

# 2

# How It All Started

*Several months earlier...*

Sophie came out of the party, drunk. In one hand she was clutching a carrier bag filled with cellophane-wrapped party food and in the other she was holding a big chunk of tinfoil-wrapped birthday cake. Around her left wrist, secured by a length of blue ribbon, was a silver balloon, which bopped against her head as she walked. On its pearlescent surface, printed in black, was the number sixty.

She tottered across the road, following her mother, and watched as her breath came out in small clouds of boozy white vapour. It was almost summertime, yet the warmth of her evaporating breath rose towards the chilled, dark underbelly of the sky. Clouds had been huddled above Horden for five days now, like a pack of sleeping dogs, suffocating May with their coarseness. Sophie thought it was high time someone woke them up and moved them on.

*Let them sleep somewhere else for a change.*

Her ears buzzed with the remembered loudness of disco music, but still she could hear the muffled clamour of other party-goers coming out of the Comrades' Social Club behind her and saying their goodbyes to one another before dispersing into the night. High heels scraped along the pavement, where many had scraped before, and a taxi door was slammed shut by someone who, presumably, also wanted the sky to waken.

The peal of a siren in the distance declared trouble for someone, somewhere, and a man started to belt out a

Proclaimers song, complete with Scottish accent, at the top of his voice. His effort wasn't enough to rouse the sky, but enough to unsettle neighbourhood dogs. One deep bark was followed by a succession of smaller yaps from numerous dogs in surrounding streets.

The mouth-watering savoury tang from the Chinese takeaway on the corner of Third Street made Sophie's stomach growl. Her dad stopped to talk to someone beneath a streetlight further up the road, she noticed, as she passed through the wrought iron gate that led to her parents' house. After a few failed attempts to get the key in the lock, her mother opened the front door and fell into the house. Sophie went in behind her.

Rodney, a ginger and white mongrel who was meant to be half corgi but looked more sheepdog than anything, jumped off the couch and sauntered over to see them, wagging his shaggy tail in polite greeting. Sophie stepped past him and tripped on the edge of a rug, then stumbled through to the kitchen.

Her mother was unloading a tray of uneaten sandwich triangles onto the draining board. She turned her head to ask, 'Where's your dad?'

'Outside, talking.' Sophie put the food she'd been carrying on the kitchen counter.

'Who with?'

'Harry House, I think.'

'Christ, he could talk the hind legs off a donkey.'

'Dad or Harry House?'

'Both.' Nora Harrington giggled and a gin and tonic mischief danced in her eyes. The eyeliner and mascara she'd put on earlier in the evening had slid down into the creases of her lower lids. She lifted the kettle from its cradle and took it to the sink, kicking her heels off at the same time. One black suede stiletto skidded across the floor and settled near the bin, the other one flew a short distance and landed next to Rodney's dinner bowl.

Sophie nudged her own shoes off and placed them by the back door.

By the time Nora was adding milk to three mugs of tea, the front door burst open and Lenny Harrington called through the house, 'Got the kettle on yet, love?'

Nora clicked her tongue and muttered, 'Do bears shit in the woods?'

Less than five minutes later all three of them were in the sitting room with an array of leftover buffet food spread out on the coffee table before them. Lenny had turned on the Al Jazeera news channel as background noise.

Nora blew into her mug, then took a cautious sip. 'Did you enjoy your party?'

'Aye, it was top notch, pet.' Lenny leaned his head back and rested his hands on the small, rounded swell of his paunch. A large badge on the chest pocket of his blue checked shirt proclaimed him to be the 'Birthday Boy' and a satisfied, inebriated glow on his face confirmed that he meant what he said.

Sophie thought he looked every bit his sixty years, though it was strange for her to acknowledge. When she didn't dwell on it so mindfully, like she was now, she thought that she could still be twenty and her mam and dad forty-five.

*How has this even happened,* she wondered. *How have we all reached this point together already?*

Lenny Harrington had always been reedy but not especially tall and although he still had all of his hair, it was completely grey now. Sophie narrowed her eyes and wondered if he would look much younger if he was to shave off his bushy Tom Selleck-style moustache. He gave her a funny look when he noticed she was staring and Sophie decided he'd probably look silly without it. He'd worn it on his top lip for as long as she'd been alive, at least. Lenny Harrington without a moustache would be like vodka and Coke without vodka. Just wrong.

'Did you see who Crazy Col's with now?' Nora said, presumably to anyone who might have noticed. 'Moira will be rolling in her grave, I bet.'

Lenny grunted and nodded in agreement. 'Not wrong there, love.'

Sophie leant forward and picked up a mini sausage roll. She began to dissect it, peeling the pastry off in layers with her teeth. Crumbs fell into her mug of tea and down her top, but she was too drunk to care. 'Who was that bloke with our Shaun?' she asked, unsure what was so scandalous about Crazy Col's new partner or why his late wife would be rolling in her grave, unless it was just the fact he was with someone else. The person she'd seen sitting with her cousin all night, however, looked nothing short of scandalous. And, what's more, he'd winked at her three times.

'The lanky bugger with the horrible teeth?' Nora said, licking pastry crumbs off her thumb. 'That's Addy Adkins. You don't want anything to do with him, pet, he's nothing but trouble.'

Sophie cocked an eyebrow at her mother's ridiculous presumption. 'I never said I did want anything to do with him.'

'Who the hell invited Addy Adkins anyway?' Lenny wanted to know.

'Our Shaun, I expect.'

'I bet the scrounging git only came to eat all of my sausage rolls.'

Sophie shook her head and laughed. 'Like there weren't enough to go round, eh, Dad?' She popped another one in her mouth and threw one to Rodney, who was drooling on the laminate flooring next to her feet.

Nora laughed. 'If that's the case, he should have shoved a few more of them down that scrawny neck of his.'

'Aye and choked on the buggers.' Lenny grumbled and reached across for a slice of quiche. It was soggy in the middle and when he lifted it off the paper plate he had wedged up against his chest, the end fell off. It bounced off the plate, but Rodney caught it before it hit the floor.

'He did a load of the allotments over in the nineties,' Lenny went on. 'I'll never forget, he nicked your grandda's wheelbarrow once and filled it with a load of potting plants and hanging baskets from around the doors to sell to some wifey in Blackhall. These days it's sheds and garages he does over. Probably houses too.'

Nora was nodding in agreement. 'No morals, that one. Dickie Henshaw reckons it was Addy Adkins who took his youngest lad's bike out of his shed, Christmas afore last.'

Lenny shoved the rest of the quiche slice into his mouth and wiped the fingers of his left hand on his jeans. He swallowed after just three chews and said, 'As your grandda would have said, Soph, that lad's a waste of a good skin.'

Sophie laughed.

'Speaking of which,' Lenny said, a hint of mischief lingering in his eyes. 'How's Gareth doing?'

Sophie became serious in an instant, as though her dad had just slapped her. 'He's on about moving to France.'

'France?' Nora put her cup of tea down. 'What does he want to go and do that for?'

Sophie shrugged. 'Apparently he wants to run a ski lodge or something.'

'And is Andrea okay about that?'

'Dunno, but I don't suppose it matters.' Sophie shrugged. 'What Gareth wants, Gareth gets.'

'Well, you'd think he'd wait a while, till Caitlyn's grown up a bit. They see each other quite a bit at the moment. How's that going to work?'

Sophie had no idea. She and Gareth had split up around eight years ago, but had maintained an amicable enough relationship for their daughter Caitlyn's sake. Gareth had since got married to a woman called Andrea, and they had two children of their own. Caitlyn was more than happy to float between both very contrasting family homes. But now Sophie wasn't sure what to expect from her ex. She picked at the hem of her top, with her eyes downcast, and said, 'I don't know.'

'You're not worried he's going to try and take her with him, are you?' Nora asked, seeing the concern on her daughter's face.

Sophie's mouth twisted to the side. She didn't answer.

'Don't be daft, of course he won't,' her mother scoffed. 'Besides, Caitlyn wouldn't want to go. She'd stay here with you if she had to make a choice.'

*Would she?* Sophie couldn't be certain. Living in a ski lodge in the mountains with her dad and two half-siblings would probably sound pretty damn tempting to an eleven-year-old. A massive adventure, like nothing Sophie could offer.

Everyone fell quiet, and the news reporter on the television may as well have been talking in Swahili for all the attention they gave her.

'Oh listen, what do you reckon to this?' Nora said eventually, touching Sophie's leg in an attempt to create an air of drama. 'Sue Taylor reckons Judith Gimmerick's middle son is going out with some lass on the telly.'

'Really?' Sophie managed to sound more interested than she actually was. 'Who's that then?'

'I dunno, I can't remember her name. Sue did tell me the programme she's on, but I've forgotten that as well.'

Sophie sighed. 'Well that was a bit of a half tale, Mam.'

Nora laughed, making a snorting noise with her nose.

She rocked forward to grab her cup of tea.

Lenny gave his wife a sideways glance and shook his head in despair. He looked at Sophie then, his expression troubled, and Sophie could tell he was still mulling over the Gareth situation.

'Do I even know who Judith Gimmerick's middle son is?' Sophie asked.

Nora looked thoughtful. 'I dunno, I thought you might. His name's Nick.'

Sophie shook her head. 'Doesn't ring any bells.'

'Her youngest son came home last year for a while. You must know him?'

'Gimmerick?' Sophie's mind searched through names and faces, trying to find a match. She shrugged. 'Dunno. What's he called?'

'John. I think he was in your year at school. Maybe the year above. Lovely looking lad. The most intense blue eyes.'

Sophie shook her head again, her expression vague. She had no idea. 'Well, that was a great story, Mam,' she said, edging forward in her seat and yawning. 'But I'm knackered, so I'm off to bed.'

It was the first time in years that Sophie was to stay over at her parents' house, in her old room. Caitlyn wasn't due back from Gareth's till the following afternoon, so there'd been no need for Sophie to rush home after the party. Besides her mother said she was making a full English the next morning: the answer to all hangover prayers.

Lenny, who was by now scrolling through the television guide, trying to find something less depressing than the news, didn't bother looking up but acknowledged her announcement with a, 'Right you are, pet.'

Nora gave her a drunken, lop-sided smile and nodded. 'Night, love. Sleep well.'

Sophie was under no illusion that she would, as climbed the stairs to her old room. She might be free of her noisy neighbours for one night, but Gareth's upcoming move to France had been the root cause of her sleeplessness since he'd dropped the bombshell just three days ago.

# 3

# Don't Let Him Keep Me

It was still dark. Something had woken Sophie. Instinctively, she felt that whatever it was was beyond her body's objections to the large quantity of alcohol she'd plied it with hours before. Realistically, though, she thought maybe it wasn't. Perhaps thirst had woken her. She'd been dreaming about dozens of glass tumblers filled with fizzy cola and ice cubes, all of them lined up before her in a row of refreshment that her body so desperately craved. Refreshment that would quell the hangover that had made her mouth feel as thick and dry as old carpet.

She licked her lips. Her tongue felt like a dying slug. She tried to lubricate her mouth, but no saliva came. When she swallowed, even though there was nothing to swallow, her parched throat hurt. Her head hurt more. Especially when she turned onto her side and fumbled in the darkness, her fingers feeling for her iPhone on the bedside table. When she found it she thumbed its screen and squinted. Its light burnt her retinas like looking at the sun.

3:01am.

*Ugh.*

She thought about going downstairs for a glass of tap water, then decided the consequences of doing so, the penalty for moving that much, would be an even worse headache, which didn't seem worth it. In the long run maybe, especially if she took a couple of paracetamols at the same time. But she was much too hungover to spend time convincing herself of the long term benefits of rehydration and painkillers, so she reshaped the duvet around herself, keeping her head very still, and hoped to recommence dreaming of fizzy pop and ice.

But that's when she saw the girl.

Over by the door. A small, dark figure who blended too well with the night. Long hair fell down past her stooped shoulders and her head was bowed. She looked forlorn, perhaps even sullen. Her presence provoked a sense of trepidation that rendered Sophie's hangover forgotten. Sophie scrabbled up onto her elbows, her heart accelerating with explosive clarity. She was about to ask the girl who she was, but the girl spoke first. 'He hid them. He hid them all away.' Her voice was like a stirring of memories that had gathered like bone-dry leaves in a dark recess; each word papery thin, but substantial enough in their mysterious context to incite a greater feel of dread. 'Don't let him keep me,' the girl implored.

Springing from the bed, kicking herself free from the sheets, Sophie groped the wall, in search of the light switch. When she found it, light filled the room and she saw there was no girl. Which was worse, perhaps, than if there had been.

*What the hell?*

Leaving the light on, Sophie eased herself down on the edge of the bed and stared at the area behind the door where she'd seen the small figure. Her whole body shook and she inhaled deeply in an attempt to regulate her breathing. Had she just seen a ghost? Or had she been partially asleep without realising? Had her subconscious projected an image that somehow strayed beyond its usual threshold, into the realm of her over-tired consciousness?

Yes. That had to be it. It was the only logical explanation.

The girl's voice lingered in Sophie's head.

*He hid them. He hid them all away.*
*Don't let him keep me.*

The words were cryptic in their ambivalence. And their method of delivery was downright creepy. Sophie shivered.

Seeing a strange child who wasn't really there lurking in the shadows of her room had been an alarming, intense wake-up call. Her nerves felt unravelled. It took a while for her to calm down, but eventually, when she felt brave enough, she went downstairs for some water. Even though she knew the layout of the house well enough to navigate past all the furniture in the dark without stubbing her toes, she turned each light on along the way. She couldn't cope with the darkness right now. Was too wary in case she saw any ghosts within the shadows.

After downing two glasses of water, Sophie lingered in the kitchen. She was all too aware of the house's stillness, and stood listening to its quiet above the gentle hum of the fridge. Rodney was lying on a faux fur blanket in front of the washing machine. His eyes were cracked open and he watched her with the mildest of interest, like maybe, just maybe, there'd be a dog biscuit on the go. Sophie bent over and fussed him for a while. The realness of his fur and the warmth of his body allowed for such a flourish of ordinariness that the ghost girl suddenly seemed like nothing more than imagined foolishness.

When she went back upstairs to her room, Sophie turned the light off and climbed into bed. Lengthways the bed fit the width of the room, perfectly. Wall to wall. Box room cosy. She wriggled to the very bottom, so the soles of her feet were pressed flat against the wall. As a kid, she'd always done the same thing. The blown vinyl wallpaper was cool on her skin. Comforting in its old familiarity.

She closed her eyes and conjured nice thoughts of swimming in a pool somewhere in the Mediterranean, the sky above some wonderful shade of blue. The body of water was cool and clear. Gentle waves lapped over her chin, touching her lips. The whole scene was thirst-quenching blue. The colour of bubble gum ice pops. The colour of raspberry flavoured Slush Puppy. The colour of John Gimmerick's eyes. Apparently.

Sophie smiled at the randomness. Who the hell was John Gimmerick anyway? Her mother seemed to know. Sophie didn't. She'd gone to Easington Comprehensive School, so maybe, she thought, John Gimmerick and his intense blue eyes had gone to Dene House or Shotton Hall.

*Well, good for him.*

She heard something then. A noise on the outer edge of noticeability, but noticeable all the same. Especially now she was aware of it.

Someone snoring.

Next door.

*The joys of living mid terrace.*

Could that have been what had disturbed her earlier? Just before she'd seen the girl?

Snoring was right up there on Sophie's list of pet peeves, alongside dinner plate scraping and people eating with their mouths open. Gareth had been a snorer.

There was a particularly loud snorted intake of air succeeded by a lengthy, raspy exhalation. This then became a new established pattern as though the snorer was purposefully antagonising and baiting for more of her attention. Sophie pulled the covers over her head and tried to zone out from the irritating sound, but could hear its invasiveness over her own thoughts. She tried hard to think about other stuff. Trivial stuff: conversations she'd had with estranged relatives at her dad's party, her mother dancing to Fergal Sharkey's *A Good Heart These*

*Days* and Aunt Margaret twirling round so fast her pleated skirt had lifted high enough to show off her knickers, which were white belly-warmers adorned, front and back, with the gusset of her natural tan tights. But the snoring persisted, scoring into her brain and killing the funniness of Aunt Margaret's faux pas.

Sophie kicked the wall with her heel, frustrated. But the snorer carried on snoring, the sound of constricted airways continuing to vibrate loudly. If anything, it gained in volume and bass. Minute after minute passed. Sophie lay awake. After a while, she decided she could feel each inhalation and exhalation vibrating through the thickness of the wall onto the soles of her feet, massaging the core of her lower legs. The humming sensations transferred up her entire body in rhythmic, not unpleasant waves. Strangely she began to feel somewhat soothed by them.

In time, Sophie managed to drift off to sleep again. She dreamt she was on Horden beach. Only it was like a parody of itself. Summertime had arrived and the sand was uncharacteristically yellow and the sky was ridiculously blue. Hordes of people had gathered, all of them sombre looking, dressed in black and grey period costume. It was as though everyone was in mourning, including herself. But for whom, Sophie didn't know.

Had some mass tragedy taken place? Or was everyone's grief for the same person?

Sophie was anxious about many things, like Caitlyn being taken away from her, a workload she doubted she'd ever get on top of and hellish neighbours who impinged too much on her home life, but all of those things filled her with a tumultuous negative energy that flitted from fretful to angry, not melancholy as such.

So what was it that she was so sad about?

She came to the conclusion that the reason for her despondency was a massive emptiness within her. And the reason for this massive emptiness was that she wasn't whole.

*Is anybody?*

*No. I don't think so.*

That was the answer then. It must be. All of the people around her were mourning the missing parts of themselves. It made perfect sense. And just knowing this made Sophie feel less alone. The fact that she had this sadness in common with all of these other shuffling, listless souls, made her feel like she belonged to something at least. The human condition.

*What a ghastly thing.*

A burly man with a curled moustache strode past, clipping Sophie's shoulder with his and spinning her round. He didn't turn to apologise and nobody else seemed to care. Sophie felt as though she was a part of some mean, bizarre Victorian postcard setting, right down to the black parasol she was carrying to shield herself from the sun. The sun which, she thought, should have an ink-painted smiling face in sinister fine lines of mocking, and a top hat that it could intermittently tip while belting out *The Sun Has Got His Hat On* in an old, crackly gramophone voice. But it didn't. It remained an inanimate plain yellow disc of card on a sheet of blue sugar paper.

Above the eerie silence of unspeaking, funereal adults, gulls barked and dogs squawked. Down near the calm, unreliably turquoise sea was a small red and yellow striped stall. In front of it was a crowd of seated children; all of them sitting cross-legged in neat rows, around ten deep. All of them still.

All of them girls.

On closer inspection, Sophie saw Caitlyn in the front row.

As if sensing her mother's presence, Caitlyn turned and waved. Sophie smiled and waved back.

Inside the stripy stall were two puppets: Punch and Judy. Punch hit Judy with his slapstick and the children, as a collective whole, laughed. Their amusement sounded forced and mechanical. Demented. Worse than canned laughter. Sophie bristled when a fresh northerly breeze came straight off the North Sea and wrapped around her bones. The dream felt close to nightmarish. Too close to real.

'That's the way to do it!' Punch declared. Over and over, he hit Judy and his high kazooing voice kept on, 'That's the way to do it! That's the way to do it!' Again and again, like the dream was a record and the needle had become stuck. Everything else faded away, except Punch's face and voice which filled Sophie's head till there was barely any room left for her to think. She found she couldn't breathe. His crooked nose curved round and down to his upwardly curved chin, till they almost touched. His teeth were antique white. His rounded wooden cheeks were rouged with paint or malevolent rage, it was hard to tell which. His angry black eyebrows framed his devious, murderous eyes. 'That's the way to do it!'

It was too much. All of it hurt Sophie's head. She crouched down and touched the sand, to steady herself. To stop herself from falling to her knees. She squeezed her eyes shut.

When she looked up again she saw the red and yellow stall falling forwards, towards the children. It was happening in slow motion and, astonishingly, all of the girls just sat there, as if waiting to be flattened.

*No!*

Sophie tried to call out to Caitlyn, to all of them. To tell them to move. To get out of the way. But she found that her mouth wouldn't form any words. She couldn't even make any sound.

Flailing her arms instead, to get their attention that

way, Sophie reeled in shock when she saw someone step out from behind the tipping stall. It was an incredibly tall man with the sun at his back. Punch and Judy were rammed onto the ends of his arms. The sight of him made Sophie so afraid, her vision faded a little at the edges.

'Hello, Sophie-cat,' the man said to her, through crooked teeth she couldn't see. 'Have you come to see another of my shows?' He laughed, a most horrible laugh that made Sophie's innards flip inside out. 'I'll put on an especially good one. A private show, just for you.'

A girl cried out, 'Don't let him keep me!'

Then all of the girls began to scream.

The man laughed.

There was a loud bang, a resonating thud, and Sophie jolted upright in bed. She didn't know if the sound had been the stall falling over in her dream or whether something had fallen over next door. Either way, her heart thumped so hard in her chest it hurt.

The girl's wretched cry was still clear in its heartfelt plea.

*Don't let him keep me.*

And the lingering, grating threat of the man's voice made the underside of Sophie's face flash cold.

*Hello, Sophie-cat. Have you come to see another of my shows? I'll put on an especially good one. A private show, just for you.*

Because it felt real. Entirely too real.

# 4

# The House Next Door

The smell of fry-up – bacon, sausages, black pudding, eggs, mushrooms and hash browns – filled the house with conflicting sickliness and heavenliness. Sophie sat down at the dining table, still in her pyjamas, and sipped from a mug of milky, sweet tea.

'Sleep alright?' Her dad was sitting across the table, reading the Daily Mail. Sophie couldn't focus on the headline on the front page because her eyes were still blurry with sleep. She had a banging headache, inside and out. Her brain felt bloated like it was too big for her skull and the skin on the left side of her scalp was tender, as though she'd lain awkwardly on her hair all night. She grunted some half-baked affirmative.

Lenny Harrington, dressed in blue jeans and a dark green polo shirt, looked as he *always* did. He chortled at her hangover face.

'How come you got off so lightly?' Sophie asked, cradling her head.

Peering over the top of his reading glasses, a grin formed beneath Lenny's moustache. 'Sixty years of practice, pet.'

Nora Harrington came trundling in from the kitchen holding two plates. She was wearing a fleecy robe over the top of flannelette pyjamas and even though winter was long dead and shallowly buried beneath a handful of warmish days, she'd probably still say she was cold if asked. Her permed blonde hair was a matted nest of stale hairspray that would need much coaxing and teasing with a comb before it would be considered publicly presentable and she still wore the remnants of last night's mascara around her eyes. She set one of the plates down in front of Sophie and handed the other to Lenny.

At the sight of the greasy food, Sophie's stomach rolled over with all the fluidity of a dead jellyfish washing ashore, but she picked up her knife and fork and began to tuck in. After a while she said, 'When you asked if I'd slept okay, I forgot to mention, I was rudely awoken by your neighbour. Snoring.'

'Must have been your dad, pet,' Nora said, casting an unamused look in Lenny's direction.

Lenny rolled his eyes as if he'd been unjustly accused, but affirmed his guilt by chuckling.

Nora remained straight-faced, sharing none of his humour. Her eyebrows were raised in disparagement; a scorn that marked forty-odd years' worth of sufferance. 'To be honest, I'm surprised we don't get complaints off Mr and Mrs Radcliffe in the end house, he's *that* bloody loud. Environmental health will be out one of these days to see how much noise pollution he's causing.'

Sophie smiled at the blatant exaggeration. 'Nah, it was definitely coming from next door.'

'It can't have been, pet.' Nora shook her head and blew on a piece of sausage. 'No one lives there.'

'Someone must be staying over then.' Sophie fingered the left side of her head, to see if the skin was still sore. It was. Maybe even swollen.

'I doubt it.' Nora looked at Lenny for his input. He gave none, except an indifferent shrug. 'Peggy Flannery, the old lady who lived there, died about three months ago. Her daughter, Fiona, who lives in Spain, owns the house. She came over for the funeral but no one's seen hide nor hair of her since. It seems Fiona's left the house for her brother, Paul, to sort out. Him and his wife were there for about a week clearing the place out. They hired a skip and chucked most of Peggy's things in it. Totally gutted the place. They're meant to be selling the house on Fiona's behalf, but I've yet to see a for sale sign go up.'

'Maybe Peggy's son's staying there then,' Sophie suggested.

'I can't see why,' Nora said. 'Paul's got a big house in Oakerside, why on earth would he want to stay next door? There isn't any furniture in there as far as I know.'

'Maybe one of Peggy's grandkids is staying there.' Sophie set her knife and fork down and pushed her plate away. She'd had enough. 'Because I'm telling you, there was definitely someone snoring next door.'

'Paul's only got one daughter and she doesn't live round here anymore,' Nora said, killing that idea outright. 'She's at uni somewhere down south.'

'Well, I dunno, maybe there's a squatter,' Sophie said, feeling suddenly agitated. She knew what she'd heard.

'Or maybe it was Old Peg herself,' Lenny said with a conspiratorial wink.

Sophie groaned. 'Yeah right, Dad.'

'Well actually, it's funny you should say that,' Nora said, reaching over for Sophie's plate to stack on top of her own unfinished breakfast. 'Peggy used to say that house was haunted.'

Lenny scoffed and picked up his newspaper, noisily opening it to where he'd left off. But Sophie felt suddenly chilled, her thoughts turning to the ghost girl in her room. 'Why did she think that?' she asked. 'What happened?'

Nora put Lenny's plate on top of the pile and stood up. 'She said she'd seen and heard stuff.'

'Like what?'

'I dunno, pet, she never went into detail.'

'Sounds like another half tale to me.' Lenny looked at Sophie and winked.

'You're a cheeky sod, you are,' Nora told him, taking the dirty plates through to the kitchen. 'Poor Peggy was adamant there was a spook in there with her. Then there was Carl and Leanne, that couple before her as well, they didn't last long in there.'

'Leanne Baxter?' Sophie asked.

'Yeah, the girl you went to school with. She once told me she'd found slime on the bedroom wall.'

'Bloody hell man, Nora,' Lenny said, with a snort of laughter. 'Better call Ghostbusters eh? Slimer's on the loose.'

'Oh piss off you,' Nora said, reappearing in the dining room. 'That poor girl wasn't happy at all in there.'

'Neither would I have been with a slug invasion and that bone idle boyfriend of hers.'

Nora rolled her eyes. 'Anyone for another cuppa?'

Sophie and Lenny both nodded.

Nora collected the mugs from the table, threading her finger through all three handles. They chinked together as she moved. 'I bet I can tell you who'd be haunting next door,' she said pointedly, while nodding towards the adjoining wall.

'Who?' Lenny and Sophie asked at the same time.

'Him who used to live there before Carl and Leanne.'

Lenny took a deep breath then nodded, looking halfway convinced. 'Ronnie Cribbins?'

'Aye,' Nora said. 'That horrible old bastard.'

'Oh God,' Sophie said. 'I remember him.'

# 5

# Ronnie Cribbins

*August 1990*

'Tinker, tailor, soldier, sailor, rich man, poor man, beggar man, thief.' Sophie bounced the three fluffy green tennis balls against the garage wall, her hands speeding up as she went through the sing-song rendition over and over again. 'Tinker, tailor, soldier, sailor, rich man, poor man, beggar man, thief. Tinker, tailor, soldier, sailor, rich man, poor man…' She dropped one of the balls.

*Shit with sugar on top!*

It was the third time she'd flunked on poor man which meant that that's who she was destined to marry, because best of three couldn't be argued with. It was the way of things. An unwritten law of nature. Like how if she stepped on too many cracks in the pavement she would die before she was old enough to leave school. And how if she didn't kiss Teddy Ruxpin before bed every night then something really awful would happen to her mam and dad. Like a five car smash up on the motorway or a mugging gone wrong where both of them ended up fatally stabbed.

But then, supposing she did keep off the cracks and stay alive long enough to reach adulthood, she might decide *not* to have a husband. Girls could do what they wanted these days, they didn't have to get married and have kids. She'd get a job and have her own money. She already thought she might like to be a journalist, like Aunt Gillian, and be highly independent. You could still get married *and* be independent, of course. And supposing she *did* get married and her husband *was* poor, that would still be okay, she reckoned. He could pick flowers from the garden for her and she'd buy him nice things. That was settled then. The future didn't seem so bad after all. Sophie dropped the other two balls and did a cartwheel across the lawn.

It was then she realised that someone was watching her. A man in the garden next door. Even though he was bent over, his elbows resting on the fence, he was about as tall as a skyscraper. All skinny and pointy with white hair and squinty eyes that were looking at her through black rimmed glasses. She couldn't tell if he was grinning or snarling, but he seemed to be directing his long yellow teeth at her.

'Hello, kitten,' he said. His voice was as scratchy and alarming as revisited nightmares. The ones that render you immobile until your mind catches up with your heartbeat. It was hoarse with phlegm and loaded with some ulterior motive that Sophie was too young to analyse much beyond a sketchy intuitive perception that he might pose a threat to her.

Sophie put her hands on her hips and scowled. Unhappy about his intrusion. Vexed that she didn't know how long he'd been watching her. It was none of his business who fate had assigned to her as a future husband – if she decided to have one. None of his business whatsoever.

'I'm not a kitten,' she said, indulging her fiery temper. 'My name's Sophie.' Her annoyance was dampened by a flash of terror. Should she have given him her real name?

*Oops.*

Probably not. He was a stranger who looked kind of odd and made her tummy feel unsettled. He could easily be one of those weird men they warned about in the stranger danger videos they'd been showing at school. And now he knew her name.

*Shit with sugar* and *a cherry on top!*

'I'm Mister Cribbins,' he said. The words rasped out of his mouth, as awful as a drain lid being slid over concrete by something emerging from the underground that defied all logic and nature. His eyes were cruelly amused. 'Your new neighbour.'

Sophie was only eight, not old enough by far to make judgement calls about strangers and their intentions. He hadn't mentioned sweets or puppies yet, which the videos at school specifically warned about, but she imagined that maybe he had either one or both of those things lined up next. She decided things had gone far enough, that it was time for grown-up intervention. Otherwise he might reach over at any moment and snatch her across the fence with his impossibly long arms, which she imagined might be able to stretch even longer at will. She backed up against the rosebushes, till thorns pricked the backs of her bare legs, and yelled, *'Mam!'*

Nora Harrington came to the front door, in no particular hurry, with a tea towel slung over her shoulder and a look of annoyance on her face. She must have been busy in the kitchen. 'What now?' she began to complain, but then she clapped eyes on Mr Cribbins and forced a smile. The sort of smile she greeted door to door canvassers and Jehovah's Witnesses with. 'Oh, er, can I help?'

Mr Cribbins stood up straight then and became the size of two skyscrapers, one on top of the other. His eyes sparkled blackly as he took in Nora standing on the doorstep in high-waisted bleached denim jeans, which hugged her small waist, and a white blouse that illuminated her face and made her naturally blonde hair look even blonder than it was.

He took too long looking at her before saying, 'I'm sure, in time, you most certainly can,' in that ghastly voice of his. Even though Sophie was only young, she could sense that he oozed wrongness. The sort of wrongness that would be black with grey vapour trails if visible.

Nora cocked an eyebrow in bemusement, her strained smile disappearing into a tight-lipped scowl. 'Excuse me?'

'I'm Ronnie. Ronnie Cribbins,' he explained, extending an incredibly long arm. 'Your new neighbour.'

'Oh.' Nora looked surprised. Then disappointed. Then disingenuously pleased. Then, surreptitiously, acting with a sense of obligation and conceding a manner of politeness, because that's what friendly neighbours are meant to do, especially ones who share walls, she stepped forward to shake his hand. She did so with a different kind of smile; a cautious one that reached her grey eyes with enough warmth to appear genuine. 'Nice to meet you Mister Cribbins. I hadn't realised we had a new neighbour.'

'Bought it privately,' he began to say, but then Keith Ferguson, a bricklayer who lived four doors down, came out of his house and banged his front door shut so hard the letterbox rattled Ronnie Cribbins' train of thought. Keith was wearing a black Fat Willy's Surf Shack vest with fluorescent text and his bare arms were the colour of the Harrington's teak television stand. As he strolled down his garden path, looking like he was carrying an imaginary roll of wallpaper beneath each arm, he whistled the tune to *Lambada*, which reminded Sophie of summer holidays and light nights and Mr Whippy ice cream dripping with monkey's blood sauce.

Ronnie Cribbins glared at him.

'Alright, Nora?' Keith called up the street when he

noticed he had an audience.

'Aye, champion,' Nora said, giving him a casual wave. 'You?'

'Can't complain.' His garden gate slammed shut behind him and within seconds Keith was starting up his burgundy Ford Sierra. It sounded like a tank and when he pulled out of the street its diesel engine could be heard roaring up Cotsford Lane bank.

'As I was saying,' Ronnie Cribbins said, with a look of annoyance that accentuated the pointiness of his pointy face. 'We bought it privately, Phyllis and I, off the family of the man who lived here before.'

'I see,' Nora said, which Sophie was pleased about because she didn't. Usually a 'for sale' sign went up when a house was for sale, then eventually a 'sold' sign. But none of that had happened with the house next door. It didn't seem all that long since Mr Johnston, the old man who used to live there, had been put in a home. He'd had dementia and used to steal the milk from their doorstep most mornings. Sophie had had to have toast instead of cereal before school at least three times a week, so she hadn't been sorry to see him go. But now it seemed Mr Johnston was being replaced by someone equally menacing, if not more so.

'Well, it's good to meet you Mister Cribbins,' Nora said.

'It's Ronnie. Please, call me Ronnie. There's no need for any formal claptrap.' Cribbins wafted a hand reminiscent of the business end of a gardening rake in the air.

'I'm Nora,' Nora said, retreating to the doorstep to guard her household from this likely villain. 'My husband's out at the moment, but his name's Lenny. And that's Sophie. Our daughter.'

Ronnie Cribbins turned to Sophie then and winked.

Sophie turned away. She felt like a gazelle in the

African plains having been marked as fair game by an African wild dog. She'd seen African wild dogs on a David Attenborough documentary just two days before. They were sneaky, always watching and waiting. Sometimes Mr Johnston had barked at her for climbing on his back wall or for kicking her football into his yard, but he'd been more like a bad tempered mongrel who liked to assert his grumpiness every now and then, whereas Ronnie Cribbins seemed much more terrible than a grumpy old dog. There was something of actual bite and cunning about him.

'So, is Phyllis your wife?' Nora asked, a little too hopefully.

Ronnie Cribbins nodded. He made a loud, unexpected grating noise with his throat, then spat a huge wad of phlegm onto the otherwise pleasant arrangement of Livingstone daisies on his border. 'She's packing a few last minute knick knacks from the old house. I'll be fetching her later today.'

Sophie crinkled her nose in disgust at Cribbins' vileness, but Nora managed to maintain a thin smile. 'I'll look forward to meeting her in that case,' she said, which Sophie thought was a bare-faced lie, because no one who was married to Ronnie Cribbins could be nice. But for some reason, which she didn't understand and wondered if she might never, she found that adults often insisted on being pleasant to one another, even when a situation didn't warrant such niceness. Adults made no sense whatsoever. In fact, they seemed as fake to her as the latest batch of Puma t-shirts her gran had acquired from the dodgy bloke with the constant supply of 'off the back of a lorry' stuff who drank in the Deps. Adults were overly complicated with a confusing set of social etiquettes and requirements. Sophie worried about how she'd ever fit into adulthood. There were too many rules that she didn't understand.

'Oh and I hope you don't mind a bit of noise,' Ronnie Cribbins said, taking a well-used, by the looks of it, hanky from the front pocket of his diarrhoea-brown corduroy trousers and blowing his nose into it.

'Bit of noise?' Nora looked defensively disconcerted by the threat, which pleased Sophie.

'My wife is disabled,' he said, stuffing the wet hanky back into his pocket. 'I'll need to install a stair lift. So there might be a bit of hammering and whatnot going on.'

'Oh!' Nora looked embarrassed. 'Of course, that's fine. I didn't know what you meant. But yes, absolutely. Do whatever you need to do.'

He grinned again; that awful sly grin. 'It's very nice of you to be so accommodating, Nora.' The way he said her name and licked his thin purple lips was as though they'd shared some private moment that Sophie had somehow missed. But then, judging by the expression on her mother's face, it looked as though she had too. 'I also plan to put an upstairs bathroom in the third bedroom,' he said. 'It'll be easier for Phyllis. And I'm going to get rid of the coalhouse in the backyard, so I can get that old, cracked concrete up and lay some nice paving. Make it more accessible for her wheelchair, you know. And I'm thinking of getting planning permission for a garage at the end of the garden. You wouldn't object, would you? I'll build it myself. I'm very good with my hands.' He winked again and showed her his obscenely large hands.

'No, me and Lenny wouldn't object to you having a garage,' Nora said. Her pleasantness was beginning to wane and her smile looked more pained than anything. Sophie could tell she was itching to get back inside, to whatever she'd been doing in the kitchen. 'Certainly sounds like you'll be full of busy.'

'Absolutely. It'll keep me out of trouble for a while.

I'll be doing all the hard, manual graft and Phyllis'll do all the decor bits and bobs. You know, primping stuff and making everything look nice, like you girls do so well.'

'I'm sure,' Nora said, pulling the tea towel off her shoulder; her cue to leave. 'Anyway, it's been nice talking to you, Ronnie, but I'll have to get back inside. Got a cottage pie in the oven for Lenny's tea.'

Ronnie Cribbins, again, licked his lips. 'Nice. Very nice.'

Then Sophie was left alone with him: she on the right side of the fence and he on the wrong side.

'I used to work in a chocolate factory, you know,' he said, after a few awful moments of them regarding each other had dragged out.

Sophie didn't respond. Wished her mam would call her inside. Or that her dad would arrive home from work. Or that the ground would open up.

'Little girls love chocolate, don't they?' Cribbins persisted. 'I used to fix the computers at the chocolate factory. You wouldn't believe how big they are. I used to have to climb right inside of them with my toolbox.' He had an idiot grin, as though his story should be hugely more impressive than it was. 'To this day, I still get free chocolate sent to me. Those big bags of mini bars. I bet you like those. Oh yes, I bet you do.'

'No. I don't like chocolate at all,' Sophie felt inclined to tell him, her face deadpan. 'Or any other kind of sweets.'

Cribbins' thin lips pinched together in a grimace, as though he knew he'd been caught out in his ploy to entice her.

Taking off down the garden path, Sophie pulled her BMX off the ground by the handlebars. She threw one leg over the frame, so her bum was on the seat and her right foot was on the pedal, ready to pump it hard should she need to, and chanced a look back. 'And I don't like puppies either,' she said. 'Just so you know.'

# 6

# The First Visit

Sophie didn't entertain the idea of going home till another three mugs of sugary, milky tea, made by her mother, had been drunk and a slab of birthday cake had been demolished. She threw on a pair of leggings and a baggy jumper, gathered her stuff together and, rather reluctantly, left the house. Flinging her overnight bag on the passenger seat of her Renault Clio, she turned the engine over, then switched on the radio. Graham Norton was on BBC2 saying something about 'rainstorms on the way'. It was the tail-end of whatever story he'd been telling, so Sophie didn't catch whereabouts in the country or when they might be. She looked up at the sky. It still seemed too nonchalant in its wishy-washy state of dirty white to summon up any sort of precipitation.

Easing the car down the front road, careful to avoid the worst of the potholes there, she pulled out onto Third Street. She trailed behind a man pootling along on his mobility scooter till it was safe to overtake, then had to pull in to let three oncoming cars pass the obstruction created by the people who'd seen fit to park on the bend in the road outside the Salvation Army. As she pulled up to the T-junction at Blackhills Road, she saw St Mary's across the road, on the left, sitting alone in its own shadow. Further along, on the right, the Victory Club, in contrast, was bustling with its Saturday afternoon regulars: smokers chatting outside, while their pints of John Smith's and Tetley's waited to be finished inside. Sophie's guts churned at the thought. She wouldn't be sorry if she never drank again.

Soon she passed the glossed black spokes of the colliery's memorial structure, which featured the actual pit head wheels from Horden's coal mine. They looked like the wet bones of a large animal, mounted at the roadside. Turning right at the mini roundabout, she drove through Seaview Industrial Estate, the North Sea to her right. The sky above the white-tipped, choppy water was shark grey, shaping up well for Graham Norton's implied storm. A solitary ship floated on the horizon. It looked in danger of being swallowed up. Sophie felt a certain affinity towards it. Intuition told her that something more than a hangover was hanging over her. Something as ominous as those North Sea clouds. The only difference, she thought, was that she would be swallowed from the inside out.

Once home, Sophie cocooned herself in a fleecy blanket which had a hood with bear ears, and lay on the couch. She turned on the television and watched Gabriel Byrne in a dog collar being hit on by Patricia Arquette in *Stigmata*. It wasn't till the film was ending that the front door opened then banged shut again. Seconds later Caitlyn came bounding into the sitting room, bringing with her a waft of fresh air. Without taking her hooded jacket off, she squeezed on the end of the couch next to Sophie's feet.

'Hey,' Sophie said, shuffling upright to give her daughter more space. 'Did you have a good time at your dad's?'

Caitlyn nodded. She was at that awkward, gangly pre-teen age, where her adult teeth looked too big for her head and her limbs were all long and spindly. She had lots of growing into herself left to do. Her auburn hair hung loose around her shoulders and her pale skin was flecked with freckles. She didn't look like Sophie or Gareth, but instead bore a resemblance to both of her grandmothers.

'What did you get up to?'

'Played on the X-Box with Olly and Niamh.' Caitlyn's eyes, the same grey as Nora's, were filled with quiet enthusiasm. 'Can I have a milkshake?'

The two of them spent all evening together, watching back-to-back films in their pyjamas. Sophie's hangover had abated, but the left side of her head still hurt to touch, as though she'd had a ponytail pulled too tightly and the roots of her hair were bruised.

'I was thinking, how about we go for a long walk tomorrow?' Sophie said at bedtime. 'Maybe Hamsterley Forest. Or Roseberry Topping. We could take Rodney.'

Caitlyn's eyes widened with an even better idea. 'Can we go for an ice cream after?'

'If you like.'

'Okay.' Caitlyn stood up and kissed Sophie on the cheek. 'Night, Mam.'

'Night, chicken. Love you.'

'Love you too.'

Sophie went through to the kitchen then, to take some ibuprofen with a glass of water. She leant against the counter and listened, already feeling anxious about what the night might bring. There were a few muffled bangs next door, but no party. Yet. Which could only be a bad thing. It meant that Darren and Tina, her neighbours, would probably kick off in the small hours and party right through into Sunday, with their shit music blaring and their idiot friends hollering. Caitlyn's room, thankfully, adjoined Jean and Barry's house, the old couple on the other side of them, so she didn't get disturbed too often by Darren and Tina's antisocial behaviour – unless they were having a particularly wild bender that spilled out into the street. Sophie had called the police on several occasions about the noise and disturbance the younger couple caused, but the police never seemed to do anything about it and, if anything, all this seemed to do was goad Darren and Tina into being even more obnoxious and difficult. Living next door to them had become a nightmare.

Sophie had been renting the house for five years. She'd always enjoyed living in the street. That is, until Darren and Tina had moved in six months ago. At first she'd resolved not to be chased from her home, but as the weeks went by and it became apparent that nothing would ever get resolved, she'd begun to think about handing the lease notice in to her landlord and looking for a new home. She was about done with living next door to people who had no work ethic or sense of community. Darren and Tina didn't have the slightest bit of respect or empathy for their fellow residents. They were the obnoxious type of people who would metaphorically shit on their own doorstep and feel a sense of malicious glee about it, if only for the sheer vindictive thrill of knowing they were causing misery to others round about. There was no reasoning with people of that calibre, Sophie knew. And, most importantly, she didn't want Caitlyn being around such dregs of society.

She went to bed and lay on her right side, to keep the pressure off the left side of her head. All was still uneventful next door, but the quietness was threatening in nature and loaded with menace, as though it would break at any moment, making way for hours of psychological torment. Sophie scrunched her eyes shut and hoped for a good night's sleep.

As it was, she fell asleep pretty quickly and landed in a dream where she and Gareth were arguing. About Caitlyn.

'You're not taking her away from me,' she told him.

'I'll do what the hell I like,' he shouted back. 'I'm Gareth Holmesworth!'

Sophie's waking self tried to object. She fought with the sheets till they snaked around her legs, constricting and tightening, but didn't wake up.

'She's all I have,' Sophie screamed. Curling her fists, she had an overwhelming urge to punch Gareth in the mouth. To shut him up. Such feral anger was channelling through her she found it hard to contain.

'It doesn't matter anyway,' he said. His face, which by now she'd grown to despise, was too much in her space. 'Because it's nearly time.'

'Time for what?'

And suddenly Gareth wasn't Gareth anymore, he was Ronnie Cribbins, his pointed face right in hers. She could feel his breath on her skin. Could smell its cigarette stench. He was too close. Much too close. 'To pay for what you've done,' he crooned. His voice was scratchy and mean, and just as frightening as she remembered it. 'I'm going to destroy you, bit by bit. Slowly. Painfully. Piece by piece. I'm going to make you suffer.'

Sophie woke up, choking on fear, and immediately was aware that something wasn't right. She could hear ringing elsewhere in the house. Bells sounding in an unhurried, persistent clangour. Like a clock's jingle that leads up to an hourly chime. Only, there weren't any chiming clocks in the house.

*Next door. It's just next door.*

But no, it couldn't be. There was no drunken clamour pumping through the walls. Darren and Tina mustn't be home. It was the first Saturday night in months that Sophie wasn't being subjected to rave music and senseless arguments. Strangely, the melodious ringing of bells seemed somehow worse. The dainty tune was haunting. Imperceptibly sinister because it had no place inside her home. When the jingling reached a finale, the mysterious clock began to chime. Sophie sat up.

*One.*

She reached over and switched on the bedside lamp.

*Two.*

A shock of light lit the room.

*Three.*

The clock fell silent after the third and final strike.

Pain ripped up the left side of Sophie's head; a crawling, stabbing sensation that forced her eyes closed.

*Owww!*

She touched her head. It hurt. A lot. At the contact of her fingers, the skin on the left side of her scalp tingled in a creeping, hurting wave that reached a crescendo of agony at the top of her head, then exploded inside her skull in a blinding headache, which only subsided after a minute or so of pulsating heat.

*Shit!*

She didn't dare touch her head again. Had never experienced pain like it before. She wondered if she might have contracted some weird cold virus from someone at her dad's party. But then, could a virus affect just one half of the head? She didn't know. She couldn't even determine if the pain was being caused internally or externally, only that it made her eyes hot with pain as her flesh crawled beneath a million fiery pins before it felt like her brain was being doused in acid.

Lying back down, on her right side, Sophie fumbled with the lamp to make everything black again. But silvery light seeped above the curtains from the streetlight outside the house, making it less than the dark sanctuary she'd hoped for and allowing too many shadows to dwell in the corners of the room. She thought about the ghostly girl she'd seen the previous night.

*Don't let him keep me.*

*Don't!*

Sophie kept her eyes open, searching the depths of shadows, watching for movement within them. Watching for shapes. Human-like ones. The sound of the chiming clock lingered in her head. The quietness of the house held onto the memory of it and threatened Sophie with something; a warning that was terribly real but unclear. Her pulse quickened. There was a noise out on the landing. Floorboards creaking. Feet barely crunching carpet.

*Caitlyn.*

A soft whump over by the closed door made Sophie stiffen. Someone was *inside* her room.

Had the ghost girl come back to share more cryptic knowledge?

*He hid them. He hid them all away.*

For a fleeting moment Sophie believed this might be true, but then she remembered the dressing gown that was hanging on the back of the door.

*That's all it was, the dressing gown falling to the floor.*

She peeked over her shoulder and saw that the dressing gown was still on its hook. The black shape of it, right there. Like the silhouette of a long, thin person, taunting her logical reasoning.

'Caitlyn?' Sophie's voice was a ragged whisper and the shadows devoured the sound of it before it reached the door. Sitting up and gripping the duvet to her chest, as though it might protect her from whatever the shadows held, Sophie raised her voice. 'Caitlyn, is that you? Are you up?'

No answer.

Sophie's skin prickled with gooseflesh. She stared at the dressing gown, cursing it for being in its rightful place and not on the floor. Because the fact it wasn't on the floor meant that something else had made the noise. Her senses were alert to danger. Her heart was thumping. Her mouth was dry. Then it moved. The dressing gown moved! Not just a quick shiver that could be blamed on a draft, it leapt across the wall and merged with the shadows in front of the wardrobe at the foot of the bed.

There *was* someone in the room with her.

*Oh God.*

And Sophie could now hear the rasping, grating breaths of someone watching her from the blackness. Right there. So close. She was aware of a new smell too; the stale stink of cigarettes. Reaching out for the bedside lamp, her fingers scrabbled around the metal base and her bare skin tightened defensively against the darkness, which she expected might bite her. Something unseen scraped the nerves between her scalp and skull till all the blackness behind her eyes became white. Then her fingers found the lamp's switch and the room became white. Sophie saw there was no one near the wardrobe. The room was as it should be. Except, her dressing gown was a crumpled mound on the floor by the door. She had heard it fall after all. So what had she seen? The tall, thin shape.

A trick of the light?

*Yes.*

A car going past outside? Its headlights playing a shadow game on the walls.

*Without a doubt.*

Yet, somehow Sophie knew this wasn't true. The light from the lamp offered no real feeling of security, it merely highlighted all that was wrong with the night by hiding all that dwelt in the dark. She had a feeling she knew who'd paid her a visit. But she didn't dare speak his name.

# 7

# Remember Me?

'Dermatitis.'

Sophie frowned. 'Really? That's what you think?'

Dr Bramwell was a short man with wiry grey hair and a grandfatherly countenance. He was wearing wool trousers and a matching jacket, both of which looked scratchy and were the same colour as a long since retired bird's nest. His white shirt was buttoned up to the throat with a septic-green tie knotted at the stiff-looking collar. He was standing to Sophie's left, riffling through her hair with his stubby fingers, emitting a faint smell of Wright's antiseptic soap.

'Yes.' He breathed heavily through his nostrils. 'There's a patch of flaky skin here.' He poked her scalp. 'Have you changed your shampoo lately?'

'Er, no.' Sophie winced at the wave of pain his finger caused, struggling with his conclusion. 'I haven't done anything differently.'

'You must have,' he assured her, his tone nothing but condescending.

Sophie gritted her teeth. 'Can dermatitis cause a headache? I mean, this really hurts and the skin's sort of numb. It's hard to explain.'

'The skin looks a little inflamed.'

*Because you've been prodding it for the past five bloody minutes.* Sophie gnawed the inside of her bottom lip, frustrated. 'It's just, I dunno, it sounds unlikely.'

'I think it'd be worth investing in some anti-dandruff shampoo,' Dr Bramwell said, dismissing what she'd just said with a flippant hand gesture. 'Head & Shoulders.

See how you get on with that.'

Sophie huffed, not at all convinced. 'Okay, I'll try it. But, is it normal for dermatitis to affect just one half of the head?' she said, trying one more time to persuade him that he might be wrong. 'I would have thought my whole scalp would be irritated if that was the case.'

Dr Bramwell shrugged and trudged back to his seat behind the large oak desk that looked very headmaster-ish. 'It's certainly unusual,' he said, with an exhalation that marked some level of mild impatience at her persistence in questioning his better judgement. 'But maybe it'll spread to the other side given time. Try the shampoo and see how you get on. If no better in a week or two, by all means come back.' He squirted hand sanitiser on his hands, rubbed them together, then started pecking at the keys of his keyboard with both forefingers, adding 'suspected dermatitis' to Sophie's medical records.

When Dr Bramwell made no further eye contact, Sophie took it as a sign that he was done talking. She stood up to leave, feeling as though she'd been brushed aside. His diagnosis seemed like a random shot in the dark, but he'd made his decision and that was that.

*Dermatitis.*

Instinctively, Sophie knew he was wrong, but what could she do? Consult Dr Google? She could, she supposed, but what would be the point? In contrast, Dr Google would probably try to convince her that she had a brain-eating parasite laid by some tropical fly that had arrived in the UK in the bunch of bananas she'd bought from the supermarket last week. She was always dubious about stuff on the internet, after all it was a vast open playing field for scaremongers, trolls and Billy Bullshitters. Dr Bramwell's dermatitis diagnosis sounded a lot less scary, but the way her head felt made Dr Google's brain-eating parasite *feel* more likely. She'd do well not to resort to self-diagnosis.

After coming out of Dr Bramwell's surgery, she went straight to the chemist for a large box of ibuprofen and a bottle of Head & Shoulders, then drove to work. Summer was yet to materialise and everything seemed so cheerless. A cold northerly wind had seen to it that she'd put on her autumn coat that morning, and a steady downpour was making a grey day greyer. Even her headache felt grey. If she touched her head or moved it too quickly though, the headache flashed white with red edges, so she tried not to do either. She took an ibuprofen with some Coke that had been in the pocket of her car door for three days and was now flat, turned off the Clio's engine, and looked up at the council-owned building where she worked. It was a converted stone house on the high street, large enough to accommodate a fleet of social workers and admin staff, but awkward enough in layout to be deemed a quirky choice by the council. Its stone façade looked sombre in the rain. Sophie snatched her door pass off the passenger seat and hurried across the car park. Swiping herself in, she stood for a moment in the back entrance lobby and dashed rainwater from her black wool coat.

'Morning, Soph.' Dominic Williams, a fellow social worker, pushed through the admin office door and breezed past Sophie. He was a large man, in both appearance and presence. Probably in his late thirties. His face always looked flushed, like he was in a constant state of physical exertion, and he wore the same black cargo trousers more often than not. His aftershave was too medicinal in its heady notes; it wasn't unpleasant, but nor was it particularly nice. 'Team meeting's not for another twenty minutes,' he said. 'Bronwyn's running late.'

'Enough time to make a cuppa in that case,' Sophie pointed out.

'My thought exactly.'

Sophie followed him up the rickety steps to the small kitchen on the first floor. 'Have you had any news on the college funding for Freddy Wallis yet?' she asked as they entered the galley space.

'Nah, not yet.' Dominic filled the kettle at the sink then flicked it on. 'I've got to go and see him sometime this week, it'd be nice if I had some good news to take.' He took two mugs from the cupboard and set about preparing Sophie's tea along with his own. 'How're things with you?' His dark eyes flicked over to her as she removed her coat.

Sophie blew out her cheeks. 'Oh you know, rushed off my feet.'

He grinned; his teeth were yellow from too much tea and coffee consumption. 'There'd be something wrong if you weren't.'

The kettle started to steam.

'Too true, Dom. Too true.' But today, especially, Sophie wished it wasn't so. She had a busy day ahead, as ever, and her bad head made her cower inwardly at the thought. The team meeting would be followed by a one to one with her manager, Bronwyn, concerning the Charlie and Christabel Abbott case. It had come to light in recent days that Charlie Abbott, a teenager with autism and ADHD, had been physically abusing his little sister Christabel, who was also on the autistic spectrum, to the point that she'd had to move out of the familial home and into her grandparents' house. The Abbott mother, a single parent who was struggling to cope, was pointing the finger at Sophie, saying she should have picked up on the issue sooner. Also, the Abbott grandmother had the first stages of Alzheimer's, so solutions had to be found and put into place as a matter of urgency. A new file had been added to Sophie's caseload too: a little girl with muscular dystrophy had moved into the catchment area with her family. Sophie had arranged a home visit straight after lunch to make an initial introduction. Afterwards a meeting at St Thomas' School with the Head of Year was scheduled in relation to one of her other kids securing a placement there, and finally a visit to Rosemount House, a local respite home where one of her newer kids, Violet Arlington, was staying for the first time. Sophie had to go and check that Violet's dietary requirements would be met and that she was settling in alright with the other kids, because she had a tendency to be overly bossy.

The kettle clicked and Dominic set about filling the two mugs with hot water. Subconsciously, Sophie moved her hand up to her head. Pain bubbled and swelled inside her skull with every movement she made. Grey then white, then back to grey. Dominic added milk to the tea and stirred, then handed one of the mugs over. His large hand was clamped around the hot circumference, so he offered the handle directly to Sophie.

'Cheers.' Sophie leaned across the counter and took it from him, trying not to grimace as her scalp spattered her brain with sharp shards of pain. Dominic seemed to notice and looked like he might say something, but then her mobile started to ring. Sophie took the phone out of her bag and looked at the screen. 'Sorry, Dom,' she said. 'Just gonna take this.'

The big man wafted a hand in the air and strode to the door with his cup of tea. 'No worries, see you in the meeting.'

She watched his broad back disappear down the stairs, the boards creaking greatly beneath his weight, and answered the phone. 'Hiya, Mam. What's up?'

'Nothing, pet,' Nora Harrington said. 'I just wondered how you got on at the doctor's.'

'Ah right. I've just got to work, so I'll have to keep it

short. Got a meeting soon.' Sophie took a sip of tea and looked at the clock on the wall. It was a cheap-looking white plastic thing and its minute hand always seemed to stammer. It was a small wonder it managed to maintain any level of accuracy. 'The doctor thinks it's dermatitis.'

'Dermatitis? Well that sounds like a load of old shite.'

'Hmmm.' Sophie smiled at her mother's choice of words, then winced when the clawing, burning pain from her scalp scattered glass into her brain again, grinding down into nerve and tissue. She tipped her head to the left, as if to relieve all weight and tension, then closed her eyes to ride out this latest wave.

'So what's the course of action?' her mother asked.

'Head & Shoulders.'

Her mother clicked her tongue. 'You should go to the walk-in centre, see what the doctor there says.'

'Yeah, maybe.' *Or maybe not.* Sophie didn't think she could muster the will to go and sit in the walk-in centre's waiting room for however long, then to be told to go and see her own GP. Which she'd already done.

'You should do,' her mother told her in that firm motherly way that all mothers seem to have mastered. 'Oh and guess what! Me and your dad are getting a new neighbour.'

'Oh?'

'Yes. I saw some bloke poking about in the garden yesterday, so I asked him what he was doing. He says he's renting it off some landlord who owns a load of properties up and down the country. He's foreign.'

'The landlord or the tenant?'

'Both, I think. The landlord's name sounded Indian and the new neighbour sounds Polish. His name's Piotr. He'll be moving in this weekend.'

'Bet that's who I heard snoring last weekend.'

'I doubt it, pet, he doesn't have the keys yet.'

'Must have been the landlord then.'

'I can't see why, he's in London. He didn't even come to see the house before he bought it, by all accounts. He'll have estate agents doing all the grunt work, I expect.'

'Well, whatever. I hope your new Polish neighbour's nice.'

'He certainly seemed it. Very polite and pleasant. He's a bit younger than you, I'd say. Late twenties maybe. Oh and by the way, Addy Adkins has been asking about you apparently.'

'*What?* Why?'

'Our Shaun told him you're single.'

Sophie rolled her eyes. 'Nice one, Shaun.'

'Remember what I said though, pet.'

'*Mam!* As if I'm bloody interested in Addy Adkins! It's not even funny.'

Nora laughed. 'It is a little bit. Anyway I'd better let you go.'

'Alright. Dad's still okay to pick Caitlyn up from school, isn't he?'

'Why wouldn't he be?'

'Just making sure.'

'See you later.'

'Yeah.' Sophie put her phone away and looked at the clock. Plenty of time for a quick visit to the loo. She left her tea and coat on the counter and dashed along the corridor. The first floor toilet was in a small, boxy room that had no window, but a fluorescent ceiling light made the space unnaturally bright. Sophie shut the heavy wooden door – an original Victorian feature – and locked the bolt. The extractor fan roared on the ceiling, its vents thick with moving cobwebs. Above the wash basin was a pine-framed mirror and looking back at Sophie was a woman who might as well have been a total stranger. Despite having the same dark hair and eyes, this other person's skin was sallow and her face was gaunt with sleeplessness and unfathomable illness, which marked her at least five years older than the real Sophie Harrington. Sophie sighed and undid her jeans, then squatted to pee. When she stood up again, pulling her jeans to her waist, the light went out, plunging the room in absolute darkness.

'Hey!' she called, above the noise of the extractor fan. 'I'm still in here!'

The room remained black; a noisy blackness that singled her out, filling her eyes and sticking to her skin like grease. She reached for the door and pounded on it with her knuckles.

'Hey, I said I'm still in here. Turn the light back on!'

Fumbling around, her fingers sliding over the grooves in the wooden panels of the door, she found the lock and tried to unbolt it. But the metal bar wouldn't budge. It was caught fast.

*Shit!*

Sophie's face flashed cold. The walls of the cramped room shuffled further inwards, threatening to crush her. She struck the door with the side of her balled fist and yelled, 'Is anyone out there? I'm locked inside!'

The extractor fan shut off and Sophie found herself enveloped in an eerie silence; a nerve-jangling collaboration with the darkness. The level of tension had risen and, just when she thought her heart couldn't beat any faster, there came a faint ringing of bells from somewhere further along the corridor. They were playing the exact same tune she'd heard in her bedroom over a week ago.

*Oh God.*

An unexpected dull whump against the door, as though someone had slumped against it, made Sophie jolt backwards. 'Hello? Is someone there?'

She heard breathing then. A ragged, hacking sound. Someone standing at the other side of the door, ignoring or enjoying her pleas.

'Can you turn on the light, please?' Sophie slapped the door with her palm, unsure if it was mostly anger or fear she felt towards whoever was out there. 'I'm locked in!'

In response, there was a harsh bark of laughter. A man's taunting jeer. Sophie's flesh tightened at the sound. Covering her mouth with a trembling hand, she stifled a sob. Then she listened in horror as whoever it was began to claw at the door; their nails scoring wood.

Someone was deliberately trying to scare her.

But who the hell would do such a thing?

That laugh. Those bells.

*Cribbins?*

Rattling the door handle up and down, her eyes still blind in the dark, she let herself go to hysteria and cried, 'Turn the fucking light on, dammit!'

Her fingers found the lock again and she strained to free the bolt, pulling at the small metal head till her nails bent and fingertips hurt.

*'Sophie.'* Someone breathed her name. The voice sounded distant, yet so close. Almost inside her head.

'Who's there?' Sophie dropped her arms and stood still, waiting and listening. Panting. Could hardly hear a thing above her own pulse. Then something touched her face. Long, probing fingers. *His* probing fingers. She leapt back in fright, losing her balance to the darkness. The backs of her legs collided with the toilet bowl and she fell sideways, almost landing on the floor. Gripping the rim of the sink, she righted herself, then touched her face where she'd felt his calloused, leathery fingers. She could smell him now too: old cigarette smoke. From somewhere within the same closed black confines, Cribbins laughed.

*Oh God!*

He was right behind her. Sophie sprang forward and banged her fists against the door in a renewed fit of frenzy. 'Let me out! Let me out!'

Straight away she felt his skeletal fingers tugging at her shirt. Groping. Pulling her back.

'No!' She thrust her elbows backwards. They met with nothing, yet still she could feel his dirty, creeping hands on her skin, beneath her shirt now, sliding up her bare torso. Gristly, cold flesh climbing higher and higher, till she thought she might pass out. Spinning round, ready to fight, Sophie felt his breath in her face; old, stale breath that belonged beneath the ground with the dead.

'Remember me, Sophie-cat?' he said.

Sophie flung her head back and screamed; a heart-stopping sound of unadulterated terror that momentarily bridged the gap between life and death.

'Is everything okay up there?' She heard Bronwyn, her manager, shouting. Then there were pounding footsteps on the rickety stairs.

Sophie grappled with the door's lock again and found the bolt slid open this time. She wrenched the door inwards and collapsed out into the dully lit corridor. Bronwyn and Dominic were rushing towards her. When they saw her, they came to a standstill just ahead and stared in horrified bewilderment.

'What's going on?' Bronwyn asked.

'Sorry, I got locked in.' Sophie was bent over, clutching her thighs and trying to catch her breath. 'Someone turned the light out and the lock got stuck.' When she saw that neither Bronwyn nor Dom was able to comprehend why she was in such a state about that, she thought to say, 'I'm really claustrophobic. Like, *really*.'

Bronwyn smiled, accepting this explanation, and brought a hand to her chest. Exhaling deeply, she said, 'You gave us all a bloody good scare, that's for sure.'

*Oh no, the scares were* all *mine.* Sophie managed a weak smile. Inside she was falling apart. Those hands.

That voice. That laugh. That breath.
  *Remember me, Sophie-cat?*
  *Yes.*
  Yes, she did.

# 8

# Angel

'Shingles.' Dr Kilburn at the walk-in centre was an attractive blonde with captivating blue eyes, nice teeth and a golden tinge to his five o' clock shade. 'That's what initially came to mind, given the symptoms you've described. *But* I can't see how it can be because you don't have a rash.'

'Could it be that the rash is yet to appear?' Sophie leaned forward, hopeful. She was desperate to attach a name and reason to whatever was going on with her head. It had been three days since she'd seen Dr Bramwell, her own GP, and things had got worse. The crawling pain and numbness in her scalp had spread down to her left ear and jawline. She worried about how far it would travel and how long she'd have to endure the pain.

Dr Kilburn's mouth twisted to the side and he shook his head. 'Doubtful.'

Sophie sighed. 'So what now?'

Sitting straight-backed, like he'd never slouched a day in his life, Dr Kilburn's attention hadn't waned once. He'd listened to what she'd had to say so far, even expressing quiet bemusement at the dermatitis diagnosis dished out by Dr Bramwell, but Sophie could tell he wasn't about to give a firm alternative opinion of his own.

'Take co-codamol for the pain,' he said, with an assertive nod. 'You'll probably find they work better than what you've been taking already. You can only take them for up to three days, but hopefully whatever this is will start to resolve itself in that time. I mean...' He shrugged his shoulders. 'It could be that you have a viral infection.'

'Okay.' That sounded feasible. And sensible.

'The sensations you describe sound like you might have nerve damage. I suggest if you feel no better by next week, you make an appointment to see your own GP again. And if your headache worsens at all in the meantime, don't hesitate to make an emergency appointment.'

Dr Kilburn was showing more concern than Sophie had expected, which was troubling. How bad could a viral infection get? And what if it ravaged her entire left side? Viruses couldn't be combated with antibiotics, you had to just ride them out. And to what end? How long did viral infections last exactly?

*How long is a piece of string?*

And could they induce hallucinations? Ones where you imagined your dead neighbour's hands assaulting you in the dark?

When she left the walk-in centre, Sophie went to her car. She sank down in the driver's seat and closed her eyes.

*What the hell next?*

She was tired. So very tired. She'd only managed to get four hours sleep the night before, thanks to Darren and Tina's music that had pounded through the walls. She'd lain awake searching for alternative accommodation on a letting app on her phone. All of the nicer properties she'd found were a little out of her price range, however, and all those she could comfortably afford made her worry that she'd be jumping out of the frying pan and into the fire.

She hadn't bothered speaking to her parents about her nightmare neighbour situation. They'd only insist that she and Caitlyn move in with them. They had two spare bedrooms after all. But Sophie didn't feel that was an option. It would give Gareth more leverage with Caitlyn. He might say that Sophie was unable to take care of their daughter, and therefore decide to challenge her for full custody. This was not something that had been a problem so far, they'd always agreed that Caitlyn would stay with Sophie and visit Gareth as much as possible, but now that Gareth was moving to France Sophie couldn't rule anything out. She knew exactly what he was capable of. So the issue of Darren and Tina remained her problem, and hers alone.

She reached across and plucked the parking ticket from the dashboard, folded it, dropped it in the door pocket and took her mobile from her handbag. Scrolling through her contacts, she searched for Bronwyn's number. It had been her manager who'd insisted that she go to the walk-in centre straight after lunch, her will strengthened by the fact that most of the team had already passed comment that Sophie wasn't quite herself this week.

*Understatement of the year.*

Sophie rarely took time off work and wasn't comfortable about her illness impacting on her already busy schedule. She didn't have time to be sick. Needed to be better already. The entire world was busy and didn't stop for anyone. Least of all her. She held the phone to her ear, listening to the dialling tone, and watched as a carrier bag whipped along the pavement like it was on some sentient mission of its own. A gust of wind peppered the car with grit. Steely clouds moved fast above.

Bronwyn answered on the sixth ring and Sophie explained the situation – that she was still in medical limbo. Bronwyn asked if she was okay to work the rest of the afternoon or if she'd prefer to take a flyer. Sophie insisted that she would go, as planned, to Rosemount

House, where she was to see Carol-Anne Higgins, Rosemount's manager, about a potential new placement. She also needed to catch up with Angel Ditchburn, a ten-year-old girl with Down's, to see how she was getting on with her Rosemount buddy, nine-year-old Lucas Sumner, who also had Down's. Bronwyn said that was fine, as long as Sophie was sure. Sophie said she was. Really she just wanted to lie down.

The journey to Rosemount House took twenty minutes, including a stop-off at the chemist to get some co-codamol. Sophie pulled up behind a silver Ford Focus at the front of the property.

Rosemount House was a whitewashed stone manor house on the outskirts of Durham. It was upwards of one hundred years old and foreboding in appearance. Inside wasn't much better. Staff had worked hard to make it a place of cheer and spaciousness for the kids, using pictures and bright colours on walls and doors to promote a feeling of vibrancy. But long, narrow corridors, too many closed off rooms and not enough windows made for a subdued atmosphere and a dismal first, second and probably forever impression. It was a house redolent of maturity and soured with age, which promised never to accept anything youthful thrown at it. Unless it was razed to the ground and built from scratch.

Checking for traffic in the side mirror before opening the door, Sophie braced herself for a blast of wind as she got out of the car. The hem of her cardigan slapped against her thighs and the wind thrashed her hair about and delved in and around the neckline of her dress, touching her skin with icy cold fingers. Shuddering, Sophie pulled her cardigan tight about her and scurried up the path to Rosemount House, trying to avoid thorny rose bushes that reached out to snag her tights.

Rosemount's doorbell trilled and sounded like a warning rather than a jingle of alacrity. One of the resident care workers, Rosalind Hughes, a large greying lady with hairy forearms, answered the door and let Sophie in. After some light banter in the chilly porch, which smelled of dead plants, Rosalind told Sophie she'd find Angel Ditchburn upstairs.

Sophie went up and found the little girl in the third bedroom on the left, unpacking an overnight bag.

'Hey, chicken,' Sophie said, standing in the doorway.

Angel looked round, a contagious grin brightening her face. She was cherubic with soft blonde hair and big blue eyes and Sophie thought, not for the first time, that the girl's name was well suited.

'Hey, chicken,' Angel said, adopting her usual tone of mimicry, like she was playing at being ten going on thirty.

'How's things?'

'Alright.' Angel held up a pair of cream fleecy pyjamas with pastel bunnies on. 'Look what I've got.'

'Oo check you out with your fancy schmancy jamas.' Sophie made an impressed face, causing Angel to blush and giggle.

'I can find out where my mam got them from if you like,' Angel offered. Again with such attempted maturity.

'That's okay, chicken. I wouldn't look nearly half as nice as you do in them.'

Again Angel giggled.

Sophie turned her head and glanced along the landing, certain she'd heard floorboards creaking. 'Is Lucas here yet?'

'Don't fink so.' Angel placed the pyjamas beneath her pillow.

'Oh well, I'm sure he will be soon. Rosalind says she's making pizza for tea. Sound good?'

'Will it be ham and pineapple?'

'Yack! I don't know, you'll have to ask Rosalind.'

There were sturdy footsteps on the stairs then and Sophie heard Carol-Anne Higgins calling out to her. She stepped back out onto the landing and waved.

'Oh there you are,' Carol-Anne said, with a wave of her own. 'Rosalind said you'd arrived.'

'About five minutes ago,' Sophie said, checking her watch but not really registering the time. 'Full of busy?'

Carol-Anne nodded, presenting a weary expression as some sort of validation. She always exuded a constant state of busyness that verged on flustered, but never quite crossed the line. She was an attractive woman, probably in her late forties, but never seemed to reach her full potential of head-turning beauty. She always looked unbrushed and unironed. Seldom did her clothes coordinate and they often looked bitty and her darks like they'd been through the wash with a stray hanky. But there was something spontaneous and devil-may-care about her that struck a chord with Sophie and anyone else who met her. The manager of Rosemount House had an addictive personality.

'Absolutely snowed under with paperwork,' Carol-Anne said. Drawing close, she touched Sophie's arm with a familiarity that spoke of easy rapport and winked. 'But I can spare some time to show you the new sensory room if you like.'

'Absolutely!' Sophie turned to Angel. 'I'll be back with you in a tick, chicken.'

She followed Carol-Anne downstairs and through the rabbit warren corridors of Rosemount House to the sensory room, which was located in the annex to the rear of the building. The last time Sophie had been in the sensory room it had been tired and in need of a serious upgrade, but now it smelled of fresh paint and new carpet. There was a whole range of colours softly glowing on the walls; light cast from various spotlights and floor-to-ceiling tubes that looked like enormous lava lamps. A new purple seating area had been installed along the back wall and a rectangular plush rug on the floor looked like polar bear pelt.

'Wow,' Sophie said. 'This is great.'

Carol-Anne's arms were folded over her chest. Having been the one who pushed for and oversaw the transformation, she brimmed with quiet pride. 'Worth the wait, eh?'

'Hell yes.'

At the front of the building, the entrance door banged shut. The sound reverberated through dingy corridors, straight to the sensory room. Then the clamour of new arrivals' voices and busy feet on old boards killed the otherwise brooding quiet of Rosemount House.

Carol-Anne looked startled. 'Crikey, I wasn't expecting Stuart back so soon.' She checked her watch and shook her head. 'But then, I hadn't realised it was this late.' She reached inside the sensory room and switched off the spotlights. 'Excuse me, will you?'

'Of course.' And Sophie was left alone, with the gentle ebb and flow of dim light from the floor lamps. Pink. Blue. Green. The calming iridescence reminded her of an aquarium she'd once visited, where jellyfish had pulsed and throbbed, radiating raw colour. She wandered inside the sensory room and sat down, leaning her head against the back wall. Purple. Yellow. Orange. Closing her eyes to steal a few moments of this ambient peacefulness, a sense of dread crept over Sophie with such alarming proximity, she snapped her eyes open again and looked about. Suddenly fearful of the black spaces in the room, she knew she wasn't alone. Even though she couldn't see anyone, she had an insurmountable feeling of being watched. Thinking back to earlier in the week when Cribbins had assaulted her at work, in the dark, she folded her arms to cover her chest: it was a conscious effort that made her even more unnerved due to the fact she was mindful of the reason she'd done it. He'd tried to grope her. He might try again.

And what was that?

A faint smell of stale cigarette smoke?

*So what?*

Carol-Anne was a smoker. She was being overly paranoid.

But then, a long thin shadow to the left of the door caught Sophie's eye. Logically, she knew it was just a dark outline cast from one of the floor lamps, but logic no longer applied. Not after what had happened to her recently. Now, more than ever, she was afraid of being trapped in the dark. Her body became so rigid her limbs ached. And her brain seared with red pain.

It was Cribbins. She was being stalked by the spirit of Ronnie Cribbins. He was terrorising her with shocking unambiguity. Those hands. That voice.

*Remember me, Sophie-cat?*

Sophie had never been a believer in the spirit world. Had never believed in much at all in fact, aside from human decency. Or indecency, as is so often the case. But now she was being forced to reconsider. And if Cribbins existed, then what about the ghostly girl she'd seen in her old room?

*Don't let him keep me.*

Could she be real? Or could it be that Sophie was simply losing her mind?

No. She felt threatened. Something otherworldly had attached itself to her. She could sense it, just like that indefinable sense of death that looms in the air after a tragic accident. An unseen, impalpable thing, but there all the same. Real enough to make the hair follicles all over your body tingle. She could feel it right now. There in the room. And there was a new sound now too. Bells ringing. Faintly. Somewhere else, within the labyrinthine innards of Rosemount House.

*Oh God.*

Each terrifying Cribbins episode seemed to be heralded by bells. It could be no coincidence. But what was their purpose? Were they intended as additional torment? To crank her panic up a notch. Or were they a warning issued by some third party? The ghostly girl, perhaps.

*He hid them. He hid them all away.*

Sophie pushed herself up. Needed to get out. But her fear transcended into a new gulf of terror and she became paralysed, frozen to the spot, when she felt that someone she couldn't see was standing right next to her. Invisible hands hovered over her bare skin, teasing baby-fine hairs with invasive strokes. And that smell. It was stronger now. Stale cigarette smoke mingled with a strong reek of dampness. Like when clothes haven't been properly dried or a leaky caravan has sat all winter in cold dankness.

Sophie couldn't move or make any noise. She wanted to ask Cribbins what he wanted and why he was plaguing her like this, but the words were frozen thoughts, her mouth unable to transmit them. She felt his fingers in her hair, a quick stroke that infuriated the damaged nerves of her scalp, making her whimper. Then the shadow by the door moved; a very subtle change of position, but a definite one nonetheless. It was as though Cribbins could be anywhere and everywhere all at once. A thought too frightening to comprehend.

'It's good to see you again, Sophie-cat.' His words, imagined or not, were spoken aloud inside her head. Sophie suppressed a cry at this new intrusion, this violation of her headspace. 'The things I'm going to do to you, you'll wish you were never born.'

Goaded into action, Sophie jumped to her feet and fled from the sensory room. She expected the door might slam shut before she got to it, but it didn't. Cribbins let her go.

In the annex, insipid grey daylight leached in through the glass-roofed ceiling, but it did nothing to lift the sense of threat Sophie felt. She panted, grasping the doorframe to steady herself, and looked about, searching for shadows. There weren't any. But further down the corridor, standing in the pale gloom of lemon walls and green carpet, was Angel Ditchburn. Watching her.

'Hey, chicken,' Sophie said, straightening up and forcing a smile. 'Is everything okay?'

Angel shook her head. 'Will you tell him to go away, please? I don't like him.'

'Lucas?'

'No.' Slowly, Angel cast a wary glance over her shoulder. Then lowering her voice, so it was barely more than a whisper, she said, 'The tall, spiky man.'

Every hair on Sophie's body reacted defensively, but she tried to appear nonchalant. 'I don't know who you mean, chicken.'

'Yes, you do,' Angel insisted. 'He's the one you came wiv today. You left him wiv me when you came down here wiv Carol-Anne. He smells funny and I don't want him in my room again.'

The little girl's words took the edge off the co-codamol Sophie had taken earlier; her scalp and ear burned with white hot needles.

*He's the one you came wiv today.*

Angel had to be mistaken. Surely she hadn't seen Cribbins too? She must be confusing a television character with real-life or had seen someone passing by outside, someone she didn't like the look of. Or maybe it was something that Lucas had said to her, because he must have arrived by now. That had to be it.

But Sophie was making excuses and she knew it. She knew exactly who the tall, spiky man was. And Angel's validation made him all the more real. His threat all the more frightening.

*Remember me, Sophie-cat? The things I'm going to do to you, you'll wish you were never born.*

# 9

# Piotr

Piotr Kamiński stood alone in the sitting room of his new home. He could hear the muffled murmur of voices coming from whatever programme or film was on next door's television. It was a comforting background noise, rather than a nuisance, in that it made him feel not *quite* so alone. It reminded him that a layer of bricks was all that separated him from other people who were doing normal stuff, getting on with life.

He'd managed to get the keys to the house two days early, so that he could get settled in before his first twelve-hour shift started on Monday night. He was completely new to the area. Nobody at all knew him. Well, nobody except Nora Harrington, the lady next door. When he'd pulled onto the drive in his Ford Focus, she'd come out of her house and offered to help him unload his boxes and bags from the boot. He'd felt a little embarrassed about his lack of material possessions, but if she'd judged him on it, he hadn't picked up any vibes of condemnation or disparagement. In fact, if anything he'd sensed there was a compassionate streak in Nora Harrington, like she was one of life's carers who would give her last pound coin to someone in need. He saw in her the type of woman who, most likely, enjoyed fussing over and selflessly helping those she deemed vulnerable.

Was Piotr Kamiński vulnerable?

Yes, in a way, he could see why she'd think so.

She'd come inside with him, into the sitting room, and openly looked about the place. Probably a touch of nosy curiosity breaking the surface of her genuine desire to help. Just last week the landlord, Mr Chaudhary, had contracted decorators to freshen up the paintwork and furnish the house throughout with practical key pieces from IKEA. Nora Harrington had expressed her pleasant surprise and told Piotr four times that he had 'a lovely home.' Then before she'd left, she'd told him that should he need anything, he need only give her or her husband, Lenny, a knock.

Now that he was alone again, he felt a little anxious. The feeling of renewed anonymity was almost overwhelming. When the opportunity had arisen for him to transfer his job from Manchester to the company's factory unit in Peterlee, he'd jumped at the chance. This was his fifth move since he'd come to England six years ago. He'd spent a large chunk of that time in Manchester and had made some decent acquaintances there. Perhaps he'd have stuck around a little while longer if he and Zoe hadn't fallen out. But things were well and truly over between them and nothing tied him to Manchester now. The time to get moving was long overdue. Piotr felt that he couldn't settle in one place for too long. He got restless. And whenever he got restless, that's when he knew that Lucja would catch up with him.

Which was always a bad thing.

# 10

# The Other One

'Lyme's Disease.' Dr Costello regarded Sophie over the top of blue-framed Moschino glasses.

'Isn't that what you get off ticks?' Sophie asked, at her wits' end because this thing, whatever it was, was getting no better and now seriously impacted on her life. Aside from Darren and Tina's all-nighters, she wasn't sleeping properly because it was too uncomfortable to lie down, to put any pressure on her head, and it took all of her effort to go to work each day.

Dr Costello nodded. She was a middle-aged woman with dyed-blonde hair, an apparent fondness for statement jewellery and a keen manner. Sophie hadn't been able to get an appointment with Dr Bramwell, unless she'd wanted to wait two weeks, so had taken an available slot with the practice's locum.

'Have you been out walking in any woodland areas in the past few weeks?' Dr Costello asked, her teeth subtly yellow against magenta lipstick.

'Er, yeah. Possibly.' Sophie tried to recall where she and Caitlyn had taken Rodney lately, anywhere there might have been ticks. 'But, wouldn't I have noticed a tick bite?'

'Typically, yes.' Dr Costello didn't look entirely convinced with her own prognosis, but she seemed concerned enough to explore the idea. 'A bullseye rash, but it's not *always* the case. I think we should rule it out, just to be safe. On your way out, ask for an appointment to see the nurse for bloods. But also, I think we need to get you in for an MRI, to see what's going on.'

Sophie dreaded to think. She imagined an MRI would identify the ghostly hands of Ronnie Cribbins wrapped around her brain. Over the past few weeks he'd hijacked her life. She was constantly aware of him in thoughts and dreams. He tailed her like a second shadow. His displays of harassment had been sporadic, but lasting enough in their psychological trauma to ensure that she slept with the light on. And the only reason she clutched the idea that she wasn't all-out losing her mind was because of the description Angel Ditchburn had given. If the little girl at Rosemount House had seen 'the tall, spiky man', then surely that meant Cribbins' terror campaign wasn't an effect of some mental defect in Sophie. It was too much of a coincidence.

Wasn't it?

Sophie left the GP's surgery feeling marginally more positive than the last time. She was no further forward in being diagnosed, but at least now action was being taken. She went straight to the office and powered through several meetings and home visits, using energy pulled from reserves she hadn't realised she had. When her shift was done she went to her mam and dad's to pick up Caitlyn, then drove home.

As she reversed into a tight space in the back lane outside her house, Sophie noticed Patricia Boyce, two doors down, taking washing in. Patricia was friendly enough, but Sophie knew to be cautious around her since she was also the street's busybody.

She was wearing a leopard print dressing gown over tartan pyjamas, and her burgundy hair was scraped up and secured with a large black crocodile clip. When she turned and saw Sophie, she hurried to the gate, waved and beckoned to her. Sophie gritted her teeth and groaned.

*What now?*

Patricia was Darren and Tina's direct neighbour on the

other side, so Sophie had a feeling that's what she wanted to talk about. Handing the door key to Caitlyn, Sophie told her to go inside then hauled herself over to Patricia's back gate.

'Police were here earlier.' Patricia kept her cigarette-hardened voice low and she made reproachful eyes at Darren and Tina's kitchen extension, which backed onto her yard.

'What happened?' Sophie glanced into Darren and Tina's yard and saw that their back door was boarded up.

'Drugs raid.' Patricia's eyes widened with the hint of undisclosed knowledge. 'Or so I thought.' She clutched at the pile of laundry that was slung over her shoulder. Her fingers, Sophie saw, were embellished with a mismatch of yellow gold and silver rings. 'They came and took the pair of them away in the back of a van.'

'Good,' Sophie felt inclined to say.

Patricia nodded and coughed into her hand. Loose phlegm rattled at the back of her throat. 'Aye, let's hope they lock them up and throw the key away.'

'We're not that lucky.'

'Well, between you and me, I think there's something bigger going on.' Patricia's eyes gleamed behind clumps of stiff spider-leg lashes. 'After the two of them had been taken away, three coppers came out the house with a computer and two laptops. They took the lot.'

'Wonder what that was about.'

Leaning in closer, so Sophie was able to smell fried food on her clothing, Patricia said, 'It's all speculation at the moment, but Bill Ringston reckons Darren's been trying it on with some fourteen-year-old girl. He reckons the girl's dad found some messages Darren had sent to her.'

'That's terrible,' Sophie said. 'If it's true, that is.'

'Too right, the dirty pig. Mind you, Tina must know

something about it, else why would they have taken her in as well?'

'I dunno. Maybe it was just a drugs raid.'

'Well, it'll not be long till the truth's out, I'm sure.'

'And in the meantime,' Sophie said, turning and edging away, needing to be away from such slanderous gossip. 'Let's hope *we* get a couple of quiet nights.'

'Yes, let's bloody well hope so.' Patricia made a face of shared sufferance. 'Oh and by the way, there was a bloke loitering about outside your house earlier. He was in your yard. Looked like he was up to no good.'

'Really? What did he look like?'

'Tall and thin. Scruffy looking really, with awful teeth.'

Sophie's face flashed cold and she felt light-headed.

*Cribbins?*

'Maybe he got the wrong yard and was meant to be next door though,' Patricia reasoned. 'He certainly looked like one of their crowd. Our Laura said she knew who he was, but I forgot what name she said.'

Sophie felt so relieved she was sure it must have shown on her face. If Patricia's daughter had recognised the man, then there was no way it could have been Cribbins. It must have been a case of wrong house after all.

As she walked to her own gate though, Patricia called after Sophie, 'Addy Adkins, that's him!'

*Fuck!*

What the hell did he want?

Sophie went inside and heated defrosted lasagne in the oven. She took an ibuprofen with a mouthful of water, then called Caitlyn down from her room.

'Got any homework for tomorrow?' Sophie said, setting two plates down on the dining table.

'Uh-huh.' Caitlyn took a seat, her grey eyes awash with quiet excitement.

'Need a hand with it?' Sophie sat opposite, intrigued by what homework could be the cause of such enthusiasm.

'It's okay, I can do it myself. I have to write a story about an adventure.'

Sophie smiled. 'Sounds fun. Any ideas what you'll write about?'

'Uh-huh. Skiing in France.'

Sophie bristled, but tried to maintain a smile of encouragement. It was an effort that ached her face and felt more like a grimace. Thankfully, Caitlyn didn't seem to notice. 'With your dad, you mean?'

'Uh-huh. He's going over there soon, to look at a place.'

So Gareth had found somewhere he was interested in. Did that mean things were about to start moving quickly? Sophie took her time chewing on a mouthful of pasta. She felt her nerves become tangled. 'How do you feel about your dad moving to France?'

Caitlyn shrugged like it was no big deal, but grinned widely. 'It's pretty cool, I suppose. I mean, it's not that far away, is it?'

Sophie felt a new flash of annoyance at Gareth. She didn't think Caitlyn understood the implications of what his move would mean. She was due to start comprehensive school in September. It was a pretty important year for her, a big transition to make, therefore she could do without the turmoil of her dad upping sticks and leaving. Moving to a foreign country when she was so used to seeing him every week. So far Caitlyn had always done well academically, but Sophie had to wonder if this disruption to her routine would send her off the rails.

'I suppose that depends whereabouts he moves to,' Sophie said.

'A place called Morzine, in the French Alps. It's only

a two-hour flight from Newcastle to Geneva.'

'But Geneva's in Switzerland.'

'I know.' Caitlyn nodded, her eyes downcast as she scooped more lasagne onto her fork. 'Morzine is just over an hour's drive from Geneva airport though.'

'Wow, you seem to know a lot about this.'

Caitlyn smiled. 'It's all Dad talks about.'

'I'm guessing he's pretty serious about it then?'

'Definitely.'

'And what about Andrea? Is she looking forward to moving to France?'

Caitlyn gave a noncommittal shrug. 'Dunno. I think so.'

'How about Olly and Niamh?'

'Yeah, they can't wait. They've been going for skiing lessons already. Dad says he's going to take me soon.'

Sophie smiled encouragingly, but ground her teeth. She was pleased for her daughter, happy to see her so excited, but she was cautious too, about how Gareth expected things to work. Would this newfound excitement of Caitlyn's turn to sadness and sullenness when she realised she'd see a lot less of her dad?

If she was honest, Sophie also felt a little bit jealous. Jealous that Gareth would be the one to provide Caitlyn with all of these new and exciting experiences. It made Sophie even more aware of her own less-than-ideal situation, thus highlighting all the ways in which she was failing their daughter. They lived in a rented two-bedroom terraced house with lousy neighbours, both of whom were drug users, perhaps even dealers. And one of them had a name that might or might not, depending on the validity of village hearsay, belong on some sex offenders register. A predator of young girls.

*Christ Almighty.*

As if their living situation wasn't bad enough, Sophie had been dragged into the middle of a shit storm at work, had some debilitating illness manifesting itself in scary ways and, whether it turned out she was losing her mind or not, she was pretty sure she was being stalked by the ghost of Ronnie Cribbins. And now Gareth was throwing this curve ball. Dying a little inside, she managed to say, 'That sounds great, chicken. I bet it'll be loads of fun.'

'I know. I can't wait.'

That night Sophie found it hard to sleep, even though she was physically exhausted and all was quiet next door. The lamp on the bedside table, a safety precaution against unwanted shadows, gave off an unobtrusive, warm honey glow, which should have had a calming effect. But Sophie lay there, mentally wired. Following her conversation with Caitlyn at the dinner table, she'd quietly fretted about Gareth all evening. Or, more pointedly, his intentions. Gareth Holmesworth was a difficult man. There was no give and take with him, he was only happy when a situation worked in his favour. He was fiercely competitive in all walks of life, to the point that Sophie had begun to think of herself as 'his challenge' when they'd been together. He was a self-confessed control freak. The kind of man who kissed with his eyes open. As their relationship had developed, he'd become increasingly stubborn and arrogant, like his opinion was the only opinion. And when challenged on this egotism of his, he had the capacity to be downright brutish. Leaving Gareth was something that Sophie still congratulated herself on, but the fact remained, he was the father of her daughter. And should this turn into a point-scoring battle, Sophie wasn't sure how well she'd fare.

It also bothered her that Addy Adkins, her cousin's reprobate friend, had been hanging around in the yard. Did he mean to burgle her, stalk her or ask her out? She didn't know which of these possibilities was worse.

When she did fall asleep, Sophie was in a state of restless anxiety, as was usual these days, and when she awoke again she knew it wasn't morning, because the room was gloating in too much darkness.

*Darkness!*

That meant someone had switched off the lamp. Lurching upright, Sophie reached across and groped for it in the dark. As she moved, pain ripped across her scalp and fear exploded inside her heart. When light filled the room again, she sat still, monitoring the room for shadows. She expected to hear bells, because something seemed off. Something was wrong.

*Addy Adkins?*

Could he have broken in?

No. There was a prickly vibe that could only be described as otherworldliness in the air, which teased her skin with malevolent intent.

*Cribbins?*

Yes. He was here. She could feel him. Lodged inside her. She shivered, imagining his long, probing fingers subtly working beneath her skin, caressing and groping muscle and tissue. Gooseflesh pricked up all over her body. She rubbed at her arms furiously, as if to rid herself of his phantom hands.

But then, there were no bells chiming. All was quiet. Was Cribbins changing the rules? Omitting to give her a courtesy warning. She sniffed the air, expecting to smell the familiar stink of old cigarettes, but the room had no definably different odour either.

'What do you want, Cribbins?' Her voice was a weak, frightened thing, which caused the unfriendliness of the room to strengthen. The lamp dimmed and shadows deepened. Swelling depravity moved within them, spilling out from behind the wardrobe, growing outwards from the corners of the room, and moving and breathing beneath the bed. 'Tell me.'

The lamp shut off; a temporary stutter which allowed the immoral darkness to absorb her for mere milliseconds before returning to its full brightness. As the shadows retreated again, Sophie found she was clutching the duvet so hard her fingers hurt. And the room had become cold. So very cold.

There was a noise downstairs. The door to the kitchen creaking on its hinges. A long drawn out sound, like deliberate taunting.

What new mental torment was this?

Sophie wanted to bury her head beneath the duvet and curl into a tight ball. But she couldn't do that. She needed to go downstairs and check there wasn't someone creeping about down there. She had to put Caitlyn's safety above her own fear of ghosts. Because what if someone really had broken in? What if Addy Adkins was inside their home?

Slipping out of bed, Sophie was mindful that the solid shadows beneath it might reach out and grab her ankles. She scurried away from the bed, out of arms' reach, but the imagined blackness of the sitting room, directly beneath, made the floorboards of the bedroom seem insubstantial against her feet. Like they might break apart beneath her weight, so the house could swallow her into its night time abyss of fear and doubt and the perversity of Cribbins' mind. Because, oh yes, she could sense him. Right there in the house. Feeding her anxieties.

*Remember me, Sophie-cat? The things I'm going to do to you, you'll wish you were never born.*

Out on the landing, Sophie paused outside Caitlyn's room. She folded her arms tightly across her chest and listened. Her daughter was gently snoring. Without switching the landing light on, Sophie turned and crept down the stairs, using the bannister to steady herself in the dark. At the bottom of the stairs she stood with her hand on the door to the sitting room. Sensing the considerable weight of the blackness behind it, she hardly dared to turn the handle. Her insides felt like a contracting mass of tight, wet knots, on top of which her heart pounded.

Was Cribbins in there? Right now? Waiting for her?

*Yes.*

There was a clicking noise behind the door. An organic sound of something moving, reacting to her being there. Like joints popping. Cartilage clicking. Connective tissue moving old limbs.

*Oh God, oh God, oh God, he's here.*

Everything fizzed black and white behind Sophie's eyes, she thought she might pass out and that her heart would rupture, because this was it, she *had* to confront him. She pushed open the door and faced the blackness, her pulse loud in her ears.

*Let's do this, you old bastard.*

The clicking noise instantly receded. Like a large spider scurrying back to its lair, Sophie saw a hunched, dark form dart away from her. It wasn't tall or thin enough to be Cribbins, or Addy Adkins, for that matter.

Grey light seeped in from the kitchen door, which was ajar. Sophie stood still, allowing her eyes to adjust to the dark. There were more clicking sounds. Synovial fluid bubbling and popping as though joints were being pulled apart. She detected movement in the corner of the room and saw the stooped and misshapen silhouette of someone standing there, watching her. Her hand glided across the skimmed wall till it found the light switch, then she smacked it down with her palm. The room was filled with harsh, mocking light. Mocking because there was no one else there. The room was empty. Just as it should be.

Something caught her eye, though. Something small. On the floor. Gleaming gold. Sophie crossed the room, tentatively, and bent to see. It was a wrapped butterscotch toffee, left there just for her.

# 11

## Real or Not?

'Possible demyelination.'

'What does that mean?' Sophie's shoulders were hunched. She fiddled with the straps of her handbag. Two weeks ago she'd had an MRI. Today she'd come for the results.

'That you'll need to be referred. You'll need to see a specialist.' Dr Costello was still scrolling through whatever document was showing on her screen. 'The report says there's an inflammatory disease, but I couldn't really speculate as to what that might mean.'

'Inflammatory disease?' Sophie sat forward, alarmed. *'In my head?'* This was going from bad to worse. 'Is this to do with Lymes Disease?'

Dr Costello clicked her mouse cursor a few times. 'No, your bloods came back negative.'

'So it's definitely not Lymes?'

'No.'

'But, surely you must have an idea of what else it could be?'

Dr Costello shook her head. Her face expressed a little too much pity, or something like it, however. 'Like I said, you'll need to see a neurologist.'

*Shit.*

Sophie left the surgery in a daze. It was after four, so she didn't bother going back to the office. Instead she went straight to pick Caitlyn up from her parents' house. The journey was an autopilot blur of other cars, white lines and obstacles she had to brake for and swerve past. The sun was shining, the sky was blue, but Sophie felt no cheer at all. She parked her Clio in front of her mam and dad's garage and when she got out she was immediately aware of Cribbins' house bearing down on her like an old nightmare. Her flesh prickled and intuition told her she was being watched. She felt what she could only describe as an attempted assault on her private thoughts.

*Hello, Sophie-cat.*

She paused at her parents' gate and stared at the downstairs window of the house next door, daring Cribbins to manifest there.

*What do you want from me?*

Someone coughed, startling Sophie from her thoughts. She turned and saw a man hunkered down on the other side of the fence, pulling weeds from the border. He was tall and slim with wavy auburn hair and the sort of pale skin that belonged to someone who didn't see a lot of sunshine. He watched her with open curiosity, his dark brown eyes underscored with purple flashes of tiredness.

Sophie blushed and offered him a cautious smile. 'Oh, er, hi.'

'Hello,' the man said; his voice heavily accented.

'It's a good day for a bit of gardening,' Sophie thought to say, before hurrying up the path. Already she was cringing at the lameness of the comment and feeling hugely embarrassed about having been caught gawping at his house. She opened the door to her parents' house, bundled inside, and left the man next door to his weeding and bemusement.

'How'd it go?' Nora Harrington was standing in the sitting room with an ironing board propped up in front of her and a pile of neatly pressed clothes balanced on the arm of the couch. Some property programme was on the television, documenting a smug middle-aged couple nosing about in a kitchen that looked bigger than the whole downstairs of Sophie's house.

'I've got to go and see a neurologist.'

'*What?*' Her mother put the iron down in its cradle and looked up in shock. 'When?'

Sophie shrugged. 'I dunno. Soon, I guess.' She didn't want to talk about what Dr Costello had said. Didn't want to talk about any of it. Not now. Not yet. 'Fancy a cuppa?' She went through to the kitchen and took two mugs from the cupboard, glad to be busying herself with a trivial task.

'Go on then,' her mother called after her. 'Caitlyn's over the allotment with your dad and Rodney. They've gone to dig up some carrots.'

When Sophie came back through to the sitting room, she set one mug down on a coaster on the coffee table and kept hold of the other. 'Is that your new neighbour out there?' she asked, going to the window to look out. She wanted to steer the conversation away from herself. Didn't want to utter the words 'inflammatory' or 'disease' within the parameters of any upcoming discussion. Didn't even want to think about what the hell demyelination might mean. Not yet. The uncertainties scared her too much.

'You mean Piotr? It will be.'

'He seems pleasant enough.'

'He is.'

Sophie moved away from the window and sat on the couch. 'He hasn't mentioned anything about any weird goings on or bumps in the night yet, has he?'

Nora gave her a curious look. 'Why on earth would he?'

'I dunno, just after what you said about Peggy Flannery. And Leanne Baxter. I was interested to know if he's had any spooky experiences yet.'

'I'm not sure he'd tell me even if he had. The poor lad's here all on his own, so I doubt he'd go mentioning stuff like that. I mean, when you're trying to settle into a place it's not going to score you many friends going round talking about ghosts is it?' Nora flashed Sophie a wry smile. 'But if you're so interested, why don't you go out and talk to him?'

'Because he'd think I'm a bloody mental case.' *If he doesn't already.*

'My point exactly.' Nora laughed.

'But, you know him already,' Sophie persisted. 'Sort of. You should definitely ask him.'

'I don't want to know about any spooks that live on the other side of my walls, thank you very much. And anyway, why the hell are you so interested? Cribbins was a bloody horrible man when he was alive, never mind...'

The back door clattered open and Rodney came racing through to the sitting room, tail wagging. Caitlyn followed shortly behind him. 'Look, Mam.' She showed a half eaten carrot to Sophie. 'Grandda gave me this.'

'And about twenty more,' Lenny Harrington said, joining them in the sitting room. 'She's eaten so many carrots, she'll be able to see in the bloody dark tonight.'

'You should have brought me some, in that case,' Sophie said before she could stop herself.

Caitlyn laughed and sat on the arm of the couch.

'We were just talking about our new neighbour,' Nora said.

Lenny eased himself down into his armchair. 'What's Polish Pete been up to now?'

'Dad!' Sophie said. 'You can't call him that.'

'Why not?'

'He's called Piotr. And you don't have to prefix his name with his nationality.'

Lenny shrugged, his expression perplexed. 'But he *is* from Poland.'

'I know, but that's neither here nor there, is it? Stephen Ainsworth's from South Africa originally, but you don't go round calling him South African Steve.'

Lenny laughed. 'No, but it's got a bloody good ring to it.'

Sophie narrowed her eyes in mild reproach and Nora shook her head.

'So what has Piotr been doing?' Lenny asked.

'Pulling weeds in his garden,' Sophie answered quickly, in order to steer the conversation away from next door's ghosts. The last thing she wanted was for Caitlyn to start having night terrors.

'Pulling weeds? Bloody hell, Nora,' Lenny said. 'Can a man not tend to his garden in peace? Leave the poor lad alone, will you?'

'I didn't know he *was* pulling weeds,' Nora admonished. 'It was our Soph, she wanted to know if...'

'Nothing. I didn't want to know anything.' Sophie jumped up and pushed Caitlyn to her feet. 'We'll be off now. You two can bicker between yourselves about Piotr's gardening habits as much as you like.' She made eyes at her mother and gestured to Caitlyn, giving a quick shake of her head. The less her daughter knew about Cribbins, the better.

Later that evening, after Caitlyn had gone to bed, Sophie watched television while trying to ignore the commotion next door. Since their run-in with the law, Darren and Tina had been a lot quieter, but their cockiness and noise levels were steadily increasing with each weekend that passed. Patricia Boyce had no new gossip about why the couple had been arrested, but someone had taken a spray can to the front of their house and scrawled the word 'PAEDO' in bold white letters in the space between their door and sitting room window. The jury was still out as to whether what Bill Ringston said was true or not.

A few seconds into a commercial break, Sophie's mobile started to ring. It was Gareth. She considered not answering, because she couldn't be bothered to deal with him. Not after the day she'd had. But she reminded herself that taking 'Gareth calls' was compulsory. They always concerned Caitlyn.

'Gareth? Is everything okay?'

'Yes.' He sounded sober and uptight. 'Are you having a party?'

'No, it's next door.'

'It's pretty loud.'

'It's Friday night.'

He was silent for a moment. 'How are you?'

'Fine.'

'Did you get your results?'

Sophie flinched. She hadn't told him about the MRI, never mind going for the results. Caitlyn must have. 'Er, yeah. Everything's fine.'

'Is it?' He sounded sceptical.

*Can't bullshit a bullshitter.* Sophie closed her eyes and rubbed her eyelids. 'Yes. So, about tomorrow. Are you picking Caitlyn up around eleven?'

'Yeah. We're gonna take her to Silksworth ski slope.'

'Okay.'

'But that's not what I'm calling about.'

'Oh?'

'I've found somewhere in France.'

'Caitlyn told me.'

'She did?'

'Yeah.'

'Well, there's a few things I need to get sorted here before we can move, but I'm hoping to get over there by the end of the year.'

'Um, okay?'

'And I'd like Caitlyn to come over for a while.'

'But, that's not possible.' Sophie's stomach turned to lead. 'She starts comprehensive school in September. It's a pretty big deal.' She heard him sigh; a haughty sound that stirred her anger.

'I'm well aware of that, Sophie,' he said, emphasising her name as though he was talking to a child. 'Calm down. I meant during the holidays.'

'The *Christmas* holidays?'

'Yes.'

Sophie was stunned. 'But…'

'But,' he cut in, 'it's Caitlyn's decision, of course. We can't make her do anything she doesn't want to.'

*Bastard!* He knew exactly what he was doing.

'Well, Christmas is a long way off yet,' Sophie said, suddenly needing to be off the phone. Her eyes had glazed over with tears of frustration and she didn't trust herself not to let them spill. 'Let's cross that bridge when we come to it, shall we?'

'Christmas will be here before you know it,' he told her. 'I was letting you know in advance, to keep you in the loop, so you know what to expect.'

*Bastard!*

Sophie went to bed even more miserable than she'd anticipated. Her head might be numb on the outside, but on the inside it was rammed with busy, painful black and red thoughts. Her heart kept an erratic pace with Darren and Tina's rave music.

*Can things get any more shit?*

She leaned across and switched the bedside lamp off, too angry to be scared. Then she stared at the dark ceiling. Every now and then she would check the shadows in front of the wardrobe, daring Cribbins to come. She wanted him to materialise, because she was consumed by a new idea that he was merely a cause and effect of her anxiety. Cribbins equated to stress.

Eventually she saw movement; a long stretch of black within the folds of darkness.

*The tall, spiky man.*

Sophie sat up, drawing courage from the music that

pounded against the walls behind her headboard, and continued to watch as his definitively black shape shifted.

'Didn't hear you coming this time,' she said. 'Not with all that racket next door.'

His long, thin body disconnected itself from the shadows of the wardrobe and he stepped forth so that he was standing independently, at the foot of the bed.

'Don't I get warning bells anymore?' Sophie was trembling with nervous anger.

There was a wet, grating noise, like laughter rasping from a mucous filled throat. It sounded so real it almost convinced her.

'I know it's not really you, Cribbins,' she said, adamantly. 'I don't believe in ghosts.'

He spread his long spindly arms outwards and began to skirt round the bed. Sophie heard his feet on the carpet and the suggestion of his gruff breaths, pumped up from shadow lungs that were buried somewhere within the centre of the blackness. Each exhalation rasped from his long-dead throat.

How could he *not* be real?

*Because he isn't.*

'You're all in my head,' Sophie insisted, her nerve faltering as he inched closer. 'You're a symptom of everything that's going on in my life, that's all. My illness. The stuff that's going on at work. Those two *dickheads* next door.' She thumped the wall behind her with the side of her fist. Sweat had beaded on her brow and upper lip. She felt feverish. Hysterical. Petrified. 'But most of all, you horrible old bastard, you're Gareth.'

Cribbins kept coming. Closer and closer. Taller and taller. Bearing down on her.

'But it's okay,' she said. 'You can take her for a week. That's all. That's all I'll let you have. A week *after*

Christmas.'

Cribbins was at Sophie's side now and she could smell the corruption on him; a meaty, rotten stench that mingled with old cigarette smoke. She held her breath and tried not to choke on it. He stooped over and his rank breath smothered her face. In that moment she wondered if she was wrong, that he was real, and almost didn't care if she lived or died.

'You're not really here,' she said, flattening herself against the headboard. She moved her head to one side, in an attempt to escape the phlegmy exhalations that were being directed at her face. 'You're not. You're *not*.' Her heartbeat was a frenzied pain in her chest and she squeezed the duvet even tighter in her fists as the darkness of him moved in even closer. Something wet touch her cheek. Cold and slimy, like a slug. She whimpered and closed her eyes, felt close to passing out. It was his tongue.

Sophie was paralysed, unable to move. Quietly hysterical. Cribbins' tongue, slick with saliva, slid over her skin, sticking to the contour of her face till it passed straight over her eyelid and meshed her lashes together. His breath was stinking. Rancid. His fingers, long bony digits covered in icy dead flesh, found her neck. Any sense of anger that lingered immediately left Sophie and was replaced with irrefutable fear like she'd never felt before.

'Oh the things I'm going to do to you,' he sighed into her ear, each word stinging the side of her face like ice burn.

'You're not real,' she sobbed, her eyes still closed.

He exhaled an amused cackle and the force of his breath was enough to move her hair. 'You'll pay for what you've done,' he said.

# 12

# Fresh Start

Piotr bagged the weeds then put them in his wheelie bin in the yard. There was still plenty of stuff he needed to do in the garden, but he'd caught the sun on his face and arms and didn't want to over do it. His armpits felt sticky and the back of his t-shirt was damp with sweat. He went inside to run a bath.

On his way upstairs, he heard voices next door. Nora Harrington and her daughter, Sophie. Piotr had seen Sophie many times before; she came on weekdays after work to pick up her young daughter. But today was the first time he'd met her face to face. The first time they'd spoken. He wasn't sure what to think of her. She always seemed flustered. Distracted. He wondered what demons chased her.

Nora had said that Sophie wasn't well, but Piotr had an instinctive feeling that it was more than illness that plagued her. Earlier when he'd looked up and found her staring at his house, he'd seen a conscious fearfulness in her eyes which made him think there was something about the house – *his* house – that scared her.

Nora had also said, several times, that her daughter was single. Sophie Harrington was older than Piotr, probably by about seven years. Not that that mattered. She was certainly an attractive woman, just too complicated for him to want to fathom. Too complicated for him full stop. Besides, he had no interest in pursuing any kind of relationship with anyone. He'd moved to Horden for a spell of anonymity and he wanted to keep things simple.

He'd adapted well to his new job. Had started an Open University course on accounting, which he studied during night shift to fill long, dead hours. And he'd settled into the house comfortably enough. It was an all round good base for this latest chapter of his life, he thought. A good place to live. So he'd do well to avoid new complications.

# 13

# Demyelination

It was two weeks since Sophie had seen Dr Conroy, the neurologist. He had agreed with whoever had written the initial MRI report that there was possible demyelination. After discussing her symptoms and running through a few physical tests – reflexes, skin pricks and heel-to-toe walking in a straight line – he'd said the best course of action was for Sophie to see him again in a few months' time and that a repeat MRI would be scheduled, to see how things were looking. As it was, Sophie thought things were calming down. Little by little she was regaining the feeling on the left side of her scalp, as well as her ear, and the pain had gone, more or less.

Before her appointment with Dr Conroy, Sophie had plucked up the courage to look up 'demyelination' online. Dr Google said it was the result of any condition that damaged the protective sheath around the nerve fibres of the brain and spinal cord. There were a few possible causes, but most online articles seemed to point at multiple sclerosis. Dr Conroy hadn't aired any specific views on the matters of demyelination, nor had he mentioned multiple sclerosis, so Sophie hadn't dared to ask. She wasn't sure she wanted him to verify it. Didn't want to make it so. The keyword in all of this, as far as she was concerned, was 'possible'. Nothing was a certainty. Her symptoms were easing, after three nightmarish months, and she was hopeful that whatever she'd had was some weird one-off viral infection.

Owing to her lessening symptoms, she was sleeping better. Especially now Darren and Tina were being quiet.

Some bloke called Loony Lewis had visited their house the weekend before last, forcing his way inside and taking a snooker cue to Darren. According to Patricia Boyce, Loony Lewis was a family friend of the fourteen-year-old girl who Darren had 'allegedly' tried it on with. Darren had lost a couple of teeth and gained a dislocated jaw and three cracked ribs in the attack. Since then, he and Tina had been lying low. There was even talk they might be moving. If that wasn't joyous enough, Sophie hadn't seen Cribbins in over a week. Not since he'd made his threat. *You'll pay for what you've done.* Things were definitely looking up.

But then Gareth called.

Sophie had just pulled into the supermarket car park after work when he rang.

'Sophie, just calling to let you know I've booked Caitlyn's flight to Geneva.'

'On Boxing Day?'

'Yes, as was agreed.' He sounded pissed off.

The previous week, Sophie had put her foot down, insisting that she should at least get to spend Christmas Day with their daughter before Gareth took her away. Especially since Caitlyn had spent Christmas Day at Gareth's house last year. Reluctantly, he'd agreed.

'For a week?'

'Twelve days.'

Sophie's jaw tightened. 'Okay.' There were still four months till Christmas. Four months for her to dwell on it. When the time came, it would be the longest stint she'd ever gone without seeing her daughter. Already she was dreading it. But what could she do?

*Suck it up.*

She got out of the car and trudged across the asphalt car park, her mood suddenly dark. Morose. The driver of a black 4x4 beeped at her when she stepped from the pedestrian zone without checking for oncoming traffic.

Jumping back, she waved in apology and allowed the vehicle to pass, then dashed the rest of the way to the trolley bay. As she rummaged in her purse for a pound coin, she was overcome by a sudden feeling of being watched; a paranoid inkling, daunting in its succinctness, which made her chest tighten and shoulders become tense. She turned and made eye contact with a stern-faced woman who was waiting to get a trolley. Sophie muttered an apology, popped a coin into the end trolley, pulled it free of the others and moved off. The trolley rattled over whatever response the other woman gave, but Sophie was too preoccupied to care, because she still had the deeply unsettling feeling of being watched. Despite the clamour and busyness all about her, she could sense an unseen voyeur. Threatening. Stealthy. Predatory. Whoever it was, their covert interest was preying on her vulnerabilities. Their invisible eyes following her every move. Sophie's skin tingled, as though the attention itself was profound enough to generate static electricity. She glanced over both shoulders, but couldn't see anyone watching.

Her trolley had a wayward front wheel and pulled too much to the right. She found it hard to keep it moving in a straight line, and on the way into the supermarket entrance, she clipped the edge of a shelving unit and sent a batch of fresh loaves flying in all directions. A middle-aged man in grey suit trousers and white trainers stopped to help her pick them up. By the time she was absorbed by the bright lights and general ruckus of the supermarket's interior, Sophie still had the uneasy feeling of being tracked. So much so, she could barely concentrate on anything else. As she entered the first aisle to the left, the areas ahead of and behind her were busy with shoppers, all of whom seemed to be minding their own business or chatting to one another. No one was showing any particular interest in her.

*You're being paranoid, Soph. It's Gareth, he's making you anxious again.*

She bent and picked up a pack of minced beef from the meat fridge. It looked like a rectangular wedge of brain matter sealed in plastic and, even though it was well within its 'use by' date, was discoloured at the edges and didn't look right.

*Demyelination.*

Feeling suddenly queasy, she put it back. Right next to the minced beef there was a stack of frying steak, presented on foam trays. Each strip of red meat looked like a slice of tongue, she thought. Dead tongues sliced from dead mouths. She thought about Cribbins' tongue on her face.

*You'll pay for what you've done.*

But what had she done? She didn't know. Was it her own anxiety that was forcing some sort of self blame for all the issues she was dealing with?

A cheery ringing of bells elsewhere in the supermarket made Sophie's breath catch. It was a different jingle to the one she'd come to dread, but she froze in terror nonetheless. Barely acknowledging an old man who complained she was in the way of the braising steak, she happened to look up. On the first floor balcony, in the homeware section, she saw a tall, thin figure duck out of view.

*Oh God, it's starting again. He's back.*

'Sophie? Sophie Harrington?'

Startled, Sophie turned and saw a woman with short pink hair regarding her with what she took to be pleasant surprise. Stuttering over names in her head, Sophie tried to place the woman's face. Eventually she said, 'Hey, Leanne.'

Leanne Baxter. What were the chances? The sheer coincidence that she should be here right now was absurd.

'Long time no see,' Leanne said, smiling.

Sophie saw that her top teeth were free from metal braces these days. She looked a lot older, her complexion too papery and creased to be complemented by the cerise pink of her hair, which used to be mid-brown and shiny. 'God, I know,' she said, nodding. 'I haven't seen you since you lived next door to my mam and dad.' And there it was, the perfect opportunity to ask Leanne Baxter about the house next door and its ghosts. Because if Leanne could verify that Cribbins was indeed real, then Sophie would know for sure she wasn't going crazy. 'It's funny bumping into you like this actually,' she said. 'I wouldn't mind having a quick word with you about something.'

Leanne's expression dulled and her shoulders became rigid. She looked almost defensive. Definitely suspicious. 'About what?'

'It's a bit random really.' Sophie wafted a hand in the air, to give the impression it was no big deal. 'Just, I was staying at my folks' the other weekend and we got to talking about the house next door.'

'What about it?' A fleeting fearfulness glinted in Leanne's eyes. Anyone else might not have noticed it, but Sophie did. It gave her hope. Hope that Leanne might have seen Cribbins.

'We'd heard that the house was meant to be haunted and I was just wondering, did anything ever happen to you in there?'

A dark-haired man with Celtic bands tattooed around his thick biceps bounded up behind Leanne. 'They don't have that offer on anymore,' he said. He was carrying two armfuls of alcohol: a crate of lager stacked on top of a crate of cider. He stopped and stared when he saw Sophie.

'Hi, Carl,' Sophie said, offering a polite smile.

He nodded in acknowledgement of the greeting, but

his eyes were hostile. Suspicious. But then, they always were. In all the time he'd lived next door to her parents, he'd never once spoken to Sophie voluntarily. Had always looked as though he'd rather chew on nettles than pass the time of day with her. Seldom had he spoken to Lenny or Nora either, so his unsociable manner wasn't reserved for Sophie alone.

'As I was saying,' Sophie said, returning her attention to Leanne.

But Leanne was quick to butt in, 'No, nothing ever did happen.' She shook her head, a little too adamantly for casualness, thus sparking Sophie's interest even more.

Carl eased the crates of alcohol into the trolley before Leanne, then looked between both women. 'What's this about?'

'Just the old house,' Leanne told him.

'What about it?'

Leanne looked to the floor.

'Oh nothing important,' Sophie said, trying to exude a certain coolness, to show Carl he didn't intimidate her – even though he was over six foot, built like a brick shithouse and most certainly did. 'There's a new neighbour in there now, that's all.'

'What's that got to do with us?'

'Well, nothing. I just mentioned it to Leanne in passing.'

'Didn't sound like it to me.' Carl's manner took on a more aggressive edge. He squared his shoulders, perhaps a subconscious effort to make himself look even bigger. 'Sounded to me like you were asking if anything had ever happened in there.'

'Seriously,' Sophie said, beginning to feel agitated, 'it really doesn't matter.'

'But it does,' he argued. 'I want to know what shit you're talking about that house.'

'Bloody hell, chill out, Carl.' Leanne reached out and

touched his arm. 'She was only asking if we'd ever had any bother there. She's looking out for the new neighbour, that's all.' She pushed her trolley forward and began to move off. 'Anyway, sorry, Soph,' she said, 'we've got people coming round for a barbecue in an hour, we'd better be off.'

Carl glared at Sophie some more before turning and following Leanne.

Sophie waited till they were out of sight before continuing down the meat aisle, unnerved by Carl's manner. At the end of the row, as she riffled through packs of unsmoked bacon, a feeling of unease washed over her again. Lifting her head, she looked about. Almost immediately her attention was drawn to the nearby escalator, where a tall, thin man, on his way to the ground floor, was watching her intently. No shame registered on his face when he saw that she saw him. In fact, he grinned and threw her a wink.

*Addy Adkins!*

# 14

# Torment

'You look tired.' Dominic Williams took a seat next to Sophie when the team meeting was done. His shirt sleeve brushed against her arm and his aftershave clung to her skin. 'Is everything okay?'

She turned to face him, unable to avoid his unwanted attention. Managing a minimal, close-lipped smile, she said, 'Yeah, thanks.'

'Is the Abbott case taking its toll?' Dom's dark blue eyes, which were small and narrow and not at all in proportion with his large, round face, were filled with something like concern.

'No.' Sophie rubbed her forehead. 'I mean, maybe. I suppose.' She wanted to be left alone. There were so many things that were causing her grief, none of which she wanted to discuss. 'There's still quite a bit left to sort out.'

Dom was regarding her a little too closely. All of Sophie's colleagues knew about the Abbott case and its complications, but they also knew Sophie was competent enough to deal with it, Dom included. Therefore, she guessed her answer must have reeked of bullshit, because he pressed his fingertips together and said, 'Is, er, everything okay at home?'

*Ugh.*

'Yes,' she said. Probably a little too quickly. 'Everything's fine.'

'And the MRI stuff?'

*Ah.*

Sophie didn't want to talk about that either, but Dom

had a determined look on his face. The type of hard resolve that indicated that since he'd detected a problem, he would get to the bottom of it come hell or high water.

'I'll be seeing the neurologist again in a couple of months, but I'm okay,' she said. 'Really. I'm feeling a lot better.' She nodded resolutely, to insist on closure of the matter, and shuffled back as if to stand. She was done talking.

But Dom wasn't. He swivelled his body, so he was completely facing her, giving the impression that he was intentionally blocking her exit with his bulk. 'So, do they know what it is yet?'

Within the confines of her head, Sophie groaned. She edged her chair back even further. 'Not really.' But when Dom carried on fixing her with the same staring, dogged intensity, she shrugged and said, 'Possible demyelination, apparently.'

'What's that?'

*A buzzword that's been forced into my vocabulary. A bit like Brexit. No one seems to know what it'll mean in the long term. Whether it'll turn out okay or be a complete fucking disaster.* She stood up, feeling lightheaded. Needing some air. Needing some space. 'I don't know, Dom.' *A random one-off or multiple sclerosis. Let's toss a coin, shall we? Heads, I win. Tails, I lose.* 'I really don't know.'

'Well, if there's anything I can do…'

'Look, Dom,' Sophie said, grabbing her handbag from the back of the chair and manoeuvring past him, with her back wedged against the wall. Her shirt made a swooshing sound as she slid along the plasterwork. 'I'm gonna take a flyer, okay? I'll see you tomorrow.' She walked off then, before he could quiz her about anything else. She wasn't sure she could take any more. It was like she was balancing on the cusp of some emotional wave that she'd been riding for too long, and she knew she was tiring fast. Anything at all might tip her over the edge. It was just a matter of time. And when that time came she'd rather she wasn't at work.

She dashed outside and bundled into her car, checking her mirrors and all around the car park for signs of Cribbins or Addy Adkins. Lately she'd become a nervous wreck. The interior of the car smelt of warm leather, because the upholstery had been basking in the sun all day. Sophie turned on the engine and cracked open the window.

Traffic was heavy at that time of the day and she almost witnessed an accident on Ropery Lane when someone pulled out too hastily onto the roundabout. As she entered Lumley New Road, with Lumley Castle to her left, the traffic eased and she got a sudden waft of cigarette smoke. The smell filled the car with such acridness that when it hit the back of her throat she fell into a coughing fit. Ill with fear, Sophie checked the rear view mirror, expecting to see Cribbins in the back of the car. He wasn't there. The back seat was empty. But she realised only then how cold it was. Despite the warmish air blowing in through the open window, her bare arms were pocked with goosebumps.

The radio crackled to life, making Sophie jump. Then just as quickly, it lost signal. About ten seconds later, music burst through the speakers and Nick Cave's deep voice was singing *Let The Bells Ring*. In a panic, Sophie fumbled with the dial, searching through the programmed stations for something else. All of the stations belted out white noise, till she was right back at that same, seemingly portentous, song about bells. With a sense of fearful repugnance over what the song might bring with it, Sophie hit the standby button. But the music went on. She tried to turn the volume down to mute, cranking the dial fully to the left, but nothing happened. On it went.

Sophie swerved to the left and pulled onto a grass verge at the side of the road, too shaken to drive any further. She continued to tweak buttons on the dashboard, then something caught her eye in the rear view mirror. A dark shape, looming. Right behind her. Inside the car.

*Oh Jesus Christ.*

Cold breath chilled her neck with rank decay and she heard the wheezy crackle of inflamed bronchial tubes, right in her ear. Her own lungs clenched painfully and she had to gasp for air. She closed her eyes, not daring to look in the mirror or to turn around. If she did, if she had to look into Cribbins' hellish black eyes right now – during daylight hours, in a public place, on a warm sunny day – she thought she might lose all sanity. It would untether itself from her consciousness and float off through the open window, to set adrift on the warm southerly wind to wherever and whenever. And, much like a wild horse, she'd never be able to coax it back. Then whatever remained of her that wasn't quite sane would simply implode. All of the myelin within her central nervous system, damaged and undamaged alike, would dissolve and an acute awareness of who she was and what she'd seen would carry through her nerve endings, distributed to, and painfully remaining in, her skin forever. Because how could you look into such dead-black eyes on a normal day and resume an ordinary life?

She felt one of his fingertips press on the side of her neck, slowly, firmly, tracing the line of it downwards. His beetle-shell nail scratched the surface of her skin. Swallowing hard, her throat hurt, like she'd swallowed a ball of gristle.

*We're having fun now, aren't we, Sophie-cat?* She heard his voice inside her head. *So many ways to torment you.*

'What do you want from me?' she dared to ask, her eyes still closed.

There was a loud bang. Sophie yelped. She realised someone was standing at the front passenger window, peering in. A man with dark, thinning hair and a deep cheeriness etched onto his face like he'd seen too many Friday nights. His knuckles were still resting on the glass where he'd rapped. 'Everything alright, love?' he asked.

Glancing over her shoulder, Sophie saw the back seat was now empty. Cribbins was gone. 'Er, yes.' She found the button to operate the passenger window and opened it.

The man rested on the door and leaned in. 'Have you broken down?'

Sophie ran both hands over her face and fought the urge to laugh hysterically. *Something like that.* Her heart was still exploding in her ears and she imagined if she looked in the mirror, she'd see the red line on her neck off Cribbins' nail. 'No. I, er, just pulled over to take a call, that's all.'

The man's eyes swept over the passenger seat and her lap in search of a phone. When he saw none, his eyes narrowed. 'Are you sure you're okay, pet? Was it a bit of bad news or something? You seem a bit shaken.'

'Yes, very bad news.' Sophie said, nodding. 'But I'll be on my way now. Thanks for stopping, I *really* appreciate it.' She dipped the clutch and shifted into first gear, then left the man gawping after her.

By the time she parked up outside her parents' house, Sophie was still trembling. And as she walked down the garden path, she felt cowed by Cribbins' house. In her parents' house, her mother was in the kitchen making tea.

'Oh hi,' Nora said cheerily. But when she looked up and saw Sophie, her brow soon furrowed and she asked, 'Is everything alright, love?'

Sophie dumped her handbag on the kitchen counter and fought hard to keep all of her emotional overload in check. 'What do you know about Ronnie Cribbins, Mam?'

Nora stopped stirring whatever was on the hob, as though the subject warranted her undivided attention. 'Why?'

'I just need you to tell me everything you know about him.'

'But...why?' Nora's lips pulled thin. She seemed discomfited that her daughter was rambling about the dead neighbour again, as though she thought Sophie had developed some morbid fascination with him.

*Oh yes, Mother, I'm definitely coming undone.* Sophie planted both of her hands on the worktop and inhaled deeply, realising she must look as dreadful as she felt. 'Some strange things have been happening, I can't explain. I just need you to tell me some stuff about Cribbins.'

'Stuff like what?'

'How did he die?'

'They reckon it was a heart attack. About fifteen years ago.'

'Did he die next door, in that house?'

'Yes, I think so.'

'What else do you know?'

'What else do you want to know?'

'Anything. I want to know what he was like.' Apart from a few hazy recollections, Sophie couldn't remember much at all about him. But she needed to know who the real Ronnie Cribbins was so she could piece together why he'd chosen her, specifically, to taunt and harass. She needed to understand.

# 15

# The Bells

**May 1992**

Nora was in the garden hanging washing. It was when she dropped a clothes peg and turned to pick it up, that she noticed Ronnie Cribbins was sitting on his doorstep, watching her. He was gripping a cigarette in the corner of his mouth and looked much too coordinated in a dark green jumper and corduroys. Nora thought he was like a giant preying mantis, all arms and legs.

'Oh, er, hi, Ronnie,' she said. 'Didn't see you there.'

'No, you wouldn't.' He stood up, his lanky limbs somehow making the movement overly quick and therefore uncanny. Leaning on the fence, he made no secret of the fact he was admiring her figure. 'There are two types of women in this world, Nora. The ones who do and the ones who don't. I know plenty of doers. But the ones who don't, I like to watch.' He dragged on his cigarette, then pointed at her, narrowing his eyes against the smoke that began to pour from his mouth. 'You, you're not a doer.'

'I'm not sure I know what you're talking about,' Nora said shaking her head and issuing an awkward, nervous laugh. She clipped the bottom of a t-shirt to the washing line and wished she could teleport herself inside the house.

'I'd like to put you on my mantelpiece,' Cribbins told her. 'So that I could look at you whenever I like.'

'Er...' Nora didn't know how to respond. Wasn't quite sure how to process that information. What the hell kind of admission was it anyway?

'You're like an ornament, see.' Cribbins took a final draw on his cigarette, then flicked the butt over his shoulder. It landed in a patch of purple and yellow pansies. 'I'd love to have you as part of my collection, but I suppose I'll have to just watch you from over the fence, like this.'

'I'd rather you didn't if I'm honest.'

'But I will anyway.' He laughed; a guttural, dirty sound. 'I know exactly where I'd put you on my mantelpiece, I've got just the spot. But I won't. I couldn't possibly.'

'No you bloody well couldn't.'

*\*\*\**

## April 1993

When Nora Harrington went to answer the door, her initial thought was that there'd been an accident. The hefty knock was the kind that heralded bad news. But, surprisingly, there was no one there. Confused, she looked about. That's when she saw Ronnie Cribbins sitting on his doorstep, holding his head in his hands.

'Ronnie?' Nora stepped outside, alarmed. 'Is everything okay?'

His pointed face was twisted; demented or pained, it was hard to tell which. 'I'm sick and tired of it,' he told her.

'Sick and tired of what?'

'The bells.'

'What bells?'

He punched the side of his head with his fist; the dull clunk of knuckle bone against skull made Nora recoil in horror.

'I can hear them, all hours,' he told her. 'Inside the

walls.'

'I, er, I don't know what you mean.'

'You're doing it on purpose.' His voice became a warning growl and the words cranked out as if from an old engine misfiring, made all the more jagged by the phlegm at the back of his throat.

'Doing *what* on purpose?' Nora crossed her arms over her chest. As much as she was perturbed by Cribbins' irrational behaviour, she felt defensive and irked enough to stand her ground. 'There are no bells.'

Cribbins looked up at her, his squinty eyes sharply black behind the grimy, finger-print marked lenses of his thick rimmed glasses. He jabbed a long finger at her, as if to strengthen the validity of his claim. 'You, woman! You're doing this. Oh yes. Trying to drive me fucking crazy, you are.'

Nora was astonished and, at first, couldn't speak. His accusation twinned with such foul language was like a slap to the face. 'It seems to me like you're doing a good job of that yourself,' she told him.

Cribbins stood up then, his spindly frame unfurling like a giant spider. He towered above her; intimidating in both size and intent. His fine white hair was mussed, from when he'd wrestled his head with his hands, and his thin lips didn't seem able to close the gap to cover his long crooked teeth. He looked perfectly mad. Nora edged backwards, into her front porch. She clutched the door with her right hand, ready to slam it shut should she need to. Never before had she been so nervous of Cribbins. Such was his display of aggressive unpredictability, she worried what he might do. What he might be capable of.

'You've got to stop it with the bells, Nora.' He continued to stare at her, but adopted a softer tone, as though he'd switched persona to become someone else entirely. Someone calm and rational. His eyes, however, remained reptile-like in their predatory regard.

'There aren't any bells.' Nora told him again, her fingertips white on the door.

Cribbins clutched his lower jaw with one massive hand. The whiskers there bristled coarsely against his fingers. He stood for a while, contemplating. Danger seeped from his every pore, making his moment of quiet deliberation frighteningly tense. 'Must be an alarm clock or a jewellery box that you have,' he said at last. 'Something like that.'

'Look, Ronnie, I don't know what you're talking about. There aren't any bleeding bells in here.'

'Don't give me that, I hear them all the time! They're driving me crazy. Fucking. Crazy.' Cribbins leant over the fence, close enough for Nora to be able to see the purple thread veins on his cheeks and grey bobbles on his knitted navy sweatshirt. His eyes possessed a human darkness that she'd only ever seen before on news bulletins and murder documentaries. 'I'm warning you, woman, if you don't stop playing games I'll make you sorrier than if the devil himself was coming to gouge out your eyes and piss in the sockets.'

Nora moved back a little further, pulling the door so it partially covered her. 'I'd appreciate it if you'd stop using language like that.'

Cribbins grinned. Tapping one of his liver-spotted temples with a long, bony finger, he said, 'I know your game. Oh yes. You're doing it on purpose, acting all innocent and trying to make me think I'm going mad.'

'Well, to be honest, I don't think that'd be too hard. You're about there anyway.' Nora said boldly, finding courage behind the door. 'No one's playing any bells in here, do you hear me? No one.'

Cribbins made a strange mewling noise and tipped his head back to look up at the sky. 'You've got to stop it,' he said quietly, after some thought. His words were a simple plea now and his mouth, Nora saw, had begun to quiver. She realised only then how anxious he looked. Maybe even afraid. 'The bells, I can't stand them. Make them go away. Just stop it with the bells, Nora!'

'You know what, Ronnie? I refuse to have this conversation any longer,' Nora said, ready to close the door on him. 'If you'd like to take it up with Lenny, I'll let him know when he gets in from work. But as far as I'm concerned, we're done.'

'Oh no. No, no, no. No we're not.' Cribbins pointed a finger at her again and licked his crooked teeth, to stop his top lip from sticking to them. 'You'd better stop it with those whoring bells, woman. I'm telling you. Else I'll come straight through those bastard walls of yours and wring your fucking neck.'

# 16

# Phyllis

'What about his wife?' Sophie asked. 'What happened to her?'

'Phyllis was a lovely lady.' Nora turned the hob down, so the contents of the saucepan reduced to a gentle simmer. A rich, meaty gravy smell filled the kitchen. 'I always felt sorry for the poor soul, she must have had a life like a dog with him. She upped and left him eventually though.' Nora took a seat with Sophie at the breakfast bar. 'I'm just surprised she didn't go sooner to be honest. I know I would have.'

'Why didn't she?'

Nora shrugged, her grey eyes becoming wistful. 'Oh I imagine it was hard for her, in all fairness. She had cerebral palsy and I think she relied on Ronnie a lot for care. I do wonder how much psychological abuse he subjected her to. You know, making her think she couldn't cope without him.' Nora inhaled deeply, her mouth pulled tight. 'Thinking back, she used to talk to me when he wasn't about, but she always seemed on edge. Nervous, like. Maybe scared that he'd come home and catch her talking to me. In hindsight, perhaps she wanted to tell me something.'

'Like what?'

'Well, I dunno. Who knows? Maybe she was just lonely. The main thing is, she got out.'

\*\*\*

## August 1992

'Morning, Phyllis.' When Nora stepped outside, she noticed her neighbour was sitting just outside her own front door, enjoying the sun.

Phyllis' face was a crosshatch of shadows, created by the large straw hat she was wearing. Her ankle-length floral dress of greens and blues was pulled up above her knees to expose downy legs that were pasty and riddled with snaking grey varicose veins. Her feet were caged in brown leather sandals. Next to her was her Zimmer frame. 'Morning, Nora.'

'Lovely day, isn't it?' In one hand Nora was holding a glass of lemonade and in the other a Mills & Boon novel that she'd been given by her sister, Gillian. She nudged a deckchair over to the fence, so she was sociably parallel to Phyllis.

Phyllis' thin lips disappeared into a wide smile and the creases at the sides of her eyes became more pronounced. 'It certainly is.'

Nora balanced her lemonade on the fence post, splayed the romance book across her bare thighs and knocked the sunglasses that had been balanced on top of her head down onto the bridge of her nose. She settled back into the firm canvas of the deckchair, ready to embrace the heat of summer. 'Are you keeping well?'

There was a slight delay before Phyllis told her, 'Yeah, yeah. You've got to just get on with things, haven't you?'

Detecting the despondency in her neighbour's response, Nora peered over the fence. 'Are you sure? Is everything okay?'

'Oh yes, it's nothing really.' Phyllis wrung her hands together in her lap and looked down. Her cheeks seemed to have coloured. 'I miss my mum, that's all.'

'Ah that's a shame.' Nora had heard Phyllis mention

her mother before, but didn't know much about the woman. 'Does she live very far away?'

'Harrogate. I talk to her on the phone every now and then, but it's not the same, is it?'

Nora's own mother had died eighteen years ago. The idea of talking to her on the phone sounded wonderful. Still, she frowned sympathetically. 'Doesn't Ronnie take you to see her?'

'Oh no!' Phyllis' expression morphed to one of horror. 'They don't get on at all. Mum can't stand him.'

Nora winced. 'I'm sorry to hear that.' But she could totally understand why.

'I don't think she's happy that Ronnie took me away from her.' Phyllis did a half-hearted laugh, which was a melancholy sound, perhaps filled with regret. 'She thinks he's all wrong for me.'

'Oh dear. I don't suppose we can keep everyone happy though, can we?'

'Hmmm.' Phyllis seemed to reflect on this.

'Do you have any other family?' Nora asked.

'No. Just Mum. And she's getting on a bit now.'

'Mother's can be protective of their daughters,' Nora reasoned, smiling encouragingly. 'Maybe she'll come round, given time.' Though she certainly wouldn't recommend that Phyllis hold her breath waiting for it to happen; she could understand perfectly well why any mother would take issue with having Ronnie Cribbins as a son-in-law.

'She won't.' Phyllis shook her head. Her eyes were somewhat glazed and her face became darkened with turmoil as she seemingly battled some deeply embedded emotion to keep it from welling to the surface and breaking loose altogether. Nora expected this was an issue that had been festering for quite some time. With no one to talk to and no one to confide in, Phyllis Cribbins was in a state of inner torment. 'She threatened to write me out of her will if I didn't see sense,' she said. 'But after about a year, she backed down and said that although she can't condone what I've done by moving north with Ronnie and marrying him, that my bed is always ready for me back home.' Phyllis' clear sadness indicated this was an offer she'd contemplated a million times over. 'Mum thinks it'll end in tears, you see.'

'As long as you and Ronnie are happy, that's the main thing, I suppose.'

Phyllis sucked in both lips and chewed on that thought for a while. Her chair creaked as she leaned closer to the fence, and in a lowered voice, quiet enough to let Nora know she was imparting a secret, she said, 'I have thought about leaving him, you know.'

'Oh?'

Looking suddenly sheepish, like she'd betrayed some basic terms and conditions of hers and Cribbins' relationship, Phyllis nodded. 'Sometimes I think that maybe Mum's right.'

'That he's wrong for you?'

'Hmmm. At times he can be...' Phyllis glanced to the end of the garden, as though she was no longer able to maintain eye contact with Nora because the guilt of her admission was too much to bear. 'Difficult.'

Nora feigned a certain amount of surprise, even though 'difficult' was a word she'd choose to describe Ronnie Cribbins herself. 'In what way?'

'Oh I think you must have an idea.' Phyllis smiled sadly. 'Ronnie can be a bit...off the wall at times.'

'I'm sorry to hear all of this,' Nora said. 'I don't know what to say. I had no idea you weren't happy.'

Phyllis was still staring at something or nothing at the far end of the garden. 'Can I tell you something else?'

'Of course you can.'

'I think if I was to go to Mum's, he'd come after me.'
'In what way?'

'I just don't think he'd let me go easily. If at all. He has a terrible temper. Mum's getting on now, she's eighty-seven, so I don't think I could put her through it. All the trouble off Ronnie, I mean.' Phyllis cast her eyes up and down the front street, her demeanour in general becoming more fidgety and irritable. Nora wondered if Ronnie was due home soon, and if Phyllis was worried that he'd catch her talking and punish her in some way for her candidness. 'Please don't tell anyone about what I've just told you, will you?'

'Of course not. I wouldn't dream of it.'

'It's just, I get lonely sometimes. There's no one to talk to. I don't have any friends round here, and Ronnie goes out a lot. I love it when Sophie calls in to see me. She's a good girl. I'd have liked a family, you know, but it just never happened. Too late in life. Mind you, I can't imagine I'd have wanted children with Ronnie.' Phyllis shuffled in her seat. 'Anyway, I'd better get inside and start the tea. He'll be wanting something to eat before he goes over the road.'

'Over the road?'

Phyllis frowned, her eyes conveying some other misery. 'He's always pops over to Nicola Pratmore's. Hers is the house straight across the road, out the back. Since her husband left, Ronnie does odd jobs for her.'

'I see.'

'Do you know Nicola at all?'

Nora shook her head. 'Not really.'

'Ronnie's always saying how good he is with his hands.' Phyllis sighed. 'He's good with his drinking as well. Always stinks of booze when he comes home.'

Nora raised her eyebrows. 'Maybe you should go over there with him. If Nicola's on her own now, she might be a friend for you.'

Phyllis laughed; a cheerless cackle that probably tasted as bitter as it sounded. 'Oh they wouldn't want me

hanging about. I'm not daft to what goes on over there.'
She was quiet for a moment, probably troubling over her
husband's large hands being handy all over Nicola
Pratmore. 'I guess it doesn't matter though, does it?' she
said at last. 'What can I do?' She gave a brief chuckle
and added, 'Except continue to put the lottery on.'

'The lottery?'

'Yes, because I tell you something, Nora, if I won
some money, I'd be off like a shot.'

# 17

# Inside

'So, did she win the lottery?' Sophie asked.

'No. Her mam died and left her some inheritance money,' Nora said. 'Phyllis sent me a letter from Brighton not long after, explaining. She didn't give me an address, but that's where the envelope was postmarked. I presumed that's where she'd moved.'

Sophie felt a swell of victory in her chest upon hearing of Phyllis' successful getaway. 'What did she say in the letter?'

'It was a bit of a farewell, I suppose. I was so pleased for her. That she'd managed to break free from him, that is, not about the circumstances that had allowed her to do it. She told me that Ronnie didn't know where she'd gone, and she asked me not to mention the letter to him.' Nora shook her head and pulled a face to show that Phyllis' request still evoked amazement after all this time. 'I mean, as if I would have!'

'Did you not hear any more from her after that?'

'No.' Nora began to swipe a stray crumb back and forth on the counter with the side of her hand. She looked distant. Pensive. Reliving some past memory. 'I suppose she was terrified that he might find out. I mean, it was a bit of a risk. Imagine if the postman had put her letter through the wrong door by some cruel twist of fate.'

Sophie thought it highly unlikely, yet possible all the same. 'Did Ronnie never try to find her?'

'Not that I know of. But then, I tried to avoid him. Especially after that incident on the doorstep, the one where he'd raved about the bells. I stayed out of his way the best I could. I'm not gonna lie, Soph, he terrified me. I mean, he was always odd and...' Nora shuddered. 'More than a bit pervy, but that day in particular he was totally volatile. Whether he could hear bells or not, something had seriously rattled him.' Nora stopped to think. 'Actually that whole business with the bells was just after Phyllis had left him. I remember now. In fact, thinking about it, I bet Phyllis leaving is what sent him over the edge. He looked totally bonkers. Like he might snap and do goodness knew what. You know when you can just sense something bad about someone? Well that day I could sense proper evil in Ronnie Cribbins. It was all in the eyes. God, his eyes.'

Sophie nodded. She knew.

'I saw him coming and going from Nicola Pratmore's a lot after the uproar about the bells,' Nora went on. 'I always presumed he was mollifying himself in her bed.'

Sophie wrinkled her nose and her mouth pulled down at the sides.

Nora noticed and gave a sardonic huff of laughter. 'I know, it doesn't bear thinking about, does it?' She reached across and put a hand over Sophie's, her grey eyes filled with concern. 'What's all this about anyway, love? Why are you so keen to dredge up all this nasty business? I shouldn't have mentioned anything about the ghostly goings on next door if I'd known it'd spook you so much.'

Sophie shook her head, hardly able to explain to her mother what had been going on without sounding as crazy as Cribbins himself. It sounded completely insane to her own logic. 'Oh it doesn't matter.'

'But there must be a reason.' Nora could see straight through her daughter's veil of nonchalance. 'Tell me.'

'I dunno.' Sophie squirmed. 'I suppose I just wanted to know if Cribbins had ever done anything to...'

There was a knock at the door. Three swift raps.

'I'll get it,' Sophie said, jumping up, pleased to be off the hook.

Piotr Kamiński was standing on the other side of the fence, leaning over as if about to knock again when Sophie opened the door. His expression turned to one of surprise when he saw her.

'Hello,' he said.

'Hi.' Sophie felt her face redden with a shameful heat caused by the memory of their first exchange, when he'd caught her gawping at his house the other day. She felt idiotic. 'Is, er, everything okay?'

'Yes. Yes.'

'Hello, Piotr.' Nora came to the door and peered over Sophie's shoulder.

Straight away, Piotr's smile became more assured. 'Nora, I wondered if you have a moment?'

'Of course, what's up?'

'I tried to hang my curtains, like how you said, but I'm not sure.' He shrugged. 'They don't look so good.'

Nora laughed. 'Alright then, let's have a look.' She patted Sophie on the shoulder and nudged her out of the door. 'Come on, Soph, give us a hand.'

Inside his house, Piotr signalled Sophie through to the sitting room, then ushered Nora in behind her. Everyone then looked to the window. The problematic floor-length curtains were heavy chenille, in a masculine dark grey. They had pencil pleat tops and at curtain rail level the thick fabric was awkwardly bunched and puckered.

'Dear me,' Nora said, with a good-humoured laugh. 'Did you hang those buggers in the dark?' She went straight to the set of step ladders that were positioned in front of the window and climbed to the second rung, then set about correcting the curtains.

Sophie stood in the middle of the room, frozen in fearful awe.

*I'm inside Cribbins' house!*

Piotr gave her an uncomfortable look, like he thought maybe he'd done something to offend her.

'Will you stay for a coffee?' he said to the back of Nora's head. 'Or tea?'

'Go on then,' Nora said, finishing with the curtain on the right and moving to the one on the left. 'I'll have a quick tea, please.'

He looked at Sophie.

'Er yeah. Same for me, please.'

When Piotr went through to the kitchen, where he could be heard filling the kettle and chinking mugs, Sophie's eyes were drawn to the fireplace. *I'd like to put you on the mantelpiece.*

Nora finished altering the left curtain and stepped back from the window to admire her handiwork. 'Sit down, love,' she said, pushing Sophie over to the couch. 'You're making the place look untidy just standing about like that.'

Sophie didn't doubt it. Piotr's sitting room was minimalistic and spotless. Not what she'd imagined for a man living on his own. Aside from the basics, like couch and television, there wasn't much in the way of homeware. No ornaments or photos. No clutter of any kind. And the large canvas on the wall above the fireplace – an arty close up of a white lily – had probably been there when he moved in, she thought; a mass produced canvas the landlord had likely got the decorators to put up in order to titivate the place.

Sophie frowned, but did as she was told and sat down.

'Don't be mean,' Nora said, sitting next to her. 'The poor lad's lonely. He's got no one here.'

Piotr popped his head round the kitchen door then. 'Sugar?'

'No thanks, love,' Nora said. 'I'm sweet enough already.'

Piotr smiled.

Sophie sighed. 'One for me, please,' she said, feeling hugely awkward about sitting on this stranger's couch, but more unsettled about the fact she was inside Cribbins' house.

'Actually Piotr, hold that thought.' Nora jumped up. 'I just remembered, I've left a pan on the hob. Len'll hit the roof if he gets back and finds it on with no one in the house. Last week I left the iron on all afternoon by mistake. He'll think I'm trying to burn the bloody house down.'

Sophie made to get up too, but Nora put a hand out to stop her. 'I'll leave you two to have a bit of a natter.'

Sophie narrowed her eyes and mouthed *don't you dare*. But Nora dashed to the front door, her eyes filled with devilment.

Piotr appeared at the kitchen door again, a teaspoon in one hand and a two-pint carton of milk in the other. 'I'll be seeing you then,' he called after her. 'And thank you for fixing my curtains.'

'Any time, love.' Nora waved as she left.

Piotr finished making the tea and the next time he emerged from the kitchen he was carrying two mugs. He handed one to Sophie, then took a seat at the other end of the couch.

'So,' Sophie said, needing to alleviate some of the awkwardness that her mother had dropped in their laps. It seemed Nora Harrington was trying to play matchmaker, and Sophie assumed her mother's mischief wouldn't be lost on Piotr either. 'You're from Poland?' The question was ridiculous. Sophie knew it as soon as the words had left her mouth. She wasn't even sure what type of answer it sought, it was more like a blunt statement. Or an accusation, depending how he took it.

'Yes. That is right.' His dark brown eyes shone with subtle humour and it was with this particular look that

Sophie felt herself warm to him.

'So how on earth did you end up in Horden?' She laughed and leant back, resting her elbow on the chair arm in a mindful effort to appear at ease.

'Because of work,' he said. Mirroring Sophie's body language, he sat back too, already looking less uncomfortable on his own couch. 'I worked in Manchester and was offered a position further north, in Peterlee. So I took it.'

'What is it that you do?' Sophie sipped her tea, her eyes not leaving his face. She was interested in what he had to say, but her attention kept drifting to thoughts of Cribbins.

'I am a security guard at a factory unit. Mostly I do nightshift.'

'Does much ever happen during the night?'

'Not really, it is very boring.' He laughed. 'But I get to do my coursework. I am studying to be an accountant. I am very good with numbers.'

A dull thump somewhere above made Sophie jolt upright and look to the ceiling.

Quietly amused by her apparent jumpiness, Piotr explained, 'Probably the floorboards settling. Or water pipes resting. Who knows? These old houses, they like to make themselves known.'

Sophie forced a smile. *Maybe not as much as their previous occupants do.*

The day beyond the window had turned almost as grey as Piotr's curtains, as though it hoped to rain and never stop. Sophie downed more of her tea and wrapped both hands around the mug. She wasn't sure if it was her imagination, but she felt a slight chill in the air. Oncoming rain? Or Cribbins? Was he watching her now? She felt watched. Piotr. That was because Piotr was watching her. 'So, do you miss home at all?' she said, keen to resume normal conversation. 'Poland, that is.'

As Piotr considered this question, his face fell into a frown. Sophie was about to apologise, in case the question was in any way offensive, but then he said, 'Where I used to live, there is not much.'

'How do you mean?'

'It is a small village in the mountains. Very remote.'

'Sounds lovely to me. What's it called?'

Piotr seemed hesitant to answer at first, but then he told her, 'Gliczarów Dolny.'

'Sorry, never heard of it.'

'For some reason, I didn't think that you would have.' Piotr grinned. Two deep dimples appeared in his cheeks and his teeth were neat and white, pleasantly contrasting against the burnt orange of his stubble. 'Let me see,' he said. 'It is not too far from a ski resort called Zakopane. Maybe you have heard of that?'

Sophie shook her head. 'Nope, sorry.'

'Hmmm.' He rubbed his chin in thought. 'Then I suppose it is not a million miles from Krakow. You have heard of that, yes?'

Sophie rocked forward in her seat and laughed. 'Hell, I'd be totally ignorant if I hadn't heard of Krakow. I'm guessing the distance between Gliczarów Dolny and Krakow is probably the equivalent of us comparing the distance between Horden and Manchester though, right? Hardly a stone's throw.'

Piotr laughed and shrugged, as if to say it didn't matter. His smile was infectious. Sophie liked him.

'So, are you totally new to the area?' she asked.

'Yes.'

'Have you made many friends yet?'

'Hmmm, a couple of people from work. And your mother and father, of course. Nora and Lenny, they are nice people.'

Another loud noise upstairs made Sophie flinch. This

time it sounded like a door being banged shut; a gunshot clamour of wood slamming against wood. The walls of the house trembled with the aftershock. Then a girl very clearly shouted, 'Take me with you!' Her voice seemed to transcend the noise of the door and, absorbed by the walls, it reached Sophie and Piotr in stereo, as if she was right there in the room with them.

At first Piotr seemed surprised, but then he relaxed back in his seat. He pointed to the wall, where the fireplace was, and said, 'Next door, they have a little girl.'

But Sophie wasn't convinced. 'What about that bang?'

'Noise travels a lot through these houses.'

'Shouldn't you check upstairs, just to make sure everything's okay? I mean, it didn't sound like it came from next door.'

Maintaining a level of indifference, Piotr stood up. 'Okay, I will go and check.'

Sophie stayed put, listening to his footsteps on the stairs. Soon she could hear him moving about directly overhead. Was it possible that the girl they'd heard cry out could be the ghost girl she'd seen in her old room? Icy fingers clawed down Sophie's spine, prompting gooseflesh to break out all over her arms.

*Don't let him keep me.*

*Take me with you.*

Could it possibly be?

Quick movement in her peripheral vision drew Sophie's attention to the fireplace. Something small and black had scurried across the mantelpiece, but when she looked at the mantelpiece directly, there was nothing there.

Piotr thundered back down the stairs and strode into the sitting room, bringing with him a faint smell of cigarette smoke. 'Everything is okay,' he said. 'It must have been next door.'

'I should probably get going.' Sophie edged forward on the couch, trying to quell the rising fear that twisted her innards and made the underside of her skin flash cold. She stood up. Needed to get going. Could feel badness brewing within the house's walls. Something terrible was vying for her attention. She could feel it. She could feel *him*. Cribbins. He was slowly manifesting. Teasing her with yet another shrewd display of intimidation.

'Oh, okay.' Piotr's brow dipped into a frown. Clearly, he was flummoxed by her abrupt desire to leave. 'Um, it was good to meet you anyway.'

'Yes, and you.' Out of the corner of her eye, Sophie saw something small and black on the mantelpiece. But again when she turned her head to look, there was nothing there.

'Is something the matter?' Piotr asked, following her gaze.

'No, no.' Sophie glanced around the walls of the sitting room – the walls of Cribbins' old sitting room – and a chill ran through her. She could feel him close, like negative energy stroking her skin. Teasing. Taunting. 'I just really need to get going' she said, dashing to the front door.

Piotr followed, looking somewhat disappointed, thinking that maybe he'd done something wrong. But Sophie was too eager to leave the house to stay a moment longer in order to explain that she wasn't fleeing him, but the man who used to live there. She was halfway down the garden path when Piotr called goodbye to her, but she was much too preoccupied with the thought of what the consequences for her having dared to enter Cribbins' domain would be.

# 18

## Confirmation

That night, after Caitlyn had gone to bed, Sophie lay on the couch in front of the television. She was vaguely aware of the flashing images of a police drama on ITV and the noise of people talking, but her attention was hardly on it; the characters' make-believe crises would never be enough to take her mind off her own problems. Not only had Cribbins shown up in her car earlier that day, but afterwards she'd gone into his house. Straight inside the monster's lair. Welcomed by the house's new tenant, Piotr Kamiński, she'd actually set foot in the place where Cribbins had lived and died, and gone on to share light-hearted conversation over a cuppa. She felt this move of hers would have ratcheted up any danger she was in, because she imagined Cribbins would be furious.

But what was it that Cribbins wanted from her?

*You'll pay for what you've done.*

What had she done? She had no idea. And, just as mystifying as Cribbins was terrifying, who was the ghost girl?

Sophie's mobile jingled with a social media notification. There was a message request from Leanne Baxter. She jabbed her finger at the screen to accept it, her hands already trembling.

*Hi hun. Sorry couldnt talk the other day. Carl was there and he doesnt like to talk about the old house. It caused a lot of trouble between us. He never believed me about any of the stuff that went on in there. To be honest I dont like to talk about it either. Too many bad memories. Let me know if theres something in particular u need to know tho. Leanne xxx*

Immediately, Sophie's thumb began to work on a reply.

*Hi Leanne, thanks for getting in touch. Sorry to hear you had such a bad time there. Apologies if it's too personal, but it really would help me out if you could tell me about what happened to you. Or if you don't want to go into specific details, could you at least tell me if it was anything to do with Ronnie Cribbins, the old man who lived there before you? Sophie x*

Sophie pressed send and rested the phone on the arm of the chair. Every ten second interval thereafter, her eyes were drawn to the screen, checking for new notifications. None came.

Darkness had crept in all around her. The final hour of sunlight had faded behind a covering of building rainclouds, leaving the house overly dingy. Shadows stretched up the walls and dominated too much space within the sitting room. Sophie felt claustrophobic. Didn't like the shadows at all. Too many unknown things dwelt in them these days. She got up and closed the blinds, then switched on the ceiling light. The safe, cream glow startled everything back into its rightful place, but Sophie didn't feel at all comforted. Beyond the television there was a brooding air of expectancy. Of something infinitely more real and chilling than the finale of the fictional murder case which was drawing to a close. She looked to the corner of the room, where she'd seen the crooked, misshapen ghostly figure weeks ago. She was pretty certain it hadn't been Cribbins. But who then?

Being perceptive to Cribbins, she wondered if it was possible that he had wedged open some gateway to the afterlife inside her head. Was there a spirit attached to her own home, who lingered and was able to show itself to her at will? Or could it be that whatever weird ailment she'd been dealing with had given her the ability to see dead people? And would this be the new norm? Would she potentially see dead people wherever she went?

*You're being ridiculous!*

Sick with nerves and eager for morning, Sophie went to bed. Her room smelt of cigarette smoke, but the bedside lamp subdued any sinister shadows and showed that there was no one else in the room with her. She wrapped herself in the duvet and lay on her back, staring at the ceiling; her thoughts a total head-fuck of malignant dead people and their cryptic messages, past wrongs that may or may not have been committed and Piotr Kamiński's face. Rolling over, she checked her phone. There was still no reply from Leanne Baxter. And many more hours till morning.

She was encapsulated in a vacuum of stillness that she was more aware of than she'd like to be. And it was because of this quietude that she thought she heard a noise downstairs. Floorboards creaking. A subtle transference of weight on boards, like someone moving slowly through the room directly beneath her. The absolute silence of the house offered no cover for these deliberate, creeping footfalls. But then, it offered all the right conditions for imagined footfalls in a cooling house too. She thought about Piotr Kamiński again and of what he'd said. *These old houses, they like to make themselves known.*

A jingling noise made her jump. Her phone screen lit up with a new notification. There was another message from Leanne Baxter. Sophie could barely breathe as she opened it.

*Ronnie Cribbins? Holy shit, I dunno. Maybe? Im not sure who used to live there before us.*

*When Carl used to work nightshifts, I dreaded nights in there on my own. Id wake up & see an old man standin over me. He was this really tall, thin bloke and he proper stunk. Like really awful. And he had this horrible laugh like nothing u ever heard before.*

*After a while he started to touch me. I know it sounds crazy but I can still feel his hands on me. It was as though he was really there. Like real flesh and bone. Only cold. REALLY cold. And one night, I swear down Im not lying, he tried to force himself on me. I had bruises all over my arms & legs. Thats when the trouble started between me & Carl. He thought I must be seein someone else and was tryin to make up this ghost story. We almost split up cos of it. Thank god my gran found us a different house and we got out of there. It was the most scary time of my life. I still have trouble sleeping these days!*

*I havent seen the old man's ghost since we left that house, but I always wondered who would end up livin there. I feel so sorry for whoever it is.*

*Hope that helps. If u need to talk, u know where I am. Leanne xxx*

*PS please dont tell anyone about this. Im trying to put it behind me. & I know it sounds totally fuckin nuts!!!*

Sophie's blood ran cold. So there it was, evidence that she wasn't going crazy. Evidence that she wasn't hallucinating. Cribbins *was* terrorising her. Only, unlike with Leanne, he was leaving the boundaries of his home in order to do so.

What was it that made her so special?

*You'll pay for what you've done.*

Clutching the phone to her chest, Sophie listened to the deep buzzing quiet of the house, convinced that after having read this damning proof about Cribbins, his ghost would be provoked into taking immediate action against her.

*Oh the things I'm going to do to you.*

She waited for the slightest creak of floorboard or groan of unoiled door hinge, and was alert to any disturbance or change in the air around her – the subtlest draft or temperature drop. So when she heard a noise right outside her bedroom door, Sophie's innards shrivelled in fright and her sanity became as fragile as sun-fractured bone. She waited, somehow clinging to consciousness, to see if she'd been mistaken. To see if the tread of dead feet on carpet might have been imagined.

Long, slow seconds passed.

Then the door to her room nudged inwards, with a short, sharp thump. Within the darkness on the landing, Sophie saw black movement. And heard the familiar *click, click, click* of old, seized joints moving.

*Not Cribbins. It's the other one!*

A new smell wafted into the room. A sweet scent that took her back to childhood and made her think of small purple sweets in a clear wrapper.

*Parma violets.*

Then suddenly she had a memory of being in Cribbins'

house. Of being offered treats from a white paper bag that had been kept on the mantelpiece, right next to a golden carriage clock. Inside the bag had been a selection of liquorice, toffees, chews and Parma violets. She remembered putting her hand into the bag and...

Quick footsteps out on the landing brought her thoughts back to the present. They were light and playful, like a child's.

'Caitlyn?'

No reply.

Sophie fought hard to breathe. Felt too scared to move. But she had to. Had to check on Caitlyn. Had to check to see what ghosts were out there. The crooked figure? The ghost girl? Sophie slid from the bed and dashed to the door, not wanting to prolong the mental torture of what she was doing and what she might find. She flung the door open, so the light from her room spilled out onto the landing, showing there was no one there.

'Caitlyn?' Her voice was a hoarse whisper and her heartbeat was a continuous buzz inside her chest, like moths imprisoned in the meaty husk of her heart, their thrashing wings denoting panic. She went to Caitlyn's closed bedroom door and put her ear against it, listening. All was quiet. Gripping the handle, she cracked open the door. Her eyes were assaulted by the intense darkness within. It took several seconds for her vision to adjust, then she could make out the shape of her daughter lying on the bed, her arm wrapped around the Steiff teddy bear that Gareth had bought for her birthday. But that wasn't all. Sophie choked on her own breath. At the foot of the bed, there was a shadowy figure of a girl, watching Caitlyn sleep.

'Who are you?' Sophie whispered, urgency making her voice sound outraged.

It was too dark to see the girl's features, but Sophie could tell she was now looking at her. There was a weighty blackness of negative energy surrounding her. An unclear angst that tended towards badness.

'If you let him keep me, he'll destroy you,' the girl said, her voice like stirred echoes in a derelict place, long-forgotten.

Sophie was both afraid and wary. She pushed the door fully open, so more light from the landing spilled into Caitlyn's room. But as it did, the ghostly girl dissolved to nothing. And a great wave of emptiness rushed over her. A feeling of aloneness that made her chest physically ache. She was left with nothing but the lingering smell of Parma violets and some instinctive knowledge that there'd be no more ghosts that night. Just the haunting impact of the girl's implied threat: *If you let him keep me, he'll destroy you.*

# 19

# Relapse

The morning after the ghost girl's second visit, Sophie awoke with a feeling of oncoming pins and needles in the soles of her feet. Hours later, the same sensation was also in her hands. The following day, her hands and feet were entirely numb, but roared with pain whenever touched. It felt as though the blood supply to her extremities had been cut off and the nerves were raging. Sophie worried her fingertips might turn black and fall off. By the next day, she had no feeling whatsoever from her chest to her lower stomach. Her entire torso was numb. An invisible band snapped into place around her ribcage, squeezing and constricting so much that she found it hard to breathe. Found it hard to move. She had no choice but to go on sick leave because she could no longer drive, was in too much pain and the least bit of exertion floored her. A walk to the end of the street was like climbing Ben Nevis. And the art of walking itself was a tricky business, since she couldn't feel her feet. Her hands had become redundant claws. She could barely get dressed or make a cup of tea.

Three months passed with no let up of symptoms; a constant onslaught of mauled nerve-endings sending messages of displeasure from the rest of her body. In November Sophie had a second MRI. Then three days before Christmas, she finally got a diagnosis.

*Relapsing remitting multiple sclerosis.*

There'd been no more sightings of Cribbins throughout this second relapse, but Sophie suspected her autoimmunity was a direct result of him.

*If you let him keep me, he'll destroy you.*

It certainly seemed like Cribbins was making good on that threat. But who was the girl he was keeping?

Sophie imagined Cribbins as an aggressive virus, aggravating her immune system and causing her cells to go into self-destruct mode. It was easy for her to think this way, that his presence had triggered the inflammation of her brain and spinal cord, because within just four months he'd managed to ravage her entire dermatome.

*Oh the things I'm going to do to you.*

On Christmas Eve, Sophie was in a dark funk. She felt beaten and miserable. Recently she'd regained the feeling in her torso and, despite there being a constant numbness in her fingertips, the pain in her hands and feet had eased. Instead, she had the distinct feeling that her limbs were generating electricity and that she'd be able to shoot lightning bolts from her fingertips at will. She wasn't due back at work till January, which meant she had the entire festive period to recuperate further. But still, what did that matter when Gareth was taking Caitlyn away in two days' time?

She put on a charade of cheeriness as she helped Caitlyn pack her suitcase, but trying to remain so upbeat when she felt so wretched inside was exhausting.

'Are you going to stay with Gran and Grandda while I'm gone?' Caitlyn asked. She was sitting on the end of the bed, running her fingers over the smooth, pink fabric of her ski jacket, which was laid out flat, ready to be packed away last.

'I don't think so, chicken,' Sophie said, placing a wool jumper in the suitcase on top of a pile of others. 'Why would I?'

'I just think you should, so that you won't be on your own.'

Sophie threw a pair of rolled up socks at Caitlyn. 'But

I won't be on my own, silly. I can go and visit your gran and grandda whenever I like. And I have friends as well, you know.' Which was sort of true, except somewhere along the line Sophie had put her entire social life on hold and hadn't seen any of them in ages. Probably too long, truth be told. Was the illness to blame? Or stress? Or was it merely down to her own peculiarity of character, her introverted nature? She wasn't sure, but half the time she just wanted to hole up in a dark, quiet room and do nothing but breathe. Lately life exhausted her.

Caitlyn started fiddling with the rolled up socks, pulling at the elastic cuff of the outermost one. Something was bothering her. 'But if you go and stay with Gran and Grandda,' she said, 'you'll have company all the time. And Rodney. You'll have Rodney to cuddle anytime you like.'

Sophie sat down on the bed and held her arms out. 'Come here, you.'

Caitlyn hesitated for a moment, then moved over and allowed herself to be hugged.

'What's all this about? You aren't worried because I've been poorly, are you? I'm okay now.'

'No.' Caitlyn's eyebrows dipped sulkily. 'It's not that.'

When Sophie had sat Caitlyn down the day before, to tell her about her diagnosis, Caitlyn had become cagey and hadn't wanted to discuss it. It was as though she didn't want to acknowledge the illness and would prefer to pretend that it wasn't an actuality. Sophie wondered if her daughter had bypassed the initial stage of shock and gone straight to feeling resentment instead. Perhaps she was indirectly angry at Sophie for having let the side down, by allowing such a disease to upset the status quo of their family. Or maybe she was worried she'd end up with a mother who was bound to a wheelchair. Caitlyn was only eleven, after all, it was a lot for her to take in.

Hell, it was a lot for Sophie to take in and she was a grown woman.

'So what is it?' Sophie asked, gently squeezing Caitlyn's upper arm. 'What's brought this on?'

Caitlyn shrugged. 'I just don't think you should be in this house on your own.'

'Why would you think that, dafty? Darren and Tina don't live next door anymore. They left weeks ago, you know that. Everything's hunky dory now.'

'It's not though.' Caitlyn's eyes became overshadowed with worry, or something close to, and Sophie caught a snippet of fear in her voice.

'Has something happened to you in here?' Sophie asked, swiping Caitlyn's fringe to the side. 'Something to upset you?'

Caitlyn's mouth pulled tight as she seemed to consider how best to answer. 'Last night,' she said, uncertainly, 'there was a man behind my curtains.'

'You mean, someone looking in at you?' Sophie whipped round to look at the window, as if she might find lingering evidence there. Already she was planning to call the police.

'No.' Caitlyn shook her head. 'He was in my room. Standing behind the curtains.'

'How come you're telling me this only now?' Sophie's grip tightened around Caitlyn's shoulder. 'Why didn't you tell me last night?'

'Because I didn't want to wake you.'

'You should always wake me if you have a nightmare.'

'It wasn't a nightmare.' Caitlyn made disdainful eyes. 'The man was a ghost. A real ghost who was really there. He was tall. Even taller than Dad. And skinny.'

Sophie's heart was crashing. She felt woozy.

'He asked if I wanted some sweets,' Caitlyn went on. 'I told him I didn't, but he said that he knows you and that it would be okay for me to go ahead and have some. I still told him no.'

Sophie felt so sick she was sure her complexion must have turned grey. 'Was that all he said?'

'No. He said that you and him go back a long way and that while I'm in France, he's gonna come and visit you lots and take care of you.' Caitlyn leant further into Sophie. 'I didn't like him, Mam. That's why I think you should go and stay with Gran and Grandda.'

Sophie kissed the top of Caitlyn's head, not exactly opposed to the idea. 'We'll see.'

'You do believe me though, don't you?' Caitlyn looked up, her eyes imploring.

Sophie didn't feel able to push the idea that her daughter had suffered from a bad dream, because it simply wasn't true. And to lie or feign ignorance would only increase Caitlyn's fear – perhaps even her doubt in Sophie.

'Of course I do, chicken.' She pulled Caitlyn into a tight hug. 'Do you want to sleep with me tonight?'

'Uh-huh. But promise you'll stay at Gran and Grandda's while I'm away.'

'Okay, I promise.'

That night consisted of the usual sleeplessness that Santa brings. Nothing to do with Cribbins. And when morning finally arrived, Sophie and Caitlyn opened their presents on the sitting room floor, ate chocolate for breakfast and played Christmas tunes too loudly. By noon, they were at Lenny and Nora's house, where all four of them sat round the dining table and pulled crackers, told jokes, recited lists of what they'd got for Christmas, as though they were contestants on The Generation Game, and fed Rodney surplus food from their plates. Because, as usual, Nora had made too much food. Lenny had red cheeks from the four bottles of ale he'd drunk, which, along with the Santa hat he was wearing, lent him quite a gnomish look. Nora, on the other hand, was merry after just one glass of white wine spritzer. She was wearing a fluffy white jumper with a reindeer on the front. The reindeer's pompom nose was positioned right on the end of her left breast and whenever he thought Sophie and Caitlyn weren't watching, Lenny would honk it.

Once dinner was done, Nora suggested they give it a while before having dessert. No one argued. Caitlyn took Rodney out in the garden to play with his new squeaky toy and Lenny retired to his armchair for a snooze. Sophie and Nora cleared the table and tackled the monumental pile of plates, pots and pans. By the time they were done, Sophie's fingers were withered like prunes.

'Our Shaun said Addy Adkins was going to send you flowers last week,' Nora said, with a certain amount of wine-induced nonchalance as she hung the damp tea towel over the radiator.

It was such a random point of conversation that Sophie was lost for words. 'Why?'

'He'd heard from our Shaun that you haven't been well.'

'But I don't even know him, why would he do that?'

Nora shrugged. 'Must still have designs on you.'

*Great.*

'Ready for some Christmas pud yet?' Nora thought to ask, as though she hadn't just dropped an Addy Adkins bomb.

Agitated that he hadn't forgotten about her, but not willing to let it ruin Christmas Day, Sophie exhaled loudly and patted her stomach. 'There might be room for a little bit. I'll go and get Caitlyn.'

In the garden, Rodney was poised at the gate watching a boy whizz up and down the front street on a mountain bike, but Caitlyn was nowhere to be seen. There was a muted cough and Sophie turned. The door to Piotr Kamiński's house was wide open, she saw. And Caitlyn was standing in the front vestibule of his house.

'Caitlyn, what are you doing?' she cried out in shock.

Caitlyn spun round and Piotr appeared behind her, holding a box of marzipan chocolates. 'Hello,' he said, showing the box to Sophie. 'A Christmas gift for you and Caitlyn.'

But Sophie wasn't listening, she was staring at Caitlyn. Her thoughts filled with the threat of Cribbins, so much so her hands and feet tingled. Her veins filled with the gushing blood from her heavily exerted heart, which threatened to burst and fill her entire body with redness that would seep from her pores. 'What do you think you're doing?' she said to Caitlyn. 'You're not to go in there, do you hear me?'

'It's okay,' Piotr said, his eyes becoming wide with consternation. 'I asked her to come round.'

'It's not okay.' Sophie flashed him a fiery glare. 'She's not to go in there.'

'But Mam…' Caitlyn began.

'Get back round here,' Sophie ordered. She could feel herself shaking. Knew she must look and sound completely irrational, but didn't care. 'Right now.'

With her shoulders stooped and head bowed, Caitlyn trudged back round to Nora and Lenny's garden path. Rodney welcomed her at the gate and followed her to the house. After she'd disappeared inside, Piotr held out the marzipan chocolates to Sophie and said, 'Merry Christmas anyway.' His tone was anything but merry and his smile had given way to a disparaged frown. 'I am sorry to have caused trouble.'

Sophie took the box from him and watched as he went inside, closing the door behind him.

'What the hell was that all about?' Nora said to Sophie, having heard the ruckus and come outside to see.

'Don't start, Mam,' Sophie said, closing her eyes and rubbing them. 'Just don't.'

# 20

# Peace Offering

Once Caitlyn had left, Sophie felt despondent. The excited chatter of her daughter had filled the house from the moment they'd got out of bed until Gareth had arrived to take her away. Now there was nothing but an ear-buzzing silence, as nauseating and unwelcome as the Christmas tree which stood in the corner: a six-foot, pre-lit, artificial abomination. A total clusterfuck of plastic needles, tinsel wreaths, silver baubles, endless glitter and mirrored plastic beads. In the weeks leading up to Christmas it had always been a thing of actual magic, but now Christmas Day was over and Caitlyn had gone, the magic had lifted and Sophie saw the tree as nothing more than a fake monstrosity. In fact, she thought she'd quite like to ram it star-first into the wheelie bin outside, because she couldn't begin to imagine being able to summon the energy or due care required to dismantle it properly and was sick of it being there already. Instead, she tore apart the two halves and, without undressing either, wrapped them as tightly as she could with bin liners and Sellotape, then dragged them up into the loft to be salvaged next year, when she'd be able to deal with Christmas again.

Right now, Sophie felt fragile. There was no greater sense of Cribbins than that which already existed within herself, but his threat lingered out in the open like impending doom. The threat that he'd visit her lots in the coming twelve days. She believed him. And she wondered if her nerves could take it. Quite literally.

*Oh the things I'll do to you.*

Her thoughts then turned to Piotr Kamiński. She wondered whether if she was to go inside his house again, she would be able to invoke old memories. To try to fathom why it was that Cribbins was so intent on pursuing her to such devastating lengths.

*You'll pay for what you've done.*

But the way she'd acted yesterday, what the hell must Piotr think? She doubted he'd speak to her, let alone allow her into his house again.

Ashamed of her behaviour, Sophie baked a cake – Victoria sponge with raspberry jam – then drove over to Horden and knocked on Piotr's door. Bold as brass. He came to the door almost immediately, as though he'd expected her arrival. But then, Sophie realised he was wearing a coat. He was on his way out. Upon seeing her on his doorstep, his dark brown eyes lacked any of their usual warmth.

Wincing, shamefaced, Sophie held out the cake tin. 'A peace offering?'

At first Piotr was hesitant, but then he reached out and took it from her. His hands were large, his fingernails tidy. A plain silver band on his thumb chinked against the metal. 'Um, thank you.' A gracious smile touched his lips, but he looked increasingly uncomfortable on his own doorstep. In his own skin. 'Would you like to come in?'

'No, no, it looks like you're on your way out,' Sophie wafted her hands dismissively, to show she didn't want to be a nuisance. 'I don't want to interrupt your plans.'

'I was only going to Wetherspoon's, to meet some people from work.' Piotr shrugged. 'They can get by without me for a while.' He shifted to one side and held the door open further. 'Please, come in. Have some of your peace offering with me. Yes?'

Sophie stepped past him, not needing to be asked twice. Needing to assert herself in order to get inside

Cribbins' domain. She caught a nose full of Piotr's aftershave – a subtle, clean smell with underlying spices – and wandered through to the familiar space of the sitting room.

'I would offer you some mulled wine,' Piotr said, following straight behind. 'But you are driving.' He clutched the cake tin to his torso and stood in front of the couch in his bulky winter coat. Sophie thought, despite his tallness, he looked quite boyish; uncertain and shy. His thick auburn hair was playfully mussed and his face freshly shaven. In contrast, his eyes conveyed some of the brutalities of adulthood and resignation thereof. They were dark shields hiding whatever ghosts lay within, yet at the same time, they were deep and rich, the colour of ale. 'Or are you staying at Nora and Lenny's?' he asked,

Sophie had promised Caitlyn that she would, but she hadn't yet spoken to her parents about it. She doubted they'd object. In fact, she knew they'd insist. 'I don't have to drive,' she said. 'I mean, I suppose I could have a drink. But then, I don't want to keep you from your friends.'

Nodding as if that was the final deciding factor for them to have wine, Piotr put the cake tin on the couch and shrugged out of his coat. 'I can see my friends some other time. I saw them on Christmas Eve. Today they can have beer without me.'

'Well, only if you're sure.' Sophie watched as he went into the cupboard under the stairs to hang his coat, then followed him through to the kitchen, where he took a milk pan from one of the cupboards. He placed it on the hob and filled it with half a bottle of shop bought mulled wine. While Piotr busied himself, Sophie took the opportunity to look around. The kitchen was compact. Wherever they stood, they could never be more than an arm's length away from each other.

'I really want to apologise for yesterday,' she said,

leaning her hip against the counter, feeling wholly comfortable in Piotr's company. 'I was bang out of order.'

'No, it is okay. I should have asked you first if it was okay for Caitlyn to have the chocolates.'

'Oh God, *that's* not what it was about. I didn't flip my lid because you gave her chocolates. That was absolutely fine. In fact, it was a lovely gesture, thank you. It's just, well…' She became quiet then. Had worked herself into a corner. She turned her head and looked into the sitting room. Could see the mantelpiece from where she stood. A feeling of dread washed over her.

*I'd like to put you on my mantelpiece. So that I could look at you whenever I like.*

'It's just what?' Piotr was staring at her now, his brow crumpled in consternation. 'I don't understand.'

Along with Piotr, the house and its essence and every single fibre within it seemed to wait for her response.

'This is gonna sound pretty crazy,' she said, wringing her hands together. 'But then, I'd rather have you think I'm crazy than some ungrateful, psycho bitch.'

Piotr's eyes sparked with caution. His stance became stiff. Guarded.

'It's this house,' Sophie told him. Her mouth twisted to the side and the awkwardness of trying to explain had made her face flush with uncomfortable warmth. 'I didn't want Caitlyn coming in here. I don't ever want her coming in here.'

'Why not?' Piotr turned the hob off. The wine was gently steaming and a rich blend of cinnamon, cloves, nutmeg and ginger filled the small space around them with a heady exoticness that seemed to push Cribbins even further away from Sophie's grasp. Sophie wished she'd waited till after they'd drank some of the wine to broach the subject. When she didn't answer immediately, Piotr urged, 'What is wrong with my house, Sophie?'

Taking a deep breath, she gathered courage enough to be forthright and said, 'What's your take on the paranormal?'

Immediately Piotr looked suspicious, like he wasn't sure if she was mocking him. 'You mean like ghosts and things?'

'Yes.'

'I am not sure.'

Sophie sensed a new prickliness about him. His eyes had darkened and when he turned his back to pour wine from the milk pan into two wine glasses, his broad shoulders were rigid. 'Has anything odd ever happened to you in here?' she persisted.

Piotr handed her a glass, which she took by the stem. His previous friendliness was shielded now by a cold caginess that caught her off guard. She didn't like it one bit. His eyes seemed to accuse her of something. 'You mean like doors rattling and things moving about when they should not? That sort of thing?'

'I suppose so.'

'No.' He shook his head, his jaw working tight. 'Nothing like that.'

The soles of Sophie's feet started to tingle, electric currents ran up the back of her calves.

*Oh the things I'll do to you.*

She blew into her glass and took a cautious sip of wine.

Piotr drank from his more easily. 'So, what? You think there is a ghost in here?'

Sophie sighed. Then nodded. 'Yes. There was a man who used to live here. I think he still does.' Wincing, she brought a hand up to her mouth. 'Shit, I'm sorry, I shouldn't be telling you this. You live here.'

To her surprise, Piotr laughed and his eyes resumed some small sparkle of warmth. 'That is okay,' he said. 'I don't scare easily. Also, I work nightshift, so most of the time when I am in the house it is day time. Not so scary, huh?'

'Hmmm.' Sophie wasn't so sure. It didn't seem to make any difference whatsoever what time Cribbins decided to indulge in a spot of haunting. It was terrifying whenever. 'I'm sorry this sounds so crazy,' she said. 'I just wanted you to know why I acted so weird yesterday. About Caitlyn coming in here. It wasn't about you.'

Piotr led her through to the sitting room, where they sat on the couch. 'So, this man who lived here before,' he said. 'Did he do something bad to you?'

And there it was, the question she didn't know the answer to. All Sophie could remember about Ronnie Cribbins came in vague flashbacks. She breathed in the warm fumes of her wine, wishing she could get drunk on them.

'I'm not sure,' she said. 'I mean, I don't think so.' She squirmed in her seat and took a mouthful of wine. The mantelpiece goaded her from across the room with its sheer emptiness. 'You must think I'm absolutely mad.'

'No, not at all. There must be a reason why he makes you feel so worried.'

*Abso-fucking-lutely, because he's stalking me.* But that was a step too far. She couldn't possibly tell Piotr that much. She'd lose him at the second hurdle if she did. And she didn't want that. *Really* didn't want that. This was a stark realisation in itself and made her mouth go dry.

'This might be the, um, therapy you need?' he said, as though having cottoned on to her ulterior motive for being there. Sophie blushed. 'What was this man's name?' he asked.

'Cribbins,' Sophie said. Her hands and feet buzzed with angry electric pulses at the mere sound of the name spoken aloud. 'Ronnie Cribbins.'

The top three buttons of Piotr's shirt were undone and when he leant back the neckline gaped open. A thick silver chain around his neck caught Sophie's eye. It dipped beneath the black fabric of his shirt and she wondered what pendant, if any, was at the end of it. He curled his fist and looked to the ceiling, his eyes sparking with devilry. 'Cribbins, are you here?' he said, grinning widely.

The whole house flinched.

All was quiet.

'If you can hear me,' Piotr went on, 'I want you to leave my friend, Sophie, alone. Okay?'

Sophie was tense. Didn't share Piotr's reckless sense of mischief at all. She could almost feel Cribbins' fury at being mocked. She expected to hear a loud bang from upstairs, then thundering footsteps as Cribbins came for her and retaliated. She braced herself.

Nothing happened.

Deep dimples remained in Piotr's cheeks. He stood and took Sophie's glass from her. 'More wine?'

When the mulled wine was finished, they drank chilled Polish lager straight from the fridge. Each can had the words 'bogaty smak' written on it, which Piotr said meant 'rich flavour'. Time passed quickly and no old memories of Cribbins resurfaced. In fact, Sophie found she enjoyed Piotr's company so much, she had relaxed into a state of indifference in regards to Cribbins without even realising until it was time to leave.

Later that night she slept in her old room, in her parents' house, with her feet touching the wall that adjoined Piotr's house. She thought about Piotr in there, right now. Lying asleep. Most likely in Cribbins' old bedroom. That particular idea made her feel nauseous.

She thought about Caitlyn too. Gareth had sent a message earlier to say they'd arrived safely in Morzine. Even though it was only in France, it seemed so far away. Like the other side of the world.

And before she fell asleep, her thoughts drifted to Addy Adkins. She reckoned she might have to speak to her cousin Shaun, to ask him to try and dissuade his friend from pursuing her, because she could do without Addy Adkins mooching about like she could do without a poke in the eye.

When she slept, Sophie dreamt she was back in Piotr's house. Standing next to him in his sitting room, in front of the fireplace. The connection between them was magnetic and strong. He took her hand and smiled. Those dimples. Then led her upstairs to his bedroom, where his mouth became hot with foreign words, uttered on the spiced warmth of his breath. He could be saying anything, anything at all, she realised, and because of her ignorance to the gravelled lilt of his voice, suddenly she wanted nothing more than to taste the words with her tongue, so she might understand him that way. She covered his mouth with hers, while he tore at her clothes and lay her down on the bed. Pulling him with her, she felt his weight on top of her. His tongue responded to hers and they communicated wordlessly in a universal, basic language of lust until...

Until his mouth felt different. Full, soft lips were now thin and hard. His warm, supple tongue was now cold and rigid. Sophie tried to pull away, but her urge to be freed was met with some resistance. Struggling, she pushed him hard and turned her head to the side, pressing herself further into the mattress to escape his mouth. And that's when she saw that it was Cribbins who lay on top of her.

Sophie awoke with a start. Her hairline was wet with sweat and her hands and feet were numb on the outside, but stuffed with nettles on the inside. A flare-up of old damage.

Cribbins was inside her head again.

Squeezing her eyes shut and grinding her teeth together till her jaw ached, Sophie screamed inside her head.

WHAT DO YOU WANT?

Cribbins gave no answer, but when Sophie passed out in a feverish stupor she dreamt about Phyllis, his wife. An old memory that brought her closer to the truth...

# 21

# Mr Sandman

**April 1993**

When Sophie left for school, Phyllis Cribbins was standing in the doorway of the house next door, gazing up at the sky. Nothing was happening up there, Sophie saw. Nothing but grey gathering more grey in an accumulation of early-spring rain. It was as though Phyllis had been waiting for Sophie especially, because there didn't seem to be any other reason for her to be there. It was too chilly for anyone to be catching fresh air without a coat, and Phyllis wasn't wearing one.

'Hey, gorgeous girl,' Phyllis said, looking down from the clouds and grinning at Sophie.

'Hi.' Sophie slung her backpack over her shoulder, then adjusted her jacket sleeves.

'Are you off to school?'

'Yep.'

'Have fun.'

'I'll try.'

'Why don't you call round here when you're finished? We can bake some cakes together.'

Sophie's eyes lit up. She loved cakes and, despite her initial reservations, because Phyllis was Ronnie Cribbins' wife, she found Phyllis to be a nice lady. Kind and caring. Probably lonely too. She always had a bag of sweets, which she offered to Sophie. And sometimes she let Sophie lick cake mixture out of the mixing bowl when they were done. 'Okay, I'll ask my mam as soon as I get home.'

'Great, you do that.'

School was a day filled with Henry the Eighth's wives, almost as many beheadings, tiggy at break time and a love note from Robert Benson asking if Sophie would like to be his girlfriend. When she finally got home, Sophie dropped her school bag in the front porch and shouted through the house, 'Mam, I'm going next door.'

'Why?' Nora Harrington was in the kitchen, creating meaty aromas with some sort of stew.

'To make cakes with Phyllis. She asked me this morning.'

'Ah okay. Well don't be too long. And don't spoil your appetite.'

'Alright.' Sophie left the house again and hopped down the garden path, then skipped up the Cribbinses' path.

The Cribbinses' lawn was overgrown and the borders were strewn with weeds. Cigarette butts littered the whole area in front of the house. Sophie didn't understand why Ronnie Cribbins didn't use a bin like normal people. It was as though he purposefully surrounded his house with his own filth in order to deter others. Like a fox, marking the boundary of his territory.

Sophie knocked on the door and waited.

Then waited some more.

A flock of racing pigeons swooshed by overhead. Then there was a short, sharp blast of a train horn in the distance. Sophie could hear the train hurtling up the coastline. Old Mr Moor appeared at the bottom of the street, slow-walking his way to the pub. Rumour had it, he had plastic hips. By the time he reached the top of the street, Sophie was still standing on the Cribbinses' doorstep. Surely Phyllis couldn't have forgotten she was coming. Perhaps she'd nipped to the loo. Sophie knocked on the door again.

When there was still no answer, she felt a pang of

concern. Supposing Phyllis had fallen over, what then? Ronnie would be out, because Phyllis only ever invited Sophie round when he wasn't home. Maybe she was lying in there, all alone, on the floor, unable to get back up. Maybe she'd broken an arm or a leg and needed an ambulance.

Sophie touched the door handle with tentative fingers. Should she go inside and check? Sensibly, she thought she should probably go and get her mother, but when the handle pushed down, she inched the door open and peered inside. 'Hello?'

There was music drifting down the stairs; some old tune with haunting female voices that were singing something about a sandman. Sophie stepped fully inside and closed the door behind her. 'Phyllis?'

The smell of cigarette smoke hung thick in the air, as though the house was an ashtray that needed emptying. From where Sophie was standing, she could see there was no one in the sitting room. The carriage clock on the mantelpiece gleamed, catching her eye. It stood tallest on a mantelpiece that was full of clutter. She went to the foot of the stairs and put her hand on the bannister. Looking up at the dingy landing, she saw the seat of Phyllis' stair lift at the top of the stairs. She supposed Phyllis might be up there ironing, or something like that, and had lost track of time. Chances were, above the sound of the music, she hadn't heard Sophie knocking and that's why she hadn't answered the door.

'Hello!' Sophie called. She stepped onto the first stair to begin her ascent, uncertainty making her movement slow.

Still there was no answer, just the same music channelling down the staircase. Onwards and upwards, Sophie crept. Her pulse began to race. The closer she got to the top, the more she felt like she was trespassing and would probably get into trouble. She thought about turning round and leaving; scarpering back down the stairs and pretending that she'd never come inside. But something didn't feel right. Something urged her onwards. She had to know that Phyllis was okay.

On the landing, the music was even louder. It was coming from the main bedroom at the front of the house, the door of which was standing ajar.

'Phyllis, are you there?' Sophie reached out and pushed the door fully inwards...

\*\*\*

She bolted upright in bed and saw it was morning. Weak daylight was leaking past the edges of the curtains, painting the magnolia walls an obscure shade of flesh and highlighting the fact that the duvet on top of her was a writhing mass of cockroaches.

'Urrrgggghhh!'

Her skin prickled. The idea that thousands of black insect legs were only thin layers of white cotton away from scraping over her flesh was too much to bear. Sophie cast the duvet away, throwing it to the floor. Then was astonished to see how the cockroaches all disappeared. Each and every one of them. As though they'd never been there.

# 22

# Plan of Action

Sophie was sitting in front of the television, not particularly watching it, when there was a knock at the door. Piotr Kamiński was on the doorstep, holding a bunch of flowers; yellow roses with white gypsophila. At first Sophie thought they must be for her mother, for some good deed she'd done, but he held them out to her and said, 'I saw Nora this morning, she told me you are not well. That is, she told me about your diagnosis. I had no idea, I am very sorry. I hope it is okay that I brought these for you.'

Silently cursing her mother for having told Piotr about her flaw, Sophie took the bouquet and thanked him. Piotr smiled. Deep dimples appeared in his cheeks and there was a subtle fervour in his dark eyes that reminded Sophie of her dream, when she'd kissed him on the mouth. Embarrassed, she looked down and focussed on the yellowness of the roses.

What did yellow mean exactly? Friendship? Wellbeing? Caution?

Nothing at all?

Struck dumb by sudden awkwardness, she didn't know what to say or do. Somewhere overhead a gull *ha-ha-ha*'d and she wished Piotr would say something. Spark a conversation. Even better if he were to do it in Polish, because she wouldn't understand and it wouldn't matter. She just wanted to hear his voice and not to have to worry about the implications or complications of whatever was going on here. But she ended up breaking the silence by asking him, 'Would you like a cuppa?'

'Er, no thanks.' Piotr put his hand on the fence, as if he meant to jump over it into his own garden. 'I will leave you in peace.'

'Please.' Sophie stepped back and beckoned for him to join her. 'I'd be glad of the company. My mam and dad are out walking Rodney and I'm getting a bit cabin feverish, if I'm honest.'

'Okay then.' Piotr kicked his trainers off in the front porch and followed Sophie through to the kitchen. 'Will you be staying with Nora and Lenny for a while?' he asked, watching as she took a vase from the window sill.

Detecting hopefulness in the question, Sophie felt pleased. But then she decided she'd probably imagined it and felt disappointed. 'Maybe a few days.' She filled the vase with water at the sink, then put the flowers inside. Next she filled the kettle and switched it on.

'And how are you feeling?' Loitering in the kitchen doorway, Piotr appeared uncertain. About the question or himself though, she couldn't tell.

'Oh I've been much worse.' Sophie smiled offhandedly, wondering why her mother had chosen that morning of all mornings to reveal her medical fuck-up to Piotr Kamiński. Did Nora Harrington sense this budding friendship was heading somewhere? And was she therefore highlighting the issue she knew her daughter would have a problem doing herself? Sophie didn't want to be defined by her illness and, chances were, she might never have broached the subject with Piotr voluntarily. Because the last thing she wanted was for him to think she was broken. Defective. Inadequate. And her reasoning for this made her feel entirely too uncomfortable.

Piotr stuffed his hands into the pockets of his dark blue Levis. His plain white t-shirt made his complexion especially pale; striking against the reddishness of his thick, wavy hair. Like a fifties idol, his entire countenance was one of quiet brooding. 'Nora said that you will be meeting with an MS nurse soon. Hopefully there will be options for you?'

Was he deciding what his own options were, Sophie wondered. And if so, could she blame him?

*Not at all.*

Steam billowed from the kettle's spout and she nodded. 'We'll see.'

'Well, fingers crossed. And if you need anything, just let me know. Like, if you need a lift, I will take you where you need to go if I am around. All you have to do is ask.'

'Thanks.' Sophie turned away. She bit her lip and filled two cups with boiling water. Although she was touched by his thoughtfulness, she also felt embarrassed and awkward; and massively confused about his intentions. She couldn't presume that he was interested in her. Could she?

*Why would he be?*

'You don't look so good today,' he told her. 'You have dark eyes, like you did not sleep.'

'I didn't.' She turned and handed him a mug of tea. 'Not very well, anyway.' She thought about the cockroaches on her bed when she'd woken. Would she tell him about those?

*Definitely not.*

She didn't know what horrified her most: the sight of them there in the first place or the fact they'd existed entirely in her head. Whether they were an extension of Cribbins or her own psychosis, it was impossible to say. She led the way through to the sitting room and when they were both sitting on the couch, she said, 'Remember what we talked about in your house?'

The same guardedness from the day before befell Piotr's face in an instant; his eyes lost clarity and his mouth became tight. 'You mean ghosts?'

'Yes, but more specifically, Cribbins' ghost. I think he's haunting me.'

'Have you seen him?'

'A few times, yes.'

Piotr considered this, watching her carefully, before asking, 'And what do you think he wants?'

'I don't know. I remembered something last night, but it's like my own mind is blocking it out. Or like *he* doesn't want me to remember. I can't explain. I have a feeling that something bad happened to me in your house.'

Focussing on the intricate pattern of the rug beneath his feet, in a zoned out kind of way, Piotr nodded. 'Trauma has a strange way of showing itself. It sounds possible.'

'You don't believe in ghosts though, do you?' Sophie said, almost glumly.

He flashed her a look that she couldn't read, but if she was truthful, she wasn't sure she wanted to. It was dark. Dangerous. 'You are not well,' he said, completely skirting the question. 'And since you have been inside of my house, it seems old memories have, um, resurfaced. Because you are at a low point and your body is at war with itself and your defences are low, what I think is that your conscious mind is allowing information to break through. Your subconscious has found a weak spot in your defences and wants to show you something.'

'Yeah.' Sophie sighed, not disagreeing with his logic. 'Maybe you're right. Maybe it is just me.'

'I think that it will help if you try to remember what it is that happened to you. It has been kept from your accessible memory for all of this time, so I am thinking that whatever it is must be bad. You can only deal with it if you know what it is you are dealing with though.' His eyes were intense, perhaps a shade darker than usual. 'And maybe you will never heal even if you do learn the truth, but at least then you will know what your demon is.'

'But how do you suggest I make myself remember?'

Piotr sipped his tea. His eyes didn't leave hers, making Sophie wonder what demon taunted him; she could see its fire blazing just beneath the surface of his gaze. A shiver ran through her.

'Okay, I have an idea,' he said. 'I am going to work soon, but tomorrow, tomorrow you must come to my house again. To look around. To go wherever you need to go.'

*Upstairs,* she thought. *It happened upstairs.*

'This will jog your memory,' he went on. 'And I will be right there with you. Everything will be okay. Yes?'

Reassured by his optimism and decisiveness, Sophie felt strong. She also felt hopeful for the first time in ages. 'Yes, it sounds like a great plan.'

# 23

# Lucja

Piotr's breath came out in white trails. The bed looked uninviting. He stripped his clothes off, dropping them in a pile where he stood, and his bare skin tightened in protest. Once he was naked, he scrabbled beneath the duvet, squeezing his eyes shut and grimacing at the shock of absolute coldness between the sheets. The radiator under the window rattled with slow warmth, but he knew it would take a while for any of its heat to reach him. He lay still and ground his teeth together, waiting for the warmness of his core to spread outwards into the bedding.

He'd just got home from work. A ten-hour shift, which for the most part had been spent doing accountancy coursework. He'd thought a lot about Sophie Harrington too. He was intrigued by her more than he should be. Perhaps drawn to the indefinable torment he could see in her. The torment associated with Cribbins.

Piotr had been living in the house for over six months and hadn't encountered the malevolent spirit of any old man. Therefore, he concluded that Cribbins must be Sophie's ghost, and hers alone. Some psychological anguish from her distant, buried past. Piotr wanted to help Sophie exorcise Cribbins from her head. He knew how harrowing ghosts could be.

Beyond that intrigue, however, the part where he helped a fellow damaged soul, he wasn't sure what lay ahead for him and Sophie. He sensed reluctance on her part. But then, perhaps it was his own unwillingness that he was aware of. An unwillingness that he tried to encourage himself to maintain. If he pursued this spark of interest, which he felt confident was a mutual thing, would it be to the detriment of his long term plans? He supposed he would just have to stay alert, to know if and when he needed to distance himself. Because as much as he wanted to…

There was a noise out on the landing. Weight shifting on floorboards. He turned his head and fixed his eyes on the gloomy swatch of space outside the room. He imagined that…

*What?*

That Cribbins was out there?

*Ha!*

When there were no more sounds and nothing moved in the darkness, Piotr silently scolded himself. Sophie had planted ghost stories in his head. All this talk of Cribbins had obviously got to him. The sound of floorboards groaning was just the sound of the house heating up. That was all. The central heating expanding old wood. Piotr Kamiński didn't believe in ghosts that haunted houses and other buildings, he knew that real ghosts were just the memories of people who haunted other people.

And yet here he was, almost spooked.

He began to turn his head, to roll the other way, but that's when he saw the dark outline of a girl standing on the landing. Watching him.

*'Lucja?'* Piotr bolted upright and threw the duvet aside, as though he was about to leap to his feet. But a brand new noise froze his limbs, making him sit where he was, exposed to the cold, listening. It was a simple but jaunty jingle of bells, which might precede the hourly chime of a clock. Cocking his head, Piotr concentrated, trying to pin point where the noise was coming from. It was ghostly and chilling in its faint melodic quality, and sounded like it might be transferring from within the very walls themselves.

The girl was still there on the landing and Piotr was suddenly afraid to move, in case any rashness on his part might interrupt whatever ghostly occurrence was taking place. He wondered if his senses had tapped into some otherworld frequency. Or by contrast, had been hacked into by an outside force. The air all around him felt charged. Filled with electric menace. And what was that smell?

Cigarette smoke.

He also sensed nervousness, but didn't know if it was his or the girl's. Afraid to take his eyes off her, in case she scarpered like a baby deer once his stare didn't hold her captive, Piotr found he could barely breathe.

*Proszę, nie idź. (Please, do not go).*

But then something tickled his bare chest and he was forced to look down. There was a large cockroach nestled in his chest hair, its legs entangled, its antennae probing. In the semi-darkness its shell glistened, tarry like a demon's fingernail. Piotr swiped at it with the back of his hand, sending it flying across the room. Above the sound of the bells, he heard its shell clack off the side of the wardrobe.

*Lucja!*

He whipped his head round and saw the girl was still there, but she was less visible because she'd taken a step back. Her silhouetted human form had shifted into a less decipherable shadow.

'Lucja?' His voice came out hoarse and frantic. 'Czy to naprawdę ty?' *(Is it really you?)*

The bells began to chime then.

*One.*

Piotr swung his legs round and scrabbled to his feet.

*Two.*

He dashed to the landing, his fingers gripping the doorframe.

*Three.*

Then the girl disappeared.

'Lucja! Nie!' *(Lucja! No!)*

The house fell silent. Wintry greyness given by the insipid dawn filtered through the front door's glass panels downstairs and seeped up the stair walls with ghostly precision. Even though it fell short of properly lighting the landing, Piotr could see there was no one else there with him. Sinking to his knees, he tore at his hair with trembling fingers. 'Gdzie jesteś?' *(Where are you?)*

Old wounds that had never properly healed burst wide open again, and his innards physically hurt with the pain of his anguish. Sobbing, he collapsed fully to the floor, laying himself exposed and vulnerable to the cold. But he could no longer feel it. All he could feel was a deep, incurable sorrow.

'Tak mi przykro, Lucja.' *(I'm so sorry, Lucja).*

# 24

# Remembering

'Where are you off to?' Nora Harrington walked into the sitting room carrying a pile of folded, white laundry.

Sophie was bent over in the front porch, pulling on her boots. 'Next door.'

'Oh yeah?' Nora smirked and made wide, knowing eyes. 'Getting cosy you two, aren't you?'

'Hardly.'

'Would it be such a bad thing?' Putting the laundry on the coffee table, Nora rested her hands on her hips; a sure sign she meant business. 'It's about time you moved on, you know.'

'What's that supposed to mean?' Sophie stood up straight, her eyes narrowing.

'Gareth moved on ages ago.'

'What the hell's Gareth got to do with me popping next door?'

'You know what I mean.'

'No, actually, I don't.'

'Gareth found someone else years ago and got married.'

'Poor Andrea.' Sophie rolled her eyes. Then matching her mother's stance, she put her hands on her hips and told her, 'And just because I'm single, doesn't mean I've not moved on.'

Still not deterred, Nora said, 'It's just, it'd be nice to see you happy again.'

'Can't I be happy without a man in my life?'

'Of course you can. But I imagine it's lonely.'

'I have Caitlyn.'

'You might now, but how long for?' Instantly, her mother seemed to regret this choice of words. Her cheeks reddened and she was quick to explain, 'When she hits eighteen, she might move away to some far-flung university.'

'And she might not.'

Nora shrugged. 'But even if she doesn't, she'll have her own stuff to be getting on with. Friends and boyfriends, that sort of thing. And it's only seven years away. Till she's eighteen, I mean.'

'Christ, is there any particular reason why you're keen to kick me while I'm down?'

'I'd just hate to see you lonely. I know you're independent, but you're too bloody stubborn for your own good. You don't have to take on the world alone, you know. You could find someone to conquer it with. Someone you can share stories and make memories with.'

'Wow, did you have sugar *and* philosophical bullshit on your Weetabix this morning?' Sophie opened the front door and when Nora didn't respond, she stepped outside. 'Right then, I'll be off.'

She left her mother staring after her in dismay and went round to Piotr's house and knocked on the door. When he answered, he looked like he'd just crawled out of bed. His hair was dishevelled and his eyes were beset with sleepless bruising. All he wore was a pair of Levis, which hung low around his hips.

'Shit, I'm sorry,' Sophie said, averting her attention from the stark bareness of his torso. 'Did I wake you? I wasn't sure what time you wanted me to come round.'

'No, no.' He rubbed his face and looked like he probably wouldn't know what day of the week it was if she asked him. Then he nodded. 'Yes, actually, you did. It is my own fault though. I remembered that I asked you to come round, but I overslept.' He moved to the side and welcomed her in. Then, running his fingers through his burnt-copper tangle of hair, he said, 'Let me go and get dressed. Go and put the kettle on if you like.' He started to make his way up the stairs, then stopped and turned. 'Actually, no,' he said. 'I will do it when I get back.'

Sophie smiled sheepishly. 'Since I knocked you out of bed, it's the least I can do.'

Piotr nodded, distractedly, and resumed his ascent.

Sophie stayed where she was and watched him. In the dim light of the staircase, his bare skin was so white it almost shone. Spectral. His body was like an opaque pillar in the gloom. A seraph-skinned paragon of moonlight itself. Her insides, Sophie realised, were churning in a way they hadn't churned in a long while. Part of her wanted to turn and leave, but most of her wanted to stay.

When Piotr came back downstairs, he was wearing a crisp grey t-shirt over the same pair of Levis. He'd dampened his hair to tidy the unruly kinks in it. 'So how are you today?' he said, seeming more awake now. His eyes more aware. 'You look good.'

*Yeah, I put on more makeup than usual and agonised over what to wear because I knew I was coming to see you, yet still I tell myself I'm not interested.* Smiling politely, she told him, 'Thanks. I am good.'

'So,' he said, going to the mantelpiece and resting an elbow on its clear surface. 'You should look around my house. Find out why Cribbins upsets you so much.'

'Yes, I suppose I should.'

He swigged a mouthful of tea, then wandered over to the window. He seemed preoccupied again. Restless. Unsettled. 'Where would you like to go first? The kitchen? We can work our way through the house if you want.'

Sophie frowned and shook her head. 'No. Whatever

happened, it didn't happen in the kitchen, I'm sure. The only memories I have of being in there are nice memories. Of baking with Phyllis.'

'Who is Phyllis?'

'Cribbins' wife.'

'So, what about in here?' Piotr gestured to the walls of the sitting room. 'Do you get any feelings in here?'

*Plenty.*

She eyed the gas fire and the area above it. Piotr's mantelpiece clutter was sparse. It comprised nothing but his car key and wallet. There were no ornaments or pictures. A far cry from Cribbins' mantelpiece. She remembered the story her mother had told her, about what Cribbins had said. *I'd like to put you on my mantelpiece. So that I could look at you whenever I like.*

'I really don't like the mantelpiece,' she told Piotr. A chill ran through her, which was absorbed by her bones, into the marrow. 'It gives me bad vibes. I remember there was a load of clutter on it. And a golden carriage clock. I don't know why, but I specifically remember the clock. It had a white face and black Roman numerals. Its glass dome was smeared with dirty marks, as though someone had touched it with greasy fingers.' *Just like the lenses of Cribbins' glasses.*

Piotr looked paler, if that was even possible. 'Did it chime?'

'I'm not sure.' Perhaps it had though, because sometimes she heard bells whenever Cribbins was close. And Cribbins, he'd heard the bells too. *The bells. I can hear them, all hours. Inside the walls. They're driving me crazy. Fucking. Crazy.*

Sophie thought back to her dream, of going upstairs to find Phyllis. In the front bedroom. In Piotr's bedroom. That's where she needed to go. 'Would you mind if I take a look upstairs?'

'Of course not.' Piotr signalled to the staircase and

allowed her to go ahead of him. He followed close behind.

The stair walls, Sophie saw, were smooth and bare. New plaster covered all evidence that Phyllis' stair lift had ever been there. Sophie could still remember the sound of it. While lying in bed each night, she'd been able to hear the low mechanical drone of it through the walls. All those years ago. She wished Piot was in front of her. Taking the lead. Because right here, right now, ascending into the unknown, she was suddenly terrified of what she might find.

*In here. This house.*

She wasn't sure she was ready. But she had no choice. This was her challenge. She needed to do it. Besides, Piotr was right behind her. So close, she could touch him if she reached back.

*Mr Sandman.*

The words to The Chordettes song popped into her head. Sudden and evocative. Her skin reacted in a rash of gooseflesh, making her shiver. Had the memory of that afternoon been real at all? Or a false recollection created in the dreamscape of her confused subconscious? Intuition told her it was a true memory. At the top of the stairs she came to a stop and struggled to breathe. Her heart whumped too fast, too loud, but she knew she had to see this through. She had to go into Piotr's – Cribbins' – bedroom. Her hands and feet roared with renewed hurt; pins and needles surged through them like electric currents. Fierce. Intense. Cribbins was inside her again, aggravating old damage. Prodding and poking exposed nerves.

She must have paused for too long, because Piotr touched her arm and said, 'Are you okay?' He was right behind her. Still so close. Then he touched her hand. At least, she saw him do it. She could feel the pressure, the busy hurt of his fingers right there, but she couldn't feel his skin on hers. Her sense of touch was completely failing her again. Yet inside her hands and feet were wasp nests.

The bedroom door was ajar, just as it had been that afternoon, way back when. Sophie reached out with her free hand and rested it against the door's white gloss surface. Fierce pain fizzed from her palm to her wrist. She gritted her teeth.

*Mr Sandman.*

Those voices. She could hear them distinctly.

And that smell.

That growing smell of…

*What?*

Up until now she'd been able to smell Piotr. The heat of him next to her, the pleasant odour of his body. But now she could smell something else. The house itself. Of how it used to smell. Cribbins' stale cigarette smoke and Phyllis' attempt to mask it with air freshener. The type that's meant to smell of flowers, but reeks of chemical nastiness. She pushed the door inwards, unsure if Piotr was still holding her hand or not. Hinges creaked and carpet swooshed. Dismal daylight spilled out onto the landing and the room fully revealed itself.

Sophie felt her knees buckle and the whole world tilted and dulled. Then she felt Piotr's hands on her arms, holding her up. He was asking her if she was okay, but she couldn't speak. Couldn't move. Couldn't do anything. Because she remembered.

She saw.

She saw.

*Oh God.*

She saw.

# 25

# What She Saw

**April 1993**

The bedroom was an attack on her senses. A grim shock to each one. A badness so profound hung almost visible in the air; a thick, sticky layer of depravity that met Sophie at the doorway and wrapped itself around her, inappropriately touching her, inside and out, and clinging to every supposed layer of skin that her body might think to regenerate. So deep was its impact.

Cigarette smoke was mingled with a sour smell: a bodily odour produced over time and excreted largely with exertion. So strong was the acrid stink, it assaulted Sophie's nose and throat, coating her tongue with an irresolvable bitterness. A taste so wrong her subconscious would never ever forget it, even if her conscious mind believed it, in time, to be overridden. Music sounded from speakers somewhere unimportant, serving as mere backing to other, more inescapable, noises: bestial grunts and the rhythmic slapping of flesh.

The worst of it all was not what Sophie saw with her eyes, but what she saw with some intuitive perception beyond her years. It was the trauma of something so terribly, horribly, irreversibly wrong that managed to tap into her psyche. A part of her psyche that should have remained unchallenged.

Phyllis was sprawled over the bed on her belly. Her eyes were looking straight at, perhaps even through, Sophie. And Cribbins was standing behind her, repeatedly smacking himself against the fleshy mound of her rear. Phyllis' clothes were dishevelled, her dress bunched up around her middle and her squashed breasts partially exposed at the gaping neckline. Cribbins wore no clothes at all. His skeletal arms were stretched forward and he gripped Phyllis' doughy hips with his large hands. Each time his scrawny pelvis connected with her flesh, his crooked, ratty mouth issued animal grunts. Behind the lenses of his thick-rimmed glasses, his eyes were fever-black. But when he saw Sophie standing in the doorway, his frenzied excitement turned to something worse than rage; his entire presence became blacker than any black mood Sophie had ever witnessed. He pulled away from Phyllis and rounded the bed in three quick strides. Like a crane fly on long legs, drawn to Sophie's fear. He towered over her, his body a framework of prominent bones that were covered in mottled, beige flesh and sparse patches of course white hair. And his penis was a large, disturbing protuberance that was wrapped in worm skin. Crouching down, he bared his long, yellow teeth at Sophie.

'Dirty little peeping Tom,' he snarled. His breath was a ferocious rattle that smelt of burnt hair and soured milk. The rank stink of it violated Sophie's airways and she thought she might start to cry and never stop again. She backed away from him. Horrified.

'Where do you think you're going, kitten?' He reached out and gripped her shoulder, his hand like a vice. Strong. Unshakeable. Infernally terrible. His fingernails bit down into her skin like dogs' teeth. 'You're a bad girl and you need to be punished. You can't just expect to come into people's homes to spy on them.'

'But...I didn't. I came to make cakes with Phyllis.'

Cribbins laughed, a chainsaw growl that spewed out more stink from the pit of his stomach. His hands clamped down harder and he pulled her closer. 'If you tell anyone about this,' he sneered. 'Anyone at all. Then

I'll tell everyone what you are. A dirty, filthy little peeping Tom!'

Sophie began to cry then. The shame. The horror. The confusion of it all.

# 26

# Otherworldly Opportunity

'Whoa!' Piotr gripped Sophie's upper arms and supported most of her weight. He managed to keep her upright, but she trembled beneath his hands as though the temperature was sub zero in the house. As though the house itself had opened up death's finite portal to her, chilling her to the core with an icy blast of exclusive revelation. When she turned to face him, he saw extensive shock in her fixed expression. A certain frozen horror. 'Sophie?' When she didn't answer, he shook her lightly and urged, 'Sophie, are you alright?'

While still not responding to him verbally, her eyes became less glazed and he could tell that she was looking at him again, rather than visualising whatever she'd seen in the bedroom. Whatever it was the house and her subconscious had collaborated to show her.

In an attempt to take the edge off whatever memory blow she'd just received, Piotr laughed nervously and nodded towards the stark, simplicity of his bedroom. 'It is not *that* messy, is it?'

Whether it was his choice of words or the continued sound of his voice which broke the spell, Sophie's face crumpled and she began to cry. Piotr wrapped his arms around her and pulled her to him; an automatic reaction of empathy that was necessary given the situation. Sophie became pliant and submitted to his embrace. Fully receptive to him, she rested her face against his chest and hugged him back tightly. Her arms around his torso. Squeezing. Needing. Fraught. Her body was racked with inconsolable sobbing and Piotr absorbed each shudder with his own body. Stroking her hair with gentle fingers, he shushed her with some murmured words of comfort. Grateful in his own way for the contact, because he hadn't known closeness in such a long time. It made him feel real. Sad, but intrinsically human. He held her close till eventually her trembling subsided.

'What happened?' he asked.

Sophie's eyes were bloodshot. They conveyed some internal terror. For a while her mouth seemed uncertain how to function, as though her lips didn't know how to form the words that would express the thoughts running amok in her head. But finally she said, 'I remembered.'

'Tell me.' Piotr squeezed her upper arms in a gesture of encouragement.

'I saw them.' Her voice came out small, dwarfed by the magnitude of all she had to say. 'Cribbins and Phyllis. I must have mentally blocked it out. For all these years. I don't know how. I can't believe…that is, he made me feel so guilty. I came up here, to this room. I didn't really know what was going on when I saw them together. It was adult stuff and I was only young. But, oh my God, what I saw. Phyllis. Her eyes. She didn't do anything. Didn't say anything. Christ, those eyes. I think he might have killed her, Piotr. I think Cribbins might have killed Phyllis.'

'How can you be sure?'

'I…I don't know. I can't. But I just know it. Her eyes, they were so lifeless. Staring. And she just lay there. She would have said something to me. Surely? She would have been mortified to see me standing there. But she didn't… she didn't do *anything*. She just lay there.' Sophie began to sob again. 'That poor woman.'

'What should we do?' Piotr looked over Sophie's head and glanced around the bedroom. *His* bedroom. Incredulous about what she was saying, that someone might have been murdered and defiled there. 'Call the police and tell them what you saw?'

'No.' Sophie shook her head, horrified by the suggestion. She also looked pained, as though delving so mindfully into her inner self had caused physical affliction. Actual hurt. 'They'd never believe me. I mean, how could I prove it? I can't even be certain. My mam received a letter from Phyllis telling her she'd moved to Brighton.'

'Then maybe you *are* incorrect. Maybe you remember it wrong?'

Sophie winced, but didn't object.

'I'm sorry.' Piotr bit his bottom lip. 'It is just…if you saw Cribbins and his wife in bed together and you were just a girl and did not understand what was going on, then I am not sure…' He shrugged. 'Maybe it was so, um, taboo, so traumatic, that you remember it differently.'

'But what if I *am* right?' Sophie said, wiping her cheeks with the back of her hand. She felt scared by the potential enormity of the information her subconscious had guarded for so many years.

'Then how do you explain the letter from Brighton?'

'Easy. What if Cribbins sent it to cover his tracks? To make my mam *think* that Phyllis had moved away. That way no one would have suspected otherwise.'

Piotr nodded. 'Maybe.'

'So how can I find out the truth?'

Piotr's own thoughts had darkened. His mind was filled with murder and death. He thought about Cribbins and his wife, whoever they were, and of the young girl he'd seen on the landing during the early hours of that morning.

*Lucja?*

The house seemed to be offering up some otherworldly opportunity; a chance to recognise and resolve past wrongs. A chance, he thought, that neither he nor Sophie could, or should, ignore. 'Maybe we could contact a, um, what do you call them? A medium?'

'What?' Sophie's eyes widened. 'To come here, you mean?'

'Yes. We could get a medium to come to my house, to see if they can communicate with her.'

'Phyllis?'

'Yes. Or whoever else exists within these walls. Whoever might like to talk.' Piotr nodded determinedly. 'Because if you truly believe what you say and if you really do think that Cribbins is haunting this house, then why not Phyllis too?' *And Lucja.*

'Okay,' Sophie said. 'Let's do it.'

# 27

# The Medium

The only medium Sophie could get to come out at such short notice was a woman she found on social media called Lunar Wax. After posting an initial query on a local newsfeed, she had had numerous recommendations. One message in particular, from a woman who lived in Cotsford Park, had caught her attention. The woman claimed that if anyone could tap into the spirit world, a local man called Sullivan Carter could. Apparently he'd spoken with her deceased son and told her things in great detail that no one else could have known. The main reason Sophie felt drawn to Carter was because, as the woman explained, he was a reluctant medium and didn't do it for a living, therefore there was less chance he'd be one of the con artists who exploited the sadness of the bereft.

As it was, Carter proved unreachable. Sophie's message request to him went unread or ignored. Given the time of year, however, and the fact she was a complete stranger calling on services he didn't even offer, his silence was hardly surprising. Nor impolite. So, given the pressing urgency of the situation, Sophie had had no choice but to go with whoever she could get: Lunar Wax, whose social media following was vast and whose profile picture was a sexy raven-haired cartoon witch character in a slinky, purple dress.

When Lunar Wax pulled up outside Piotr's house, forty minutes late, in a brand new black X-Trail, Sophie was watching from the sitting room window.

'She can't be short of a quid or two,' Sophie pointed

out.

Piotr grumbled and made his way to the front door. 'Hopefully it is a sign that she is good at what she does.' His expression wasn't at all hopeful though.

'Oh I'm sure she's very good at what she does,' Sophie said, following him with her eyes. 'But whether that's mediumship or bullshittery, we'll have to wait and see.'

'Hmmm.'

Sophie then joined him at the door and they watched Lunar Wax get out of her car and saunter up the garden path; her pace altogether too leisurely considering how late she was. Not at all like her social media profile picture, she was petite in height and build – almost childlike – with bleached hair that belonged somewhere back in the eighties. Early nineties, at a push. It was wispy and fine like candy floss, and her styled quiff was so laden with hairspray, the entire front section of her hair moved as one entity in the wind. She wore a green duffle coat over the top of skinny blue jeans, which hung baggy around her ankles, and tasselled suede pixie boots that looked like something Sophie would have worn as a kid. Slung over her shoulder was a purple crushed velvet backpack.

*Bag of tricks?*

Sophie had initially put the older woman at fifty-five or thereabouts, but up close she realised she was probably ten years off the mark, and not in Ms Wax's favour. She had a toothy countenance and loose-fitting, leathery skin, which gave the impression that she'd shrunk at some point but her teeth and skin hadn't. Her eye makeup was as crude as wax crayon scribblings and she wore perfume so cutting, Sophie imagined her sinuses were shrivelling in objection.

'Hi there, I'm running a bit late.' Lunar Wax made a conceited effort to look especially harassed and in no way apologetic, as though whatever the reason for her shoddy timekeeping it should remain unquestioned. In fact, such was her air of haughtiness, she probably expected them to put it down to something as massive and uncontrollable as the moon's cycle. Sophie had a feeling she considered herself that important.

Piotr welcomed her inside, his expression unreadable. She walked straight through to the sitting room, the heels of her pixie boots clip-clopping on the laminate flooring, and looked about at the walls and furniture; gauging spirit activity or being openly nosy, it was impossible to say.

'Right then, lovelies,' she said, turning to face Piotr and Sophie. 'I take it you're Piotr. And you're Sophie. I'm Jocelyn. Jocelyn Barns.'

Piotr tugged on his bottom lip, his dark eyes clouding with confusion. 'I thought you were Lunar Wax.'

The woman laughed; a raucous throaty sound that was more startling than infectious. She set her backpack down on the couch and opened it. 'That's just social media branding, sweetheart. My stage name, if you like.'

Sophie didn't. Suddenly it made this whole thing seem too gimmicky. Too false. She'd been under no illusion that Lunar Wax was the woman's given name, but had at least expected that she'd keep up the charade and become that persona throughout their dealings that afternoon, at least for the sake of professionalism. Because who the hell was Jocelyn Barns? She certainly wasn't the person Sophie had made contact with, which made Sophie feel somehow lied to, lured in by fake assurances of eccentricity.

'I like to tell people my real name as soon as we meet in person,' Jocelyn said, as though sensing Sophie's mistrust. 'It creates an air of honesty and the spirits, they like that.' Fully switching her attention to Piotr, she asked, 'So, you believe you have a spirit?'

Piotr shrugged, like he was having second thoughts about whether he did or not. He was standing in front of the mantelpiece, fiddling with his fingers and twirling the silver ring on his thumb round and round. 'I am not sure.'

'Oh but I am, pet lamb.' Jocelyn started to root about in her backpack till she found a small satin pouch. Her lips drew back from her teeth in a smile that might have been a grimace. 'As soon as I walked into this house I could sense more than one presence.'

Even though her intense stare seemed to demand a reaction from him, Piotr didn't respond. He rubbed his chin and maintained a neutral expression, his dark eyes guarded. Hesitant.

'So how do we go about speaking to them?' Sophie asked.

'Just a sec.' Jocelyn shook the satin pouch over her palm and a small rounded stone fell out. It was dark green with red spatters and looked as ominous as a poisonous frog. 'This is my bloodstone,' she explained, showing it to them. 'To ward off bad spirits. We may begin now, if you like. My spirit guide will direct the spirits towards me.'

'Your spirit guide?' Sophie expected all mediums must have their own ways of doing things, but she had no idea what any of those methods were.

'Yes, his name is Jeremy Fox,' Jocelyn said, stroking the bloodstone in her hand, as though it was a living thing. 'He's been giving me guidance ever since I was ten years old.'

'And how did that arrangement come about?' Sophie asked, managing to keep all sense of sarcasm from her tone.

'We connected in the spirit world before I was saved by hospital staff and brought back to life. I fell off a horse and died, you see. Well, technically the horse threw me off, if you want to get all pedantic about it.'

'Not really.' Sophie glanced at Piotr. He looked uncomfortable. Uptight even.

'Should we sit?' he asked.

'You can if you like, sweetheart,' Jocelyn said, motioning to the couch. 'But I prefer to stand. I like to wander. To go wherever I can hear them best.' Putting this theory into practice, she walked over to the window, where she ran her hand along the length of glossed sill, as if absorbing some psychic energy from it. Then rubbing her hands together, she breathed in deeply. 'I've got someone coming through already. A lady.'

Despite her already growing doubts, Sophie's breath caught. *Could it possibly be?* 'What's she called?'

Jocelyn shushed her with a moderate scowl and closed her eyes in concentration, thus revealing the full extent of waxy pearlescent blue that covered her eyelids in crinkled layers. 'I feel like she's telling me …Shirley? No, wait. Susan.' Opening her eyes again, she looked from Piotr to Sophie. When neither of them expressed anything but vagueness, she said, 'I could be wrong though, she seems very agitated. She's stumbling over her words and not making a great deal of sense.'

'But it is definitely a woman, yes?' Piotr asked.

'Yes.' Jocelyn tilted her head back and spoke, as if to the ceiling, 'What was that, Jeremy? She told you what? That she used to live here? Oh. Okay. Could you ask her to speak more slowly, please, so that *I* can understand? Get her to focus. Ask her to…ah yes, I can hear you now, lovely. Stay with me. Stay focussed.' Jocelyn stopped talking and appeared to listen to something that no one else in the room could hear. She looked at Sophie and said, 'This lady, she says that she knows you.'

'Oh?'

A smile that seemed too smug to be anything but settled into the creases of Jocelyn's slack mouth with some presumed exclusive knowledge. 'Yes, and she says she's very happy that you two are together at last.' She pointed a finger at Sophie and Piotr and waggled it about as if binding them together with invisible thread. 'She says you deserve each other.'

Neither Sophie nor Piotr thought to correct this overconfident inaccuracy of hers.

'She's presenting me with the image of a baby boy,' Jocelyn went on, grinning like an idiot. 'But not until after there's been a white wedding.'

Sophie chanced a sideways glance at Piotr. He avoided looking at her, but she could feel doubt emanating from him almost as strongly as she could feel it herself; a dejected sense of embarrassment at having invited this crank into his home.

'I don't know any Susans or Shirleys in the afterlife,' Sophie said, wanting to get things back on track.

Jocelyn closed her eyes and her lips began to move in silent speech. After a while she said, 'I'm sorry, she won't confirm her name. It might not be Susan or Shirley.'

'Well, is anybody else here?'

'Not at the moment.'

'But I thought you said there's more than one presence?'

'Yes, but they're not talking to me right now. They're not here in this room with us.'

'So where are they?'

'I don't know.'

'What about upstairs? Can we go up there?' Sophie thought about Cribbins and Phyllis in Piotr's room.

'As a rule of thumb,' Jocelyn said, her drawn on eyebrows crumpling with some sort of petulant disapproval, 'I never go upstairs in clients' homes.'

'I really can't see any harm in you having a quick look though,' Sophie argued. 'This is really important.'

Jocelyn licked her teeth and looked at Piotr for his input. It was his house after all. He nodded his consent, but the dourness of his expression implied that this granting of permission for them to go mooching about in his private room was not a willing one.

'Alright then.' Jocelyn inhaled deeply through her nose to convey an air of persecution, to let them know she was even less keen. 'I'll take a look. A very quick look.' But as she made her way across the sitting room, the door that led to the stairs crashed shut, barring her way to the upper realm of the house. It caused a gunfire crack of wood against wood, which made everyone jump.

'Goodness me!' She leapt backwards, clutching the bloodstone to her chest.

'It is okay,' Piotr said, holding his arms out in assurance. 'The bedroom window is open, that is all. It causes a draft.'

But Jocelyn was having none of it, she shook her head adamantly. 'No, it's the spirits. They don't want me up there.'

'Really, there is nothing to worry about,' Piotr reiterated. He went to the door and opened it easily, then peered up the stairs. 'It was just a draft.'

'No, it was a sign.' Jocelyn backed away from Piotr and the door. 'And I have to respect the spirits' wishes.' She clenched the bloodstone tight in her fist, as though hoping to melt it and absorb it into her body. 'Something bad happened up there. Jeremy says so.' She closed her eyes and swayed on her feet. 'I can feel it now. There's evil all around us.'

Sophie felt her skin bristle. She caught Piotr's eye. His eyebrows rose in shared consternation.

Now hugging herself, appearing somewhat possessed, Jocelyn's eyes snapped open again and her mouth became a rictus of pain. 'And children...there are children here as well!'

'How many?' Sophie was stunned. Her thoughts turned to the ghost girl.

*Don't let him keep me.*

'I don't know, but I can hear them. They're all chattering. They sound very scared.'

'Did they die here?'

'I don't know.' Jocelyn had paled considerably. 'Jeremy is trying to find them, to coax them out so that I can speak with them.'

A crashing noise upstairs made it sound as though the ceiling directly above them had split open and the contents of Piotr's room were about to fall on their heads. They all flinched and looked up. When nothing else happened, Piotr took off up the stairs, his feet urgent, taking two at a time.

'I can't do this anymore,' Jocelyn told Sophie. 'Not here. Not in this house. No. I'm sorry. I can't continue with this contact. I can feel...I can feel...' She put a hand loosely over her eyes, as if the insipid daylight in the room hurt them, and Sophie saw how much she was trembling.

'You can feel what?' Sophie urged.

But Jocelyn was having some sort of funny turn and no longer seemed compos mentis. Her eyes were rolled back and her whole body had begun to convulse. Words which meant nothing to Sophie were spilling out of her mouth in some convoluted, demented chant. Sophie could do nothing but stare, open mouthed.

Piotr jogged back down the stairs and re-joined them in the sitting room. 'Everything is okay up there,' he said.

'No. It's not!' Jocelyn jolted out of her state of trancelike gibberish and became suddenly riled in her state of panic. She jostled the bloodstone back into its pouch and cried, '*Nothing* is okay up there. And I need to leave. Right now.'

'You can't,' Sophie said. 'You only just arrived.'

'I won't charge for a full session.'

'But you haven't told us much of anything. And what you did tell us didn't mean a thing.'

'Please.' Jocelyn swung her backpack over her shoulder and stepped past Sophie. 'I understand your frustration, but I really can't do this. I just can't.' She crossed the room towards the front door, to leave, but as she did the interior door that led to the entrance vestibule and stairs began to move of its own accord again. Only this time it creaked shut slowly. Deliberately. Teasingly. Jocelyn stopped walking, her eyes becoming wide. Slow seconds passed, then her hand flew up to her mouth and she groaned. 'There's a girl. Right there. By the door. I can see her. Clear as day.' Jocelyn seemed more surprised by this than she probably should have, given her claims of mediumship.

Both Sophie and Piotr looked at the empty space that Jocelyn gestured to. This time neither of them thought that she might be bluffing, because the air all around them had altered. It was cold. And charged. Undeniably supernatural in its sudden transformation to become something so perceptively different. Their realities had crossed paths with a dimension they didn't yet belong to, and Piotr, Sophie saw, was more ashen than ever.

'Ask her what her name is,' he said to Jocelyn.

# 28

# The Children

'She's trying to tell me something,' Jocelyn said. 'Something about sweets, I think. Lollies. No. What was that, lovely? Lolly? A lollipop?' Jocelyn closed her eyes. Her breath came out in trails of subtle white, as the warm moist air from her lungs met with the increasing coldness of the room. 'No? I don't know what you're trying to tell me, sweetheart. Jeremy, can you confirm? What is she trying to say? I don't understand.' Jocelyn's hands were trembling. She massaged her temples as if to manually clear her thoughts. 'A box of lollies? No. Lolly. Just one lolly? A box with just one lolly in it? Oh, I see! Okay. Lolly Box. Your *name* is Lolly Box.' Jocelyn opened her eyes and looked at Sophie then Piotr. 'Does that name mean anything to you? There's a girl here called Lolly Box.'

Sophie shook her head and Piotr asked, 'Are you sure that's her name?'

Jocelyn held up her hands. 'That's what she says. Though I can't be certain, she seems highly irritable.'

Piotr rubbed his neck till the skin turned pink. 'Could it be Lucja?'

Sophie looked at him, confused. Wanted to ask who Lucja was, but Jocelyn shook her head and said, 'I don't think so, no.'

A door banged shut somewhere upstairs. Then footsteps thundered overhead, rattling floorboards and plasterboard. Sophie blanched, dreading what might happen next. No one spoke; all three of them afraid that any further sound they made would prompt every bad spirit in the house to confront them directly, and if that were to happen none of them would know what to do. They were dabbling with the unknown, after all, and despite what Jocelyn Barns claimed to see and know with her sixth sense, Sophie didn't believe there were any steadfast rules when it came to resolving issues of the deceased. Especially Cribbins. Because the realm of the dead, she imagined, was a complicated place, much like the land of the living. All of it depicted in greys, none of it black and white. Seldom would it be a case of uttering some prayer as a quick-fix solution, like they do in the movies, to prevent the disgruntled dead from further harassing the living, because real life was never that simple. As with all human conflict, this was about different ideals and psychologies at war. The living were bad enough, but who the hell was there to police the dead? Who was going to keep a morally debased spirit like Cribbins in check?

Sophie believed Cribbins had the upper hand in this situation. By far. Without doubt. He lived between both worlds and had the luxury to move freely between them. Whenever he needed to recharge, he had a hiding place where Sophie couldn't reach him. Whereas when it came to Sophie, he knew exactly where to find her at all times. There was no escape.

Then what about Lolly Box? Could she be the ghost girl Sophie had seen?

And who was Piotr's Lucja?

Things had become a lot more confusing.

Jocelyn made a strangled, mewling noise – a shriek but not quite – and pointed at the fireplace, where the whole hearth area was swarming with cockroaches. A black stream of them emerged, one by one, from beneath the artificial coals of the gas fire and crawled upwards, en masse. Dozens were marching across the top of the mantelpiece already.

Sophie thought about the ones on her bed; the phantom insects that had disappeared as soon as she'd shaken the duvet. She wondered if these ones on the fireplace were another of Cribbins' tricks. A sick mind game to keep her scared. She imagined that if she were to run her hand along the mantelpiece the cockroaches would all vanish, leaving the cream surface clear, unmarred, but she wasn't willing to put her theory to the test. No way.

'Ask the girl how many other children there are,' Piotr said to Jocelyn, seemingly too distracted by the possibility of Lucja to care about the cockroaches.

'Okay.' Jocelyn closed her eyes and scrunched her face in concentration. 'How many other children are with you, Lolly?' She grunted in acknowledgement of something she was being told, something that neither Sophie nor Piotr could hear. 'What was that? Oh. You're not Lolly? Then who is?' Her brow crinkled in frustration at her apparent inability to decipher what the ghost girl said. 'Lolly is another girl who's here with you? I see, but slow down, lovely. Who are you?'

Sophie and Piotr watched Jocelyn, transfixed.

'You must calm down,' Jocelyn said. 'I know the bad man is here, but I'm here too. I'm here to help. Do you know who he is? Can you tell me his name?'

Sophie could feel Cribbins' building presence. Her brain buzzed and nerve endings fizzed with the overpowering black aura of his wickedness. All the badness within him that she'd not yet been exposed to now threatened to impound her sanity.

'He's tall?' Jocelyn said. 'Okay, very tall. And thin?'

Sophie felt lightheaded. *The tall, spiky man.* She made eye contact with Piotr. He seemed less convinced. Then, as though the house itself was addressing this lingering doubt of his, the ceiling lightshade fell loose from its fitting and caught him on the back of the head. A crashing blow that brought him to his knees. The pendant burst into pieces upon impact and small shards of glass scattered everywhere.

'We're making him angry,' Jocelyn wailed, covering her face with her hands. 'He's here. In the house. I can feel him.'

Sophie stooped to help Piotr. She touched his head with careful fingers, brushing small fragments of glass from his hair. 'Shit,' she said, when she saw that her fingertips were wet with his blood. 'Are you okay?'

Piotr's eyes were slits of pain as he rose to his feet. He hissed through his teeth and told her, 'Yes, yes, I am fine.'

Sophie was about to object, to show him evidence to the contrary – the blood on her fingers – when the entire fire surround, with all of its shifting black army of cockroaches, started to shake. It made a low rumbling sound like distant thunder and shuddered so violently it seemed likely that the entire heavy fitting might come off the wall. Piotr groaned at this new display of malevolent mischief and moved out of the way in case it did. He pulled Sophie with him. Cockroaches scurried across the carpet in all directions, as though they'd suddenly broken free from whatever spell had kept them drawn to the mantelpiece.

'It's him,' Jocelyn said, eyeing the fireplace. Abject terror made her waxy face colourless. 'He's not happy about me doing this. He doesn't want me speaking to the children.'

Sophie was gripping Piotr's arm, but hardly realised she was doing it. 'What did he do to them?' she asked.

'I don't know, but I feel like this man, whoever he is, I feel like he murdered them.' Jocelyn clutched a hand to her chest, as though her heart might fail her. 'The little girl, the one I spoke to, she's gone now. She's too afraid. And the others, they won't come out. He's angry, very angry that we know about them.'

The mantelpiece fell still. Everyone looked warily at one another, waiting for something else to happen. When nothing did, Jocelyn adjusted her backpack and marched to the front door. 'I'm sorry, I can't do this. I need to leave. This isn't right. It's all too much for me. Jeremy? Where are you, Jeremy?'

'Before you go,' Sophie said. 'Tell me the man's name.'

'I don't know what it is.' Jocelyn's bottom lip had begun to tremble. She gripped the handle of the front door, eager to leave. But something seemed to be stopping her. Regret, perhaps? Regret that she'd be leaving Sophie and Piotr to deal with the supernatural shit storm she'd helped to stir up. 'The little girl didn't tell me. I got as much information as I could. There's nothing more that I can do.'

'You could speak to *him*,' Sophie suggested.

'Oh no. No, no, no.' Jocelyn pulled open the front door. Sunlight splashed into the passageway, but offered no sense of security from the things that, in an ideal world, should dwell only in darkness. 'I couldn't possibly do that.'

'Why not?'

'I don't want to.' Jocelyn looked back to the sitting room, where Sophie and Piotr still stood. 'I can see him right now,' she whimpered, her voice so low it was a strain to hear the words. Her unblinking eyes were glazed with such deep-rooted fear, Sophie thought she might be experiencing some final death throe. 'He's standing right behind you.'

The hairs on Sophie's neck prickled and her fingers tightened on Piotr's arm. Fighting the urge to turn and look, she said, 'Describe what he looks like.'

Jocelyn gulped and took a step outside onto the doorstep, as though it was a safe zone. 'He's tall and thin, just like the girl said.' She looked to the floor then, as though experiencing some inner conflict. 'I don't know if I should tell you this, but he's just given me a name.'

Sophie's heart felt like it might break through her ribcage. 'What name?'

'Caitlyn.'

By the time Sophie had time to absorb the enormity of Cribbins' threat, Jocelyn was already racing down the garden path.

'Jocelyn!' Sophie cried, running after her. 'You can't leave. Not yet.'

'I have to.'

'But Caitlyn's my daughter!'

Jocelyn paused at the door of her X-Trail and gave Sophie a heartfelt look of pity. 'I'm so sorry, I really am.' She pulled open the door and jumped inside.

A blast of lavender air freshener hit Sophie in the face. 'But...what should I do?' She put her hand on the car window, appealing to whatever compassion Jocelyn Barns might have.

Rolling the window down, the medium looked on the verge of hysteria herself. 'I don't know, I've never encountered a spirit like this one before. I don't know what to do myself. I've laid myself wide open. Even Jeremy has gone. That's never happened before. I don't know where he is. I can't hear him.'

'But what about Caitlyn?'

'I don't know.'

'Can't you talk to Cribbins some more?'

'Who?'

'The man in there. Ask him what he wants.'

'Absolutely not.'

'Please.'

Jocelyn shook her head vehemently and started the car's engine. 'I can't talk to him. I just can't. I *won't*. He's evil. A violation of the senses. You don't know what it's like to have him channelling through your head, to have him come so close to your soul. He's evil. Pure evil.' She released the handbrake and pulled away, then accelerated too fast down the back lane.

'I do know what it's like,' Sophie said, watching her go. When she turned back to the house, she could see a tall, ghostly figure at the doorway, waiting for her. Piotr.

# 29

## Piotr's Anguish

'Gareth?' Sophie felt a rush of relief when her call was answered on the third ring. 'Is Caitlyn there? Is she okay?'

'Of course she is. What the hell's wrong?' Gareth sounded mildly annoyed.

'Can I speak to her?'

'If you must.'

'Look, I'm sorry, I just had…I dunno, I had a bad feeling. I just needed to know that she's okay.' Sophie heard some light clunks as Gareth handed the phone over.

'Mam?' It was Caitlyn's voice.

'Hey, chicken. How's it going?'

'Great. It's cool over here, you should see it. And it's snowing again.'

Sophie laughed. 'Good. I take it you're having fun?'

'Yeah, totally. We've been skiing and snowboarding, and Dad took us all on the cable car yesterday. It was, like, *really* high.' Caitlyn went quiet then. 'Is something wrong, Mam?'

'No, I'm just missing you, that's all. Needed to hear your voice.'

'Oh. Okay. Well Dad's taking us to the beginners' slope again soon, so I'd better go and get ready. Speak to you later, okay?'

'Okay. I hope you have a lovely time, and you be careful.'

'Will do. Love you, Mam.'

'Love you too, chicken. Put your dad back on for a

minute, please.' Sophie heard the phone being passed over again, then Gareth's voice, 'Uh-huh?'

'Keep a close eye on her, Gareth.' Sophie fiddled with her bottom lip, nervously, and regarded the mantelpiece. It retained no evidence of the cockroaches that had swarmed all over it not yet an hour ago.

She heard Gareth sigh, then he said, 'Of course I fucking will, she's my daughter.' His voice was low and Sophie imagined he must have skulked away from the kids, so they couldn't hear him. 'And, let me remind you, this is *my* time with her.'

'Don't, Gareth.' Sophie massaged her forehead. 'I didn't call to pick a fight. I just…I…just keep her safe, yeah?'

The phone went dead. He'd hung up. She could imagine him frowning. Insulted. His jaw set tight. His blue eyes glaring. Cold.

'Is everything okay?' Piotr asked. His brown eyes were filled with concern. He was on his hands and knees in front of the fireplace, picking up pieces of glass from the carpet and collecting them in the centrefold of a magazine; the hi-res photograph showed a sprawling green landscape. It could be anywhere, Sophie thought. As close as Wales or as far as New Zealand.

'I'm so sorry for all of this,' she said. She slid down off the couch, onto her knees. 'Here, let me help you.'

'No, no.' He waved his hands to shoo her away. 'You might cut yourself.'

Knowingly or not, Sophie supposed he was probably right. Her fingertips were still numb. 'Well can I get you anything? A dustpan or something?'

'No, it's okay. I will sort it.' His eyes were intense, impatient; she hadn't yet answered his question. 'So, is everything alright?' he urged. 'Caitlyn, she is okay?'

'Oh, yes. Yes. She seems fine.'

'Good.'

They both fell quiet for a while, lost to their own thoughts. Outside the wind had picked up. It whistled a taunting tune through the letterbox and keyhole of the front door, and bayed behind the sturdy brickwork of the chimney breast like a restless, penned animal. Sophie glanced about the sitting room, checking along the skirting boards and in corners for lingering cockroaches. For any sign that they had existed. The fact that Piotr and Jocelyn had also seen them meant they weren't some personal neurosis of Sophie's, which was good news, she supposed. But was there such a thing as group hysteria? And if so, had she caused it?

'What did Jocelyn say to you?' Piotr said, stopping to dust tiny glass particles from his palms. 'When you followed her out to her car.'

'Nothing. The silly woman just scarpered.'

'Do you think maybe she did see Cribbins?'

'I don't know.' Sophie was still dubious about Jocelyn Barns and all she'd said. 'She didn't give us any hard proof did she? Like his name or a more detailed description.'

Piotr didn't argue Jocelyn's case and resumed picking up glass. Sophie watched him with interest. His hands systematically brushed the carpet and his t-shirt rose to reveal the waistband of grey marl boxer shorts each time he stretched forward. 'What did you think about the other stuff?' she said. 'The stuff about the children. Lolly Box and the other little girl.'

'Honestly? I am not sure.' Piotr glanced across at Sophie. 'I hope she was talking nonsense, that there are no children here, but...' He left the sentence hanging. Became thoughtful.

Sophie took a deep breath. 'Can I ask you something?'

'Er, yes. Sure.' Piotr shrugged, but his attempt at indifference was overshadowed by stiff unease, like he already knew what was coming.

'Who is Lucja?'

He ran a hand over his face and closed his eyes. Piotr seemed to fall into himself, becoming lost to some other time and place that only he knew. He stayed like that for almost a minute, then exhaled deeply and said, 'My sister.'

Sophie could see his heartache almost as clearly as she could see the dilated blackness of his pupils. Sighing, she said, 'Can I ask what happened?'

Concentrating on a section of carpet next to his right knee, Piotr became absorbed by the past and all of its horror. Even though his physical body was kneeling next to Sophie's on the sitting room floor, he was no longer there in the house with her. 'She was eleven, the last time I saw her,' he said, his voice monotone with numb resignation. 'It happened nine years ago. I was nineteen. I was supposed to collect her from school after work. My parents, they were at a family gathering. That was all they asked me to do: pick up Lucja and take her home.' Piotr seemed to get stuck on that memory.

'Didn't you go for her?' Sophie reached over and touched his arm, to remind him she was still there.

'No.' Piotr looked at her, but she doubted he saw her; his brain not registering the here and now. 'I had made other arrangements. There was a girl I knew. I had arranged to meet her. I forgot about Lucja.' He grimaced in pained self-loathing, and Sophie could tell that this was a wound that would keep opening up, repeatedly getting infected with guilt and remorse. Never fully healing. No matter where he went or who he became.

She tried to think of something to say, anything that might lessen his sense of accountability, anything that might make him feel in some way less plagued by himself, because everyone fucks up now and then. Everyone forgets to do something that they really shouldn't. Forgetting to pick up his kid sister didn't make Piotr a bad person. But all the words that came to Sophie's mind sounded weak and insincere, too flippant to vocalise. So instead, she asked, 'What happened to her? Where did she go?'

'There were a couple of witnesses,' Piotr said, miserably. 'People who saw her waiting outside of the school. When I did not show up, she must have started to walk. Nobody knows for sure. Nobody knows what happened to her next. She never arrived home. In all this time, we never found out where she went or who took her. Whether she is dead or alive.'

'So there's still hope that she's out there?'

Piotr shook his head and placed a hand on his chest. 'I can feel here, right here, that she is no longer with us.'

'I'm so sorry, I don't know what to say.' Sophie put her hand on his and gently squeezed. Now racked with guilt of her own, she worried that all of her talk and insistence about ghosts had stirred Piotr's past into a tumultuous storm inside his head. Was the reason he'd come to Horden to escape his past? And had she inadvertently made it catch up with him so soon? She couldn't begin to imagine what mental torture he must have put himself through during the past nine years. The what ifs and the self-recrimination. Had he thought the ghost girl Jocelyn Barns had spoken of might be Lucja? And that the communication would serve as some sort of closure, however terrible that confirmation might be? That Lucja was indeed dead. 'It must be so hard,' Sophie said. 'The not knowing.'

'But I *do* know. I cannot explain it, but I do.'

Sophie shuffled forward on her knees and wrapped her arms around him in an awkward hug which wasn't well received. She only intended to offer some small sliver of comfort, but his body was taut and unreceptive. 'I'm sorry to have roped you into this whole Cribbins business,' she said, dropping her arms and sitting back onto her legs. 'I never would have if I'd known.'

Rocking back, so the space between them was even wider, Piotr looked mildly vexed. 'Why not?'

'Because this is your house. Your home. It wasn't fair of me. You live here, for God's sake.'

Piotr rubbed beneath his eyes with the heel of his hand, wiping at tears that weren't there. 'Like I said before, I do not scare easily.'

'Being scared and physically hurt are two different things entirely. I mean, bloody hell, Piotr, that lightshade fell on your head. You actually got hurt. It could have been so much worse.'

'The lightshade fell, big deal.' Piotr touched his head. His face had clouded with growing frustration. 'Jocelyn Barns was a fake. You said it yourself, she did not tell us anything.'

Sophie wanted to believe he was right, even appreciated his rationale to an extent. But then, what about the legion of cockroaches they'd seen? And her own experiences with Cribbins so far? She and Piotr were both being haunted by some element of their past, but now Sophie's present and future were being jeopardised. She couldn't brush aside the fact that Jocelyn Barns had mentioned Caitlyn by name.

When Piotr had finished clearing all of the broken glass from the floor, he sat next to Sophie on the couch and said, 'I am sorry.'

'What for?'

'I overreacted. Before. I just...I am not sure what I can do. How I can help you.'

Throughout the house the wailing wind found gaps and holes through which to reach them. Its voice prophesied loneliness and heart-aching anguish.

'That's okay, I'm not sure what to do myself.' Sophie took her mobile phone from her bag and opened a new window in the web browser. 'Although I do think we should start by seeing if we can find any information about that little girl, Lolly Box.'

The search brought up nothing but links to confectionary websites offering wholesale boxes of lollipops. Sophie tried searching for 'Lolly Box missing girl' instead. This time lots of headlines about child abductions and murders came up on her screen, but nothing specifically about a girl called Lolly Box. Scrolling through a few pages before giving up, Sophie sighed. 'I dunno, maybe there is no Lolly Box. Maybe Jocelyn Barns did make it all up.'

Piotr didn't agree nor disagree. He put his hand over hers and squeezed. His wretched expression made Sophie somewhat pleased that he'd be working night shift that evening, so he wouldn't have to spend the night alone in the house with Cribbins. Or the ghost of his kid sister, Lucja.

# 30

# Autoimmunity

Piotr called at the house for Sophie.

'Are you ready?' The last time she'd spoken to him, four days ago, he'd offered to go to the hospital with her. She had an appointment to meet Ruth Barton, the hospital's MS nurse, to discuss what her options were. Originally she'd planned to go alone, but was pleased to find Piotr on the doorstep, still willing to fulfil his kind offer. She would be glad of his company. She'd missed him a lot. Since the day Jocelyn Barns had been to Piotr's house, he'd been doing lots of overtime at work and Sophie had seen nothing of him. He'd texted a couple of times to ask how she was doing, but that was all. She'd begun to wonder if he was working extra hours just to avoid her.

Following the medium's visit, Sophie, herself, had been inspired and overcome with a desire to be proactive in her fight against Cribbins. She'd bought some crystals online – a bloodstone and an amethyst – both for protection. She carried them everywhere, even slept with them under her pillow. Not that she'd admit that to anyone. She'd also begun to meditate, thinking that to purge herself of as much negativity as she could certainly wouldn't do any harm. Strangely, it seemed to be working. Well, something seemed to be working. The crystals. Meditation. Or both. Because all was quiet on the Cribbins front. Eerily quiet. She welcomed his absence, but deep down feared what his silence might mean.

Was he building up to something bigger?

For now, theories about Cribbins would have to wait though. Today was all about herself. She was about to be presented with a set of medical choices, which would require much thought and consideration. Because whatever course of action she decided upon would impact on her future. It could be the difference between whether she stayed mobile or ended up in a wheelchair. And the latter of the two possibilities terrified Sophie just as much as Cribbins did.

Piotr waited outside on the doorstep while she pulled her boots on. He was clean-shaven and nicely dressed: blue jeans and a white t-shirt that showed at the neckline of a charcoal chunky knit jumper. His wavy, auburn hair was organised chaos. He looked good, despite the long shifts he'd put in over the past few days. Ignoring Sophie's protests that she would take her car, he insisted he'd drive them to the hospital. He had his car key in his hand already and wore an adamant expression that suggested he wouldn't back down.

How could she refuse?

He was kind and thoughtful and if he insisted on insisting so vehemently about driving, then who was she to argue? There were worse ways to spend her time, Sophie thought, than being chauffeured about by Piotr Kamiński.

Usually Sophie was decisive and spontaneous. She would pursue any matter of interest. So had she been in good health, she thought she might have made a move on Piotr by now. But then, she suspected her ill health might be the reason he hadn't made a move on her. Of course, the alternative explanation was that Piotr just wasn't interested. Oddly, it was easier to allow herself to think he was reluctant to invest his future in someone with an autoimmune disease than it was to think he wasn't attracted to her.

They spent the thirty-minute journey to the hospital

casually chatting about work and British weather, then Poland. In particular, Gliczarów Dolny, the village Piotr was from, and the Tatras Mountains. It was only when they got to the hospital waiting room, where they sat close together, that Sophie decided it was time to address the elephant in the room.

'So,' she said, pulling her hair to one side, subconsciously smoothing it. The sleeve of her coat made a swishing sound against the wool of Piotr's jumper as she moved her arm. 'How've things been in the house?'

Immediately, Piotr stiffened. He gave her a sideways glance. 'Fine.' His response was curt, indicating a reluctance to discuss the matter any further. Evidently, his house being haunted was a closed case as far as he was concerned.

Disregarding his unwillingness, Sophie asked, 'Nothing else has happened then?'

'Like what?'

'Like any more falling lightshades?'

'The house is fine,' Piotr said, almost huffily. 'Nothing else has happened.' When she continued to look at him, he sighed. 'I will let you know if anything else does happen, okay?'

'Okay.' She nodded, accepting his word, happy to believe that he would.

A young nurse with dark blonde hair pushed through the swing doors at the end of the corridor. Her flat shoes squeaked on the lino as she approached. She greeted an elderly man, the only other person in the waiting room, in a way that suggested he was a known regular. The man stood up and slipped into easy chatter as the nurse led him back towards the swing doors, leaving Sophie and Piotr alone.

'I know you don't believe me about Cribbins,' Sophie said. 'And that's okay. To be honest, I'm not sure I'd believe you if it was the other way round. It's all a bit much. A bit too crazy. And I'm sorry for going on about it. I only asked you about the house just now because, get this...' She swivelled round to face Piotr fully, risking a smile and daring to feel hopeful. 'I've had no new experiences either. It's like Cribbins is leaving me alone.'

Piotr smiled too; relief making the dimples appear in his cheeks. 'This is great news, Sophie.'

'Yes. Yes, it is. But...' Her optimism gave way to a frown.

'But what?'

'I still think he killed Phyllis. I can't just forget about that, can I?'

Piotr's smile faded too. 'I think you are getting worked up about this way more than you need to. You were just a child. You do not remember what happened properly. You will never know for sure. And even if you did, what can you do about it? Cribbins is dead anyway.' Sophie made to argue, but Piotr held a hand up to stop her and said, 'Just let it go. All of this stress, can you not see? It is not good for you.'

'No, it's not.'

'So forget about Cribbins. He cannot harm you.'

'Hmmm. Tell that to Leanne Baxter.'

'Who is Leanne Baxter?'

'Never mind.' Sophie took a long, deep breath and rested her head against the wall behind. 'He *is* harming me though, Piotr. He's trying to destroy me, bit by bit. He's the reason I'm here.' She lifted her hands to indicate the hospital. 'He's done all of this to me. Each relapse, it's been him.'

'No.' Piotr shook his head. A strand of his hair fell down over his right eye. He brushed it upwards, using his fingers like a comb. 'You have multiple sclerosis, it has nothing to do with Cribbins. It is just bad luck. Bad luck that you did not deserve.'

Sophie's jaw became tense. 'And just what *is* multiple sclerosis?' Her question was loaded with a distinct warning, for him to tread carefully.

But Piotr was unfazed. 'You know this already. Your immune system is attacking your own body.'

'And why does that happen?'

He shrugged. 'I am not a medical expert.'

'Nobody knows. Not for certain.'

'I am sure they do.'

'I'm not. There are too many factors involved. I mean, is it genetic, dietary or environmental? Nobody seems to be able to pinpoint the exact cause. Is it something that lies dormant from birth which can only be triggered by an external source, like a specific type of viral or bacterial infection? They say the majority of people who have MS live in the northern hemisphere. Did you know that?' Sophie laughed, humourlessly. 'Maybe it's lack of vitamin D and I should blame my goth days, when I used to hide away from the sun in pursuit of the palest skin possible. But then, I'm sure not all MS patients live in sun-starved places or keep themselves cooped up indoors. Hell, maybe it's when the immune system gets bored in such clean, modern times, and goes looking for something to do, creating all kinds of mayhem along the way.'

Piotr stared at her, wide-eyed.

'It's all too sketchy,' Sophie went on. 'All I know is that my symptoms started right after that night I stayed at my folks' house, when it was my dad's birthday. It was the first time I'd stayed in my old room in years. I dreamt about Cribbins. I saw him. On the beach. In a Punch and Judy stall. Christ, I think I even heard him through the wall. Snoring. Mocking me. I think that night he managed to get inside of me, infiltrating my immune system like a virus and causing the initial inflammation at least.'

'A ghost cannot cause inflammation of the brain,' Piotr said, refusing to believe.

'Says who? It's too much of a coincidence.'

'But still, it *is* a coincidence. You must have remembered about Cribbins and what you saw. It upset you. You were already stressed about Caitlyn and work and the shitty neighbours you had. Maybe it was all of this other stress that lowered your immune system in the first place, then you caught a bug at the party which triggered the MS.'

Sophie looked away from him and focussed on a poster about quitting smoking. 'You're wrong, Piotr. It is Cribbins. You don't know what it's like. I can feel him inside of me. He's so aggressive.'

'MS is aggressive.'

'Don't patronise me.'

Piotr held up his hands in apology. 'That is not my intention. I just want you to forget about Cribbins and to focus on the MS. Then everything will be okay, you will see.'

'At this moment in time, I find that very hard to believe.'

'Why? Just remember, things could be a lot worse.'

Sophie was taken aback by his apparent frivolousness. His words felt too much like an insult. 'Don't say that.'

'But it is true, what you have is not fatal.'

'It's not curable either.'

'It will be, in time.'

'I love your optimism, Piotr, but please don't belittle what I'm going through. Not now. It doesn't help.'

'I'm sorry. I just thought that it might help if I could make you see things a bit more positively.'

'Positively? You think I haven't considered everything a million times over since this whole thing started? Yes, okay, I fully accept that things could definitely be a whole lot worse for me, but you know what? I'm struggling with this diagnosis now. Me. Aren't I allowed that much? It's new. I'm still reeling. I feel like I'm stuck in a nightmare, a nightmare I just want to wake up from. But I know there's no waking up. This is it, the hand I've been dealt. The way it has to be now. And I'm terrified.

'I mean, I get it, you aren't sure what else to say. That's why people say things like *'it could be worse'*, to try and cheer me up. To keep me chipper. But when you've spent months on end with no feeling in your hands and feet and various other body parts, not knowing if the feeling will ever return, not knowing when the next attack might strike, or how serious it will be, or if you'll wake up blind one morning, then you'll forgive me for taking offence at such glib comments, however well intended. I understand the sentiment, I really do, but it doesn't help. Not yet. It's too soon.'

'Sorry.' Piotr reached out and took her hand in his. 'I had no idea you felt this way. You never said.'

Sophie sighed, squeezing his fingers between hers. 'No, I'm sorry. I didn't mean to rant at you, I'm just spun out. Overwhelmed. I need time to adapt emotionally. Sometimes I have to vent, to get all of this off my chest, because I don't know who I am anymore. I don't know who I'll become. It's like I'm in a state of grieving for my old self, my old carefree life. I feel like I've been living in a dark, unfamiliar place for months. Left alone. To deal with the darkness. And there's been no light. None at all. No one to tell me how things will be. Sometimes I just need someone to listen, that's all. And I don't always expect a response, because there's nothing really to say.'

'I'm here,' Piotr said. 'I will listen.' He kept a firm hold of her hand and Sophie knew then, beyond any sliver of doubt, that he was someone she would do well to keep close.

'Thank you,' she said, relishing the warmth of his hand in hers. 'I'm strong and I'll adjust, I just need time. Right now it's too new. I've had a taster of what MS can do and it makes me feel physically sick.' Her eyes darkened. 'And I've also had a taster of what Cribbins can do.' She felt Piotr's hand slacken in hers, but she gripped it tight to stop him from letting go. 'I know you don't believe me,' she said. 'But I swear to God Cribbins is real.'

# 31

# Cribbins' Reign of Terror

Sophie was mentally exhausted, as well as soaked, by the time she and Piotr got back to the car. She slumped in the passenger seat and listened to the rain hammering on the roof. Rainwater rolled off her coat. She imagined Piotr's jumper would be cold and heavy against his skin. His hair looked much darker and his face gleamed with wetness. He hadn't said much since they'd left Ruth Barton's room and he remained quiet now, leaving Sophie to her thoughts while he mulled over his own.

Ruth Barton, the MS nurse, who Sophie had warmed to immediately because of her no nonsense, let's get down to the business of kicking MS' arse right now approach, had run through two options. Oral medication that Sophie would need to take every day for the rest of her life, which would, hopefully, reduce the number of further relapses and decrease the severity of each one. Or a one-off intravenous treatment that would wipe out the parts of Sophie's immune system that had turned bad, so that when the cells reformed they'd return in their original, clean state. A bit like a system reboot. The hoped-for outcome was that the progression of MS would be halted. The treatment, however, didn't come without its own set of risks. There was a list of possible side effects; some of them easily manageable, some of them potentially fatal. Ruth had assured Sophie that she'd be closely monitored for five years, to nip any such side effects in the bud, and that the chances of developing any of the really nasty stuff was very low. There was a significant chance she'd develop thyroid disease, but that would be easy to control. And Sophie figured she'd rather contend with an over- or underactive thyroid than MS. In theory it seemed like a no-brainer, that the one-off disease modifying treatment was the best course of action. To hit MS hard and fast, as Ruth had put it. Because with MS, time is brain. But still, it was a huge decision to make. One she needed to take away, to fully digest and understand. She had Caitlyn to think about. Couldn't outright ignore the most dangerous of the possible side effects.

Right now she didn't want to talk about it though. She needed time to reflect. Thankfully, Piotr seemed to understand this. He turned the engine over and switched the heaters on full. It wasn't long till Sophie could feel their warmth blasting onto her face.

Already it was getting dark outside. Through the windscreen the car park was a mottled greyness filled with moving white headlights and red rear lights; the hospital grounds were a hive of visitors and patients coming and going. Piotr flicked the windscreen wipers on and moved out of the parking bay. He filed from the car park in a queue of cars forced to wait at the traffic lights, then once they were out onto the main road they drove steadily past the wrought iron fencing of the crematorium and its neighbouring graveyard. Some of the gravestones looked extremely old; large slabs of rain-soaked, weathered limestone beneath which, Sophie imagined, each person was most likely forgotten about, by now little more than the subject of vague family anecdotes that had been rehashed and passed down the line.

Rain continued to blast the windscreen in torrents. Piotr began to whistle. A cheerful tune that Sophie, at first, only noticed on some content, subconscious level, but as he continued she jolted upright and looked at him in horror.

That tune.

*Mr Sandman.*

He was humming *that* tune.

A new brooding tension prickled Sophie's fear enough to make her heart thump in her ears. 'Piotr?'

She watched as his gaze slid away from the road. He turned his head and grinned at her, baring straight white teeth. Something about his expression was altogether too sly. His eyes unfamiliar, yet familiar in their misplaced blackness.

'Are you okay?' Sophie pushed herself against the passenger door.

'Did you miss me, kitten?' he said. 'It's been what, four days?' His voice was no longer accented with a Polish lilt and it came out as a gnarly sound that clawed its way up his throat from a larynx that sounded much older than he was. He jerked the steering wheel to the left and pulled the car into a bus stop; a sudden movement that jolted Sophie towards him.

'Piotr, what are you doing?' Fear made her own voice tremulous.

'Would you like me to show you what I did to Leanne Baxter?' He reached over and gripped her thigh, his fingertips biting into the flesh beneath her jeans.

Sophie yelped and tried to prise his fingers away. 'Stop it!'

Lurching closer, Piotr's dark eyes were ablaze with unfounded fury and his lips were drawn back in a feral snarl. His breath was hot and angry in her face. 'Oh the things I've yet to do to you.' Both of his hands came up and he grabbed her by the neck; all of his fingers pressing hard at the back and his thumbs squeezing deep into the flesh of her throat. Sophie gasped for air while struggling to break free. She tugged at the sleeves of his jumper and batted his arms with her own.

'Or would you like me to show you what I did to Lolly

Box?' he said, thrusting his face closer, so their noses almost touched.

Sophie managed to clear her right arm and landed a hard slap across his face.

Immediately Piotr shrank away from her and froze. 'Sophie?' His eyes became his own again, no longer maniacal, and he looked at her in vague horror. 'What happened?' He touched his cheek where it stung and regarded his splayed hands as if they belonged to someone else. 'What did I do?'

At first Sophie couldn't find any words with which to respond, she just sat there shaking her head and clutching her throat. But then she relaxed away from the passenger door and said, 'It wasn't you.'

'What do you mean?'

'Cribbins, he took you over.'

'But...I do not understand.' In the semi-darkness Piotr's face was pallid around the shadow of his slapped cheek.

'Neither do I.'

'You think I was possessed?' He ran a hand through his hair, his whole manner agitated. Restless. He looked just as vulnerable as Sophie had felt moments before.

'You talked just like him.'

'Cribbins?'

'Yes. You sounded different and you said some stuff that only he would say.'

'I have never blacked out before.' Piotr shook his head, stupefied. 'And I am not a violent man. I would never raise my hand to a woman. Never.'

'You don't have to explain. I believe you.' Sophie felt the threat of tears warming her eyes, but she didn't think she'd cry. Not now. 'I know it wasn't you.'

They made the journey home in relative silence and when Piotr parked on his drive, they got out of the car and barely said goodbye to each other. By bedtime,

Sophie was more anxious than ever. She hadn't heard from Gareth all day, so she had no idea how Caitlyn was doing. And she could still feel the pressure of Piotr's hands around her neck whenever she thought about it, which was often. It seemed Cribbins had merely been biding his time after all. Choosing a new tactic to surprise and scare her with.

Yet, what if it had nothing to do with Cribbins? What if Piotr had wanted her to believe he was possessed, but really he was nuttier than a jar of Sun-Pat?

*No.*

She couldn't believe he'd be capable of doing something like that to her.

*Why not?*

How well did she really know Piotr Kamiński, the aspiring accountant from Gliczarów Dolny who'd neglected to pick his kid sister up from school nine years ago?

*Not very.*

He was the attractive redhead next door with the kind eyes and outwardly warm personality, who probably kissed like he meant it, with his eyes closed. He exuded deep thoughtfulness, which suggested to Sophie that he'd have the ability to lose himself to his own imagination and longing with ease. But he was also a deeply troubled man who no longer had any contact with his family or friends in Poland. Should that have served as a red flag?

*Possibly.*

What had really happened to Lucja Kamiński?

Sophie ran her bare feet over the blown vinyl wallpaper at the end of the bed and imagined she could feel a faint thrum through the wall, as though the house itself was breathing. At the outer edge of consciousness, in some defunct part of herself, where everything was dark and obscure, she was aware of Cribbins. She could smell him too. Only, his sour stench was actually spilling out into the room.

The wall continued to breathe and Sophie imagined the wallpaper was the membrane of Cribbins' lungs and that her feet were permeable to his evil, therefore able to absorb him into her fully.

*No!*

She felt too hot and threw the duvet back, but her sweat quickly turned to chills. Pulling the duvet back up to her chin, she thought she saw black cockroaches scurry across the Artex ceiling. Could have sworn she'd heard their legs tick-ticking across the plasterwork. Or was it the sound of a second hand? The second hand of the golden carriage clock on Cribbins' mantelpiece.

*One. Two. Three.*

She waited for the bells. Waited for them to chime.

No bells sounded.

She was febrile. Delirious. On the verge of fever. Kicking out at the wall, she turned onto her side and brought her knees up to her chest, so that her feet no longer touched the wall. She needed to break the connection. Needed to break contact with Cribbins. But it was too late. Perhaps it always had been. Because he was there with her already. Possibly since childhood. She knew he was about to do something terrible. And she wasn't wrong at all.

*Would you like me to show you what I did to Lolly Box?*

# 32

# Lolly Box

**1977**

Lolly didn't know how much time had passed, but she expected she'd be in serious trouble with her mum and dad if she was to go home. She knew she'd have missed dinner by now; Mum's mince and dumplings. She remembered seeing the carton of mince thawing on a plate on the draining board before she'd left the house that morning, which almost always meant mince and dumplings. Her favourite. She should be starving by now, because she hadn't eaten in hours, but all she felt was sick. Nauseous. Her belly churned with underlying hunger, but the need to eat was overpowered by a horrible, gnawing feeling of unease and dread.

On the whole, it had been a strange day. Exciting at first, then downright terrifying. She'd lied to her mum. That had been her first mistake. A funfair had arrived at a neighbouring town and all the other kids at school had been talking about it, saying how great it was. She and her best friend, Melanie, weren't allowed to go without adult supervision, but neither set of parents was prepared to take them. The lure of hook-a-duck stalls, bags of pink and blue candy floss, shooting games and carnival music had been too strong to resist though, so they'd lied to their mums, saying they were going to the park to play on the swings, then hopped on the bus to go to the fair.

Lolly's second mistake was to lose Melanie. She'd nipped off to find the loo and when she came back to where she thought she'd left her, next to a donkey derby stall manned by a fat balding man with brown teeth and a bellowing voice, there was no sign of her best friend anywhere. There were so many people. In all directions. Everyone moving about. Bustling. Barging. Too much noise. And, stupidly, Lolly and Melanie hadn't agreed on a meeting point in the event of them becoming separated.

Lolly had wandered around for what felt like ages. Then eventually, deciding to stay put in one place so she had a greater chance of spotting Melanie's blue pointelle cardigan among the constant throng of other people, she'd stood next to a striped yellow and red stall. Inside the stall, some unseen man was conducting a puppet show. A bunch of small kids had gathered to watch. They all gazed up slack-jawed as a crocodile tried but failed to devour a string of wooden sausages. The man's voice was maniacal, the puppet show aggressive. Lolly wasn't keen on any of it, but she felt in some way safer around the younger kids, knowing that their parents would most likely be watching from nearby.

Being on her own in such a busy place, without her friend by her side, made Lolly feel vulnerable. Earlier, when she and Melanie had got off the bus and strutted through the gates to join the carnival rabble, amidst exotic sounds and delightful smells, she'd felt like she was twelve going on sixteen. But now, singled out, she felt like she was twelve going on six. Timid. Shy. Unsure of herself.

By the time the puppet show had come to an end and all the kids had moved off, Lolly still hadn't spotted Melanie and was left all alone. That's when tears threatened. Because she knew they should have been catching the bus home soon, so as not to get caught by their parents for not being at the park. She considered going to the bus stop, to see if Melanie was there. But then she worried that in all likelihood Melanie would still be at the fair, searching, just as she was. And she really didn't want to have to leave without her best friend. Besides, Melanie was smaller, so Lolly imagined she must be even more afraid.

Lolly had been about to leave her spot by the yellow and red stall, to do another sweep of the stalls and port-a-loos, when the strange man had appeared, right in front of her. He was so tall, he had to crouch as he spoke to her. On first impression, Lolly didn't think he looked like anyone's dad; someone who might help her. He was too old and didn't look like he would have the patience for children. He didn't look like anyone's granddad either. He was too young and his pointed face was unkind. She should have known better. Should have trusted her initial gut instinct. But when he'd told her he knew where her friend was and that he could show her, she'd believed him. Perhaps because she was so upset and wanted it to be true more than anything else in the world. In hindsight she knew that trusting the strange man had been her third and final mistake. The worst mistake she'd ever made.

She'd gone with him, willingly at first, believing she'd be reunited with Melanie. He'd led her away from the crowds, away from prying eyes, to a burgundy Cortina in a nearby street, behind a derelict pub. And that's when he'd stolen her.

Since then, time had been a long stretch of terror. Lolly's face was tight from all the crying she'd done. Tears had dried to salt over and over again, making her cheeks taut and her eyes blurry and puffy. She was tired of crying, exhausted from being scared, wanted to be in the sanctuary of her own bedroom, playing her favourite music and writing poetry. Poetry that nobody else knew she wrote. Not even Melanie. But instead she was trapped in the man's sitting room, tied to a hard dining chair that made her backside ache.

Since the man had carried her into the house, from the boot of his Cortina, he hadn't touched her. He came close, but not quite. Every now and then he would come into the room and stand over her, his face right in hers, his breathing hard and heavy, looking at her as though she was some exciting curio. But he hadn't so much as laid a finger on her. His breath stank and Lolly especially didn't like his eyes. Behind thick-rimmed glasses, they were as black as the hearse that had taken Grandma Box away. They were the kind of eyes that belonged to someone who'd find pleasure in drowning puppies in weighted down sacks. His lipless mouth was a mean slit, like an old wound that had healed but still gaped. And he pulsed his fists a lot, which made Lolly think he might hit her.

She had no idea where she was; close to home or a million miles away. At first the room she was in had existed in ghostly hues of grey, because thick discoloured nets covered the window, blocking a lot of what daylight there was beyond the awful walls of the man's house. Then before it had got completely dark outside, the man had drawn thin curtains across the window, to block out the night. The quality of light in the room was now a sickly yellow, cast from a ceiling bulb which made everything look jaundiced.

Lolly could hear the man now; he was coming back to see her. The way he dragged his feet on the carpet was almost certainly a cruel trick to taunt her, she thought. As though he found immense joy in terrorising her. Sometimes he would bring a glass of water for her to sip from. It was always room temperature and tasted like it had been scooped from a fish tank. Last time she'd refused to drink any of it, and thankfully he hadn't made her. He hadn't tried to feed her yet. She hoped that he wouldn't. She couldn't imagine wanting to eat anything he might have to offer, no matter how hungry she got.

The man had told Lolly three times that he thought she was pretty and that he would like to put her on his mantelpiece. She had no idea what he meant by that. Or why anyone would think to put a person on their mantelpiece. Mantelpieces were for ornaments and knick-knacks. Lolly was a girl, a real-life living person who would not fit comfortably on any mantelpiece.

She was confused and had never been more scared in her entire life. Not even when she'd got separated from her mother at the Bullring Rag Market when she was much younger. Being lost in the busy marketplace for five minutes had felt like five hours, but being in this stranger's house was much worse. A few hours already felt like days. And there was no one here to help. The nice lady from the knitting stall at the Bullring Rag Market wasn't around to take her hand, to help find her mum. There was just the bad man, with his foul breath and wicked eyes. The bad man who wouldn't let her get up, not even to go to the toilet. Lolly had wet herself ages ago, which had made her cry even more. She hadn't wet herself since she was very small, so she felt shame on top of everything else.

The door to the sitting room creaked open and the bottom of it scraped across the top of brown patterned carpet, creating a swooshing sound. Lolly's innards clenched. She crossed her fingers behind her back, hoping beyond hope that it might be someone else: a policeman, her mum, her dad or a concerned neighbour of the man's who might have seen him carrying her inside. But no. It was him. The man. He stepped into the room like a human insect, his arms and legs incredibly long. Lolly whimpered and tried to cower away, the dampness of her jeans adding to her misery as she moved.

'I'm going to clear a space for you on my mantelpiece,' the man said, with cruel delight.

Lolly had lost count of how many times she'd pleaded. Each time she'd been ignored. She thought she'd give it one last try. 'Please, I want to go home. I won't tell anyone. Please, mister. Just let me go.'

The man shook his head. A wet, purring sound issued from his throat as he chuckled. He squatted down before her. The gristle in his knee caps crunched. This close, his sweat smelt like cooked liver. Lolly thought she might be sick. There was something in his hands. Something metal. He uncurled his fingers to show her. A pair of pliers. Like the ones in her dad's toolbox.

'I'm going to declaw you,' he said. 'Then you can stay here with me, kitten, right there on my mantelpiece. You'll be mine to look at whenever I like.'

'But…I don't want to stay here. And I'm not a kitten,' Lolly said. She began to sob and her words came out barely comprehensible. 'I don't have claws either.'

'Oh but you do. All girls have claws.'

Lolly was too young to try to rationalise the situation or understand this monster's intentions, yet she was afforded some instinctive perception that death was right there in the room with them. And it was with this realisation that she knew she would never see her mum or dad again.

The man untied her left hand from the spindles at the back of the chair and brought it round to inspect her nails. His skin was papery and dry, like dead leaves, against her own. Lolly tried to pull away, but his large hand crushed hers till she cried out in pain and stopped struggling.

'Keep still, kitten,' he said, clamping the lightly rusted ends of the pliers to the tip of her index fingernail. 'I'd tell you that it won't hurt, but that would be a lie.'

Lolly felt lightheaded. Thought she might pass out. Hoped he was teasing. Prayed that he was just trying to scare her even more than he already had. Which she wouldn't have thought possible till now. But he yanked his arm back and, as he did, she felt the deepest, sharpest pain she'd ever known. The ripping, tearing of skin and tissue sent a blaze of agony from the tip of her finger right up to her shoulder. Shock filled her core with heated, rushing redness. Then she saw black. Then nothing.

When she came round, Lolly felt delirious. Hellish. Feverish. Her entire left hand was a wet, pulsing red thing, which felt three times its usual size. The man had placed it in her lap, where it rested like a skinned animal, bleeding onto her jeans.

He'd untied her right hand and was now holding it in his. Watching her with his hearse-black eyes, he licked his bottom lip hungrily and patted her hand, as though encouraging her to wake up. To watch. But it was all too much. He latched the bloodied pliers onto the end of her thumbnail and Lolly blacked out again.

Next time she awoke, Lolly wished that Grandma Box would come and get her. Because this was too awful. Too painful. The man's large hands were now around her neck, pressing hard. Squeezing her windpipe. Taking her life. She gasped for air, but couldn't draw any into her lungs. It felt like there was a fire raging inside her throat. She tried to cough, but couldn't. Then she heard bells. A light, tinkling sound. The golden carriage clock on the mantelpiece. Zoning out from the man, Lolly listened to the bells. As she did, a more resolute blackness blossomed within her. She imagined the clock was chiming the end of her life, the melodious tune safeguarding her straight to the golden gates of heaven, where Grandma Box would be waiting.

Lolly Box died on the stroke of three.

# 33

# News

Sophie joined her parents for breakfast the next morning even though she wasn't hungry. There was an air of casual indifference around the dining table, but Nora's eyes narrowed with concern and something like mild suspicion, as soon as Sophie sat down. 'Are you okay, pet?'

As it happened, Sophie felt like hell. The dream she'd had about Lolly Box, real or not, would haunt her forever. She picked up her mug of tea and forced a smile. 'I'm fine.'

'Feeling a bit cold?' Nora gestured to the scarf round her neck.

Sophie cringed, brushing the woollen fabric of the scarf with her fingertips. The bruising on her neck from Piotr's hands was faint but there all the same. She had absolutely no desire to try to explain how it had happened. Didn't want to have to tell her mam and dad that their new neighbour had tried to strangle her in his car the day before, but that really there was no need to get up on the ceiling about it because it was their old neighbour, Ronnie Cribbins, who'd possessed him, so it hadn't been Piotr at all. Not really. She'd covered it up with the only scarf she had with her, which wasn't exactly dining table attire. 'Just some odd sensations going on in my neck, that's all,' she lied.

During her last relapse, Sophie had resorted to tying a dressing gown belt round her ribcage, to trick her mind into thinking it was the belt she could feel and not the MS hug, where the muscles round her ribs had contracted for no apparent reason. That way it felt less weird and disconcerting. Her mother knew this.

Nora gave Sophie a sympathetic smile and patted her hand, then said, 'Have you decided yet?'

'On what?'

'Treatment.'

'No.' And she really didn't want to have to right now. So to stop her mother from pressing the issue, Sophie said, 'I don't suppose either of you can remember a case on the news or in the papers about a little girl called Lolly Box going missing?'

Lenny, who'd been skimming the sports pages of the newspaper till now, peered over the top of his reading glasses to look at her. 'Lolly Box? What kind of a name's that?'

Sophie shrugged. 'I dunno, but I take it that means you've not heard of her?'

'When would it have been, pet?' Nora asked, wiping the corners of her mouth with her thumb and forefinger. There was a pile of toast crusts on her plate and the tablecloth in front of her was speckled with crumbs.

'I'm not sure.' Sophie picked up a cold piece of toast from her own plate and just looked at it. 'Late sixties? Seventies? Might have been the early eighties.'

'Hmmm, I'm not sure. I don't think I have heard that name before.'

'Me neither.' Lenny seemed to consider it for a while longer. 'Lolly Box, eh?' He shook his head. 'Queer name that.'

Nora hummed in agreement. 'What makes you ask, love?'

'Oh it was just something I heard someone talking about,' Sophie said, not wanting to go into specifics. 'It doesn't matter.'

'Actually, speaking of little girls.' Nora grinned and her grey eyes flashed with quiet excitement. 'What time will Caitlyn be home tomorrow?'

Sophie sighed. Since the previous afternoon she'd sent Gareth six text messages and tried calling him a dozen times. She'd left three voice messages asking for him to get back to her as soon as possible, but so far he hadn't, which was unusual. 'Their flight's meant to arrive at Newcastle at about quarter past three, but I've not heard from Gareth in almost two days now.'

'Oh, well I'm sure there must be a valid reason,' Nora said, looking thoughtful. 'Maybe they've been out and about in the mountains and have run into some areas with no signal.'

'Yeah, I suppose.' Sophie leaned forward, putting her elbows on the table. She felt agitated. 'It's just, I can't understand it, I specifically told him to…'

'Give the lad a break,' Lenny interrupted. He folded his newspaper and slapped it down on the table. 'If he's got no signal, he's got no signal, has he? As much as I think Gareth's a bloody pillock, he's always been responsible enough with Caitlyn. He'll be looking after her, so stop being silly. Getting yourself all worked up like that, it's daft. She'll be home tomorrow.'

'I know, I know.' Sophie sat back and exhaled loudly. 'It's just…well, he *is* a bloody pillock.'

Lenny laughed and Nora nodded. 'You're not wrong there, love.'

Sophie look up expectantly when she heard the familiar rattle of Piotr's front door banging shut. She hoped he might knock, to see how she was, but he didn't. Instead she heard the engine of his car starting up, then the sound of it drifting away down the street.

'No Piotr today?' Nora observed.

'Guess not.' Sophie tried to make a blasé face, like she wasn't bothered either way, but instantly knew she'd failed.

Nora's eyes wandered to the vase of yellow roses and

white gypsophila in the middle of the table. 'Is everything okay between you two?'

'Yes, why wouldn't it be?'

'I dunno. You haven't been arguing, have you?'

'Christ, Mother, you'd think we were a couple or something. We're just friends, he doesn't have to pop in to see me all the time, you know. He has a life of his own.'

Raising her eyebrows in response to Sophie's sharp tone, Nora stood up and gathered plates. 'Alright, don't get your knickers in a twist, lady. I was only asking.'

'And I was only saying.' Sophie's phone started to ring. Gareth's name was on the screen.

*Finally.*

Accepting the call, she blurted, 'Gareth? Is everything okay?' But mother's instinct told her it wasn't.

'Sophie?' The line was faint. Not great at all. 'We're having a bit of a nightmare here. The weather took an unexpected turn. Some freak storm hit us and we've been snowed in for the past two days.'

'Oh God, is everyone okay?'

'Yeah, but we're still snowed in and there's no way we'll be able to make it to the airport for our flight home.'

Sophie's blood ran cold. 'But surely there must be some way you could try…'

'No. There's not. It's pretty fucking bad. We've been listening to the radio and apparently the storm brought a few trees down on the main road. Nobody can get in or out of the village at the moment.'

'Shit, how long do you think it'll be before it gets cleared?'

'I've no idea, but we've got plenty of stuff to eat and drink. And there's a gas heater on standby, in case the electric goes off. The kids are having a blast. They think it's great.'

'What about school?' Sophie said, her jaw locking tight. Gareth sounded way too cheerful about the situation. 'Caitlyn's meant to be starting back at school on Monday.'

'So are Olly and Niamh,' he snapped. 'I can't help it, there's nothing I can do. School will just have to wait till I can get them back to the UK.'

'How come you haven't called in two days to let me know?' Sophie felt angry, to think that all of this had been happening and she'd had no clue.

'I've had no signal.'

'How come you do now?'

'Because I'm not at the frigging house. There's a break in the snow, so I ventured out on foot to try and find some fucking signal just to let you know what's going on.'

'Oh right. Er, thanks,' she said, feeling no gratitude whatsoever. It was his fault Caitlyn was stuck in the middle of a freak storm in the first place. Though she knew her thought process wasn't exactly reasonable, she just needed to assign some blame. Needed to be angry with someone. 'Where's Caitlyn now?'

'Back at the house, making a snowman in the garden with Olly and Niamh.'

'You should probably go back and make sure she's okay.'

'Of course she is, Andrea's there.'

Sophie's stomach lurched. Just how well would Gareth's wife be watching their daughter? Caitlyn had never spoken badly of Andrea, in fact if anything she only ever had nice things to say about the woman. But still, would Andrea be watching Caitlyn as closely as she would be her own kids? Because what if Cribbins posed any kind of threat to Caitlyn in France? He'd more or less issued a threat when he'd spoken her name to Jocelyn Barns. Sophie felt sick with worry.

'Well, thanks for letting me know what's going on,' she said. 'But you should probably get back to the house before it snows again anyway.'

'Yeah, I will. And I'll be in touch when I have signal again,' he told her. 'But until then, we're fine. We've got everything we need, right there at the house.'

*Haven't you just.*

# 34

# Piotr's Turmoil

A ten-hour shift loomed. Piotr should have spent all morning in bed, but he hadn't been able to sleep. He'd tossed and turned all night. He'd thought about popping next door to see Sophie, but hadn't been able to summon the will. He felt massively awkward about the previous day and wasn't sure what to do. Too many questions and scenarios played out in his head.

Did he need to say sorry again?

Should he be worried about Lenny and Nora? He couldn't imagine that Sophie would have told them what had happened, but he couldn't know for sure. Should *he* tell them? Possibly. He certainly didn't want to shy away from the awful thing that he had but hadn't done.

Also, he wasn't sure if he should make an appointment to see a doctor, in case he was losing his mind. Because what if it happened again? And what if next time the outcome was worse? He could have seriously hurt Sophie.

Should he buy her more flowers? A gesture of apology that might be considered more sincere than words? Or would it merely cement his guilt?

He didn't know the answer to any of the questions. Wasn't sure about anything anymore. He wasn't thinking properly. So, when he'd got out of bed and got dressed, he'd decided to go for a drive.

At first Piotr had no idea where he was headed, he just needed some outside stimulus for a while, to keep his thoughts from drowning him. There was a hard frost on the ground and traffic was light. He took the coast road through Blackhall and decided, last minute, to pull off at Crimdon. The static caravan park on his left looked deserted and the car park at the top of the beach banks was empty apart from one other car. A dirty, blue Ford Focus with a Kennel Club sticker on the rear window and dog snot on the side windows.

Piotr parked up, facing the steely grey sea way below, and switched off the engine. The sky was the same colour as his anxiety, and looked to be nursing a storm. A gull swept by overhead, allowing itself to be carried seaward by the wind. Piotr thought about Sophie again. He was racked with inner turmoil, which made him feel massively conflicted. Which, in turn, made him desperately unhappy. He liked her a lot, but wasn't sure what he'd be getting himself into in the long run if he was to pursue this line of interest. It wasn't so much the MS that bothered him, it was the fact she was convinced she was being stalked by a dead man. What was he supposed to do with that knowledge? Ignore it? Accept it? Refute it?

But then, who was he to scoff? Hadn't he thought he'd seen the ghost of Lucja?

*Yes, but only after Sophie had got into my head.*

Besides, there was the issue that Sophie believed Piotr's house was haunted. Was obsessive about it in fact. So how could things ever work out between them if every time he invited her round she'd be on edge, thinking about Cribbins? And what if things were to go to the next level? Piotr would never be able to take Sophie up to his bedroom. Not after what she'd seen in there. She was obviously suffering from some delayed post-traumatic stress; a deep-rooted shock that had never been addressed till now. And his bedroom was a boiling pot of horror that would perhaps send her over the edge into some lasting hysteria.

He couldn't deny the oddness and scariness of what

had happened the day before, on the way home from the hospital. Sophie was convinced he'd been possessed by Cribbins and, as crazy as that sounded, it was Piotr's preferred answer. But what if he'd tripped out? What if the stress and anxiety of his own life had got too much?

He wondered if he should just let whatever had developed between him and Sophie fizzle out. It seemed they both had too many unresolved issues. The timing wasn't right for either of them. He had too much coursework to complete and future career prospects to think about. She had her own work commitments, as well as serious health problems to deal with. Not to mention the potentially messy situation with her ex and daughter. Did he really want to get caught up in all of that?

Or was he merely making excuses? Weak ones at that.

And then, what about the dodgy looking goon with the bad teeth and black tracksuit who'd waited outside of Piotr's car the day after Jocelyn Barns had visited? Seemingly he'd known when Piotr would be off to work, which meant he must have been watching for some time, studying Piotr's shift patterns. But for how long? Could have been days. Maybe weeks. A disturbing thought. The man had got right in Piotr's face, trying to intimidate him, and told him in colourful language that he was to stay away from Sophie. He hadn't looked like the type of person Sophie would be involved with, but then, what did Piotr know? He hadn't known her all that long.

So, was Piotr interested enough in Sophie to risk provoking the wrath of the village thug? The man didn't scare him per se, but Piotr didn't know what circles he ran in or the type of people he knew. Making an enemy of one unscrupulous person in a place where he wasn't known might end up getting Piotr into a lot of trouble.

*Gówno! (Shit!)*

# 35

# Into The Night

*Don't let him keep me.*

Sophie sat up in bed, alarmed by a sudden clarity of thought.

*Of course, that's it!*

The ghost girl had given Sophie cryptic messages and within them was the answer which she now thought she understood. Cribbins had killed the girl as well as Lolly Box – maybe others too, according to Jocelyn Barns – but he'd never been found out.

*He hid them. He hid them all away.*

But where?

*In Piotr's house.*

Sophie didn't expect to be able to find actual bodies anywhere within Piotr's house, but she did expect to be able to find whatever Cribbins had kept on his mantelpiece.

*His trophies.*

Mementoes of each victim, she reckoned, because that made most sense when she tried to apply logic to Cribbins' warped mind.

*I'd like to put you on my mantelpiece so that I can look at you whenever I like.*

He had objectified the girls. He would consider whatever keepsakes he'd taken from them an extension of the girls – his possessions. And Cribbins was hugely possessive over that which he thought was his. She thought about the muddle of stuff she'd seen often, as a child, on his mantelpiece alongside the carriage clock; the very same carriage clock that had witnessed the death of Lolly Box. But nothing revealed itself with any clarity. She wondered if it was Cribbins' hidden grisly collection that kept him tethered to this world, which gave her hope, in theory. Because if she could find the items, she reckoned she would be able to banish him. By exposing him to the police and giving resolution to each girl's family. By giving peace to the girls themselves. Thereby releasing the house and the world of his evil presence.

Feeling wired, Sophie reached for her phone. Since she'd heard from Gareth she'd checked the weather forecasts for Morzine, as well as the whole of France and Switzerland, quite obsessively. She was aching to hear news about when Caitlyn would be coming home. She saw that there were no new messages from Gareth, but Piotr had sent her a text message over an hour ago, at 11:30pm:

**I hope I have not woke you...I have something to tell you.**

Sophie called him immediately, her heart racing. 'Piotr, I just got your message. Are you okay to talk?'

'Er, yes.' He sounded unsure.

'What happened? You said you've got something to tell me?'

The line went quiet. Sophie was about to ask if he was still there, but then he said, 'I'm sorry I have not been in touch with you sooner, I just... after what happened...if it happened once, it could happen again.'

'So you were just gonna stay away and ignore me? Were you planning on never speaking to me again?'

'I...I'm not sure. I did not know what to do.' Piotr went quiet again, but the silence on the line was weighted with such turmoil it was loud in Sophie's ear.

'Is everything okay?' she asked. 'Was that all you

wanted to talk about?'

'No. There is something else.' The tone of his voice didn't bode well.

Her heart lurched. 'What is it?'

'Jocelyn Barns, she called me tonight.'

Sophie certainly hadn't expected that. A shiver ran through her. 'Why?'

'She said that while she was watching television earlier this evening, Lucja came to her.'

'Oh.' Sophie hadn't expected that either. 'Did she give you a message?'

'Yes, she told me that Lucja said that she does not blame me for what happened.'

Sophie didn't know what to feel about that, or how to respond. Was the medium homing in on Piotr's grief for her own gain? He'd plied her with his sister's name after all. 'Did Jocelyn give you any other information? Anything that might validate that what she said could be true? I mean, did she say what happened?'

'She said that Lucja's English was very broken and that she could not understand everything she tried to tell her.'

Sophie was trying to remain impartial for Piotr's sake. She wanted more than anything for him to be able find closure, but at the same time she didn't want him to be taken advantage of. 'So how do you feel about what Jocelyn said?'

'That she is telling the truth.' He said this with such conviction that Sophie knew he'd made up his mind and there'd be no swaying his decision. 'She gave a description of Lucja.'

'And it was so precise that it made you believe beyond a shadow of doubt?' Sophie was still sceptical.

'Yes. Lucja had a birthmark which covered the left side of her face. Jocelyn knew this.'

'But, what about newspaper articles when Lucja went

missing? Couldn't Jocelyn have seen anything like that
online?'

'I suppose it is possible, but she also told me about
Lucja's favourite stuffed animal. A grey rabbit called
Konrad Królik, who she slept with every night. Jocelyn
could not have known this.'

Sophie shivered again. Goosebumps tightened her
skin. 'Did she say anything else?'

'No, but I believe her, Sophie. I believe that Jocelyn
Barns is telling the truth.'

'Okay.'

'And because of what she told me about Lucja, I think
we must believe that Lolly Box is real.'

'I know she is,' Sophie told him.

There was a short delay, then Piotr said, 'How did you
find out?'

'Cribbins showed me.' Before he could ask what she
meant by that, Sophie said, 'I think he kept belongings
of each of the girls, like souvenirs. We need to find
where he hid them.'

'Can we not just tell the police about Lolly Box?'

'With what evidence? That a medium saw her in your
house and that I had a dream? No. I think we'd look
pretty foolish.'

'Then what else do you suggest?'

'I dunno. How about the loft in your house? Is there
anything up there? Any old stuff?'

'No.'

'You're certain?'

'I looked in the attic when I first moved into the house.
There was nothing but dust and an old television aerial.'

'How about under the floorboards? Or hidden in a
cupboard, behind some panelling? The more I think
about it the more I know Cribbins' collection has got to
be in your house. That's what the girl has been trying to
tell me.'

'What girl?'

'Never mind.' Sophie's pulse was racing with adrenalin. The fact she had Piotr fully on board made her feel strangely elated. 'I think these souvenirs of his allow him to stay here. In your house.'

'Then I will look, see if I can find anything.'

'I'll help.'

After hanging up, Sophie thought about Lolly Box and the nameless ghost girl. She wondered how many other girls were there with them; bound to the house next door, for as long as Cribbins was there to keep them. Sophie knew she had to be the one to release them. The one who would set them free and send Cribbins to Hell, where he belonged. She was shocked at the knowledge that she'd lived next door to a murderer of little girls when she herself had been a little girl. Had Cribbins deemed it too risky to add her to his collection on his mantelpiece because he lived so close? Or were his child-killing days over by that point? And what about the carriage clock? The bells of Lolly Box. Had they been too much for him to bear? Were they a representation of his guilt?

Her feet touched the wall, but she couldn't feel Cribbins tonight. Sophie didn't trust his silence or the air of expectancy that accompanied it. He was up to something. She tossed and turned. Turned and tossed. Sleeping lightly on and off for quite some time, till something woke her again. She lay still for a moment, listening. Then reached over and felt for her phone on the bedside table. 4am. No new texts from Gareth or Piotr.

There was a loud bang and the wall at her feet vibrated, as though the whole house had been shunted by next door.

Had Piotr come home from work early and slammed a door? Or was it Cribbins?

Sophie sat up, alarmed.

A faint scuffling sound beyond the wall made Sophie scrabble to the bottom of the bed. She put her ear against the blown vinyl wallpaper and listened. At first she heard nothing, then a child spoke a few muffled words that she couldn't make out. Leaping from the bed, Sophie managed to find her fleecy robe in the dark and threw it on over her pyjamas. She slipped her mobile phone into one of the robe's pockets and crept downstairs, unsure what she meant to do. On the other side of the wall, she heard quick steps on the stairs in Piotr's house. Were the girls tracking her whereabouts, trying to maintain her attention? Were they restless, because they knew that she understood what she must do in order to help them? Were they eager for her to get on with things?

*But what can I do right now?*

There was a crashing sound to the rear of the house, like a bottle bin falling over in someone's yard.

*Piotr's?*

Sophie crept outside, into the back lane. All was quiet and, as far as she could tell, there was no one else about. The night itself had a haunted quality, like it was too preoccupied by its own shadows and mystery to summon even the slightest of breezes. A sleepy orange glow, cast from the street light about six houses down, tinted everything it touched and strengthened the solemnity of the overall stillness with a Hallowe'en aura. Walking to Piotr's gate, Sophie saw that his yard housed shadows within shadows. But what she saw most of all was the yawning black opening of the back door, which stood open. Like an invitation. Beckoning the night and everything in it to step inside the house.

*Right this way.*

Sophie knew then that she had to go in.

# 36

# Inside

Sophie looked up and down the street before passing through the gate, into the yard. Shadows edged closer, like curious animals. She should really call Piotr, then the police, because his house had probably been broken into. But the idea that it was the girls who were allowing her access to his house to show her something important, right now, kept her moving forward.

She lingered at the open doorway and peered inside. All she saw was exulting darkness and her own breath coming out in ghostly trails. No noise issued from within, but the house kept a different kind of silence to that of outside. It was a silence filled with held breaths, which meant someone might be lurking in one of the rooms. Somewhere. A burglar with a bat or some other sort of weapon. Sophie's bladder twinged. She really should call Piotr.

She stepped into the kitchen and swung the door closed behind her, slowly and quietly. All of her senses were alert. Highly tuned to danger. Inside the house it was just as icy as it was outside. Coldness from the kitchen floor tiles seeped through the thin soles of her slippers, stinging her feet. She picked up a heavy wooden chopping board from the counter, anticipating using it as a weapon should she need to, then crept to the open doorway of the sitting room. It was too dark to determine whether anyone was in there, but she didn't think so. Gut instinct told her the room was empty. She felt along the wall for the light switch, then dared to flip it down. Brightness filled the room in a shock of light from the bare bulb that hung down from the ceiling. Piotr hadn't yet replaced the broken pendant. There was no one in the room, Sophie saw, but she gasped when she saw the wall above the couch. Someone had scrawled a message in large, angry black letters. Each letter was spidery, where the paint had run. The message read: **SHES MINE!**

Even without the apostrophe, the meaning was perfectly clear. Sophie looked about. Everything else in the room appeared to be intact. Untouched. Had Cribbins done this to warn Sophie off the girl? Was it because she was so close to revealing the truth?

*Don't let him keep me.*

*She's mine!*

There was a noise. Upstairs. Directly above her. Subtle creaking. Not floorboards. Maybe the bed. Mattress springs.

*Oh God.*

Then there were quick, light footsteps on the stairs, moving upwards. The girl. Was she trying to lead Sophie up there? She went to the door that led to the stairs and edged it open, cringing when its hinges made a high, grinding noise that certainly alerted the entire house to her whereabouts, even though she suspected everything within it already knew.

Music drifted down the stairs, filling the vestibule with a haunted ambiance of vintage surreal.

*Mr Sandman.*

Sophie's skin tightened defensively to inner chills that rendered her paralysed. She couldn't possibly go up there. This was exactly how it had happened all those years ago. But she had to. The girl wanted her to. There must be a reason. Gripping the bannister, Sophie made her way up to the gloom of the landing, where thick black shadows closed around her like hawk-moth wings, touching her skin with velvety closeness. She gripped the doorframe to Piotr's bedroom. She had to go inside. Had to see. Her breaths were quick and shallow. Her hands trembled.

*Oh God.*

Nudging the door open, she saw that everything in the bedroom was draped in black shadow. A thick funereal voile, opaque enough to obscure, but not dense enough to hide the dark shape that moved within the murk. The music was even louder here. And the air was frigid in every sense. There was a foul stink too, of sour sweat and stale flesh.

Sophie found the light switch and, in an instant, the room was filled with light and revisited horror. Cribbins was standing behind Phyllis, who was bent over the bed, face-down. Just as she had been all those years ago. Her head was twisted to the side, her face vacant, and her dead eyes watched but didn't see. The music stopped and Cribbins looked up. Grinning at Sophie, he stopped grinding into the back of Phyllis and lifted the upper part of her lifeless body. Gripping her face by the chin, he moved her jaw up and down. Then mimicking her voice, he said, 'Hello, gorgeous girl. Shall we bake some cakes today? Is that what you came for? To bake some cakes with lovely old Phyllis?' He let go and Phyllis flopped back down onto the mattress, her limp body making a dull smacking sound. 'Or did you come up here for some young, foreign cock? You'd like that wouldn't you? Well, maybe you can close your eyes and just pretend.' Cribbins laughed and flashed her a lewd wink. He moved away from Phyllis' body and grabbed his own penis.

Sophie could feel her nerves coming undone, but she stood her ground and stayed where she was. 'I'm not afraid of you, Cribbins.'

His expression darkened and he skirted the bed, so that he was standing directly in front of her now, just six feet away at the most. Footsteps on the landing made Sophie turn. Despite the light from the bedroom, she could see the dark outline of someone standing there. The ghost girl. Sophie reached out and swung the door closed, so the girl was spared the prolonged sight of Cribbins' nakedness.

'Where are they?' Sophie said, turning back to him. 'Your mantelpiece keepsakes.'

Cribbins laughed; a raucous cackle of phlegm in his throat. He took a step closer, but didn't answer.

'I'm not afraid of you,' Sophie reminded him, still resisting the urge to turn and flee. 'You're weak and pathetic.'

He lunged at her then, his large hands around her neck before she could escape them. His flesh was cold and clammy and his strength was shockingly bull-like. He grappled Sophie down onto the bed, his face so close that his nose touched hers. Breathing through his mouth, his breath was as repugnant as sewage. It coated Sophie's skin and hit the back of her throat. Retching, she struggled beneath the dead weight of him. Trying to get away from those hands. That breath. Turning her head, she saw that Phyllis was right next to her on the bed; mouth agape and eyes dead.

From somewhere else, perhaps nowhere at all, the bells of the carriage clock began their familiar jingle. Cribbins' hands loosened around Sophie's throat and distress lessened the depravity in his eyes. His cruel mouth slackened to a quiver and he lifted his hands to his ears. 'No! The bells. Tell her to stop. You tell her to stop playing those fucking bells. *I can't take anymore!*'

Seizing the opportunity, Sophie brought her leg up and kneed the sunken pit of his abdomen. He doubled over and snarled in pained surprise. She pushed him away and scrabbled to her feet. The bells kept sounding and Cribbins cowered on the floor, his body becoming transparent as though the bells were somehow negating his presence. Somewhere in the house a little girl laughed. Then there was a familiar clicking noise. Old joints moving. And Sophie watched in awed horror as Phyllis' body came to life. The older woman pushed herself upright; her movement irregular, her limbs spasmodic. Her dead eyes became focussed, aware, and she snapped her mouth open and shut, as though testing that her jaw still worked.

'I tried to tell you,' she said to Sophie, her voice a dreadful croak. 'I wanted to tell you where he hid them.'

'It was you who left the toffee for me, wasn't it?'

'Yes.'

'Why didn't you tell me then?'

'I couldn't. He wouldn't let me.' Quaking with terror, Phyllis glanced at Cribbins. As she did, she seemed to fade to little more than a memory. Bullied and controlled by him even in death, she looked more forlorn than Sophie could ever remember her having been in life.

'But you can tell me now, can't you?' Sophie cried, afraid that she'd disappear altogether.

'Yes. She'll help.'

'The girl?'

Phyllis nodded. 'She'll keep playing the bells. That's what she does, she and the other girls. Ronnie doesn't like that. He doesn't like her. But I do. I'd have been lost without her for all this time.'

'Did you know your husband was a child murderer?'

'No!' Phyllis' face scrunched in horror. 'I didn't know. All those years, I had no idea of the things he'd done. Those girls. Those poor girls.' She began to sob then. 'I love children. You have to know that. I want you to know that.'

'I do know, Phyllis,' Sophie told her. 'I just had to check. I wanted to know for certain. You were always very kind to me. And now I'm going to set you free. You and the girls.'

Phyllis managed a smile. It was sad. Bereft of joy. But edged with hope. 'Thank you, gorgeous girl.'

'Tell me where he hid them.'

# 37

# Hiding Place

Piotr was exhausted by the time his shift ended. He packed up his coursework and put it in his backpack, then went outside to the car park. The sun was still two hours away, so the morning was as black as night. The factory floor workers who were on early shift had clocked on just before Piotr had clocked off, so most of the parking bays were filled. He'd left his car in the bay closest to the side door, so didn't have far to walk.

It was even colder inside the car than it was outside, and the heaters didn't start to blow warm enough to make a difference until he was almost home. When he parked in his driveway, he looked straight ahead at the house. Reluctant to go in, he just sat there. It would be cold inside, he knew. His bed sheets even more so. Piotr didn't leave the heating on while he was out. Couldn't afford the gas bills if he did.

*Well, it will not warm up if you just sitting here looking at it.*

Bundling out of the car with his backpack, he dashed up the path, thinking he would have a hot drink before bed. But as soon as he opened the front door he could tell something was wrong. The house was way colder than it should be. And there was a draft blowing straight through the ground floor rooms. His heart pitched. He lurched inside and closed the door behind him, then felt the wall for the light switch in the sitting room, bracing himself for what he'd find. As it was, he was stunned to see a display of vandalism on the wall.

**SHES MINE!**

And beyond the kitchen door, he could see that the back door was wide open. There was a figure standing outside in the darkness of the yard.

*Sophie?*

Filled with confused concern, he raced through to the kitchen. 'Sophie, what are you doing?'

She turned to face him, her face pale. Only then did he notice that she was wearing a fleecy cream robe over blue pyjamas.

'What happened?' he urged, his heart beating uncomfortably fast. 'Are you okay?'

'She was here. I spoke to her.'

'Who?' Piotr went to the door and looked about the yard. Saw no one.

'Phyllis.'

'What are you talking about? And what is going on. My house. That writing on the wall.'

Sophie grimaced. 'Oh God, Piotr, I'm so sorry I should have called you. To warn you. I didn't realise the time. I heard the ghost girl through the wall, when I was in bed. Then there was a loud bang. I came out here to make sure everything was okay, and that's when I saw that your door was open. I was gonna call you. Call the police. But I had to check, to see the girl. But then I saw him. I saw Cribbins. In your room. With Phyllis. And I didn't realise the time.'

'But...why are you standing in the yard?'

'Phyllis told me where his trophies are.'

Piotr shook his head, wondering if Sophie had lost the plot and if she would take him with her if they continued down this route. He glanced about the blackness of the yard again. 'Out here?'

'Yes. Beneath the paving.'

His eyes widened. 'You want me to rip up the yard?'

'I'll help.'

Piotr ran a hand over his face and sighed.

'It's the only way to put an end to all of this,' Sophie implored.

'Okay,' he said, resignedly. 'Let us dig the yard up if that is what you want. Then afterwards you can tell me who is the thug who broke into my house.'

# 38

## The Truth

'What thug?' Sophie was astounded by the absolute conviction showing on Piotr's face. 'I didn't see anyone. I thought it was…' *What? Ghosts letting me inside and Cribbins' handiwork on the wall.* It sounded crazy. And maybe it was. 'I don't know.'

'He was tall with brown hair. And bad teeth,' Piotr said, pointing to his own teeth as he spoke.

'*Addy Adkins?*'

'He told me to stay away from you.'

'When?'

'Last week.'

'Why didn't you tell me?' She was outraged. How dare Addy Adkins warn anyone off her, let alone Piotr? She was also perturbed. What kind of maniac broke into someone's house to vandalise their property all because of some creepy obsession they had with someone else? Her mam and dad had warned that he was trouble, but Sophie hadn't expected him to be quite so unhinged.

'I didn't think it was important,' Piotr said, inspecting the back door's busted lock. 'But since he is taking his threat to another level, should I be concerned?'

'I don't know. That is, I don't really know him.' Sophie rubbed her forehead. Agitated. Troubled. 'He hangs around with my cousin. I'll have a word with Shaun. God, I'm so sorry.'

'Let us worry about it later. For now, we need to find Cribbins' things. Yes?' Piotr went to the cupboard under the stairs and brought a spade outside. It was still dark, but light flooded out from the kitchen window. He shooed Sophie away, wouldn't let her help. Sent her back inside, where it was marginally less cold.

At first she stood in the doorway, watching as he tried to wrestle the first paving slab up. It proved tricky to remove and, as he struggled to get enough leverage to lift it, he chipped a corner of the concrete off with his spade and muttered a word she didn't understand. Once the first slab was out of the way, moving subsequent ones became a much quicker process.

'Shall I put the kettle on?' Sophie offered, needing something to do.

Piotr gave her a look which suggested it was an absurd question for an absurd situation. But she went and filled the kettle anyway and set about making two cups of tea. She shook with adrenalin and cold, and watched miserably through the kitchen window as Piotr pulled up paving slabs and stacked them in the far corner of the yard. He'd come home from a ten hour shift to *this* and she dreaded that perhaps, just perhaps, she was wrong: that she'd imagined the whole thing and Phyllis was living in Brighton.

The whole house was colder than a mortuary's cold chamber. She thought she should probably go and put the heating on. The thermostat was on the wall at the bottom of the stairs; she'd noticed it the other day. As she crossed the sitting room she rubbed her arms. The house was laden with such ambiguous malevolence, she realised then that her flesh was tingling with more than just cold. Something else was there in the room with her, prowling beyond her peripheral vision. Watching. Preying. She knew she'd walked straight into danger.

Behind her, the door to the kitchen slammed shut. She came to a stop, hardly daring to turn, to look, but when she did, she saw Cribbins, fully clothed now, standing with his back to the door. A gaunt, frightening figure of substance, blocking her way to the yard. Guarding his trophies. She could smell him now too, his infernal stench of old smoke and stale sweat clogging the room with profound bitterness.

'Naughty, naughty,' he said. The syllables of each word churned from his greased throat and he wagged a finger at her. 'I should have killed you all those years ago.'

Almost too afraid to ask the question in case it provoked him to rectify his mistake, but genuinely wanting to know all the same, Sophie said, 'Why didn't you?'

Provoked, Cribbins lunged forward. His arms and legs were quick and long, and he was upon her in an instant. He pushed her backwards, towards the fireplace, and clamped a hand over her face to stop her from screaming. As he flung her down to the floor, Sophie's head banged against the edge of the hearth. It was a sharp blow which brought a fleeting smell of blood to the back of her nose or the suggestion of it inside her head; imagined or real, she couldn't tell which. Cribbins straddled her torso and she felt her lungs deflate as his weight crushed down on her ribs.

'I've asked myself the same question many times,' he said, saliva bubbling on his teeth each time his lips pulled back. 'The bitter sweet irony is, on that very first day I saw you in the garden, I wanted you for my mantelpiece. But now? Now I just want to cave your skull in and set fire to your body, then piss on your ashes. I want you to pay for all you've done to me. I want you to suffer, eternally. You and your kitten.'

Sophie closed her eyes against the spittle that flew from his mouth. 'No! You leave Caitlyn alone, you bastard!'

Cribbins chuckled and stooped closer. So close that his breath was as intimate on Sophie's face as only a lover's should be. She could smell the badness of his guts and see the implied menace of his hell-black eyes. 'Oh I didn't mean Caitlyn,' he crooned. 'Not yet, anyway. I meant that kitten right there.' He turned his head.

Struggling to breathe, Sophie craned her neck to look past him. There was a small figure watching them from the gloom of the vestibule at the foot of the stairs.

The ghost girl.

*Don't let him keep me.*

'That's who you've been looking for, isn't it Sophie-cat?' Cribbins said, the catarrh at the back of his throat creating a nauseating purr. 'Only, I don't think you realised it, did you?'

Sophie didn't understand. Wasn't sure what he meant. But when the girl moved into the light of the sitting room, Sophie felt faint. Her eyes glittered as her consciousness sparred with the utter disbelief that preludes mental overload. She couldn't comprehend, on any level whatsoever, what she was seeing.

The girl was herself, as a child.

'If you let him keep me, he'll destroy you,' the girl said. Her voice was like a dark requiem of regret and her eyes were haunted. Disturbed. Changed. 'I already told you that.'

'But, I…I don't understand,' Sophie said.

'That part of you right there,' Cribbins said, pointing at the girl. 'She's been with me ever since the day you came poking your nose where it didn't belong.' His frown deepened. 'And oh how she's tormented me.'

The girl laughed. It was a sound so filled with maniacal glee, Sophie was both shocked and frightened.

'Wicked, isn't she?' Cribbins said, reacting to Sophie's surprise. 'She's been hounding me for all this time. On and on and on and on. What an ordeal it's been. She killed me, you know. Enticed that little girl, Lolly Box, from her hiding place and befriended her. Some of the others too. Together they made no end of mischief.

Tormenting me with those fucking bells mostly. I got rid of the clock, with the other stuff, yet still it chimed. All hours. Drove me fucking mad. Exhausted my nerves. Gave me a fucking heart attack from the stress of it all.'

'It's less than you deserved,' Sophie spat.

Cribbins laughed. 'You should have seen what she did to that friend of yours earlier. Addy Adkins?'

'He's not my friend.' Sophie struggled again to free herself, but Cribbins stayed firmly in place. His hands squeezed her arms harder, as though he hoped to puncture her flesh with his fingertips. She imagined bruises blooming already.

'I would have applauded her if she wasn't so loathsome,' Cribbins said, his jaw set tight. 'Because I'm sure he'll have many sleepless nights to come.'

Sophie's eyes widened. *What had she done?*

'Oh yes,' Cribbins said, 'even declawed, she's an evil little hellcat, that one.'

The girl was near the window now. Sophie looked at her hands, which hung by her sides, and saw they were nail-less and tarnished with dried blood. The girl regarded Cribbins with cool, dark eyes.

'What did you do to Addy Adkins?' Sophie asked the girl.

The girl simply grinned.

'Here, let me show you,' Cribbins said, wrapping his hands around Sophie's neck.

The kitchen door burst open at that exact moment and Piotr stumbled into the sitting room. 'Sophie, guess what?' His face was flushed with excitement, but as he took in the scene before him his expression morphed to one of horror. Reacting quickly, he swung his spade up and round in an arc and brought its flat underside crashing into the side of Cribbins' head. Cribbins quivered, then faded to nothing.

Sophie felt an immediate wave of relief as the weight

of Cribbins lifted. She rolled onto her side and wheezed for breath, clawing at her throat as she did so.

'Are you okay?' Piotr dropped to the floor on his knees.

'Yes, yes, but look...' Sophie pointed to the window. 'The girl, she's me.'

Piotr looked, but saw no one. 'What do you mean?'

Sophie sat up and frowned. 'Oh, she's gone. The girl I kept seeing, she's me.'

'I don't understand what you are saying.'

'The day I saw Cribbins, just after he'd killed Phyllis, part of me lingered here.'

'But, how is that possible?'

'I don't know. I guess I was so traumatised, part of me was damaged. Like a chunk of my psyche detached itself and stayed. Me and Cribbins, it's like we're bound together or something. And the only way to be free of each other is if he kills me or if I...I dunno...if I send him to Hell? I need to nail the bastard. We need to find...'

'His trophies?' Piotr said. 'That is what I came to tell you, I found a container in the yard.'

'*Really?* What's inside?'

'I am not sure. Come on, we will open it.' Piotr grabbed Sophie's hands and made to pull her off the floor, but Cribbins reappeared; a gangly scarecrow-like ghoul who flickered into existence as easily as he'd flashed out of it just moments before. He lashed out one long arm, punching Piotr in the face. Piotr staggered backwards and landed on the couch. Then Cribbins was on top of Sophie again, this time his bony knees pinning her arms to the floor.

'I'll kill you, you cunt!' But as his hands found the soft flesh of her neck again, a tennis ball slammed against his cheekbone and his head snapped to the side. The ball ricocheted off the wall above the mantelpiece and

Cribbins' eyes widened in shock. He whipped his head round.

The girl was by the window again, her face contorted in anger. 'Tinker, tailor, soldier, sailor, rich man, *poor man*,' she said, in an angry sing-song voice. She threw another ball and this time it smashed into Cribbins' mouth, making it bloody. 'You can't have me anymore,' she screamed. 'I'm Piotr's, not yours.'

Sophie looked at Piotr, stunned. Then she understood. And had the situation allowed, she might have laughed. Evidently her younger self was still holding onto the unwritten law of 'best of three' and believed Piotr to be her 'poor man'.

*Ha!*

Cribbins cringed and seemed to shrink physically in face of the girl's demand. His weight became less real on top of Sophie. So, using her legs for leverage, Sophie lurched upwards in an erratic body-pop, managing to send him sprawling. As she scrabbled away in an awkward crab position, the girl pounded Cribbins with another tennis ball.

'I'm not yours,' the girl told him. She came forward and put one foot on Cribbins' throat and pressed down till he gagged. 'Not anymore. You can't have me!'

Cribbins' eyes flickered to Sophie, fury-black, as though he might be able to control this small but wayward part of her psyche by intimidating her directly. But Sophie shook her head and said calmly, 'No. No you can't.'

Then Cribbins was gone. And so was the girl.

The house fell quiet. Sophie collapsed down onto her back and stared up at the ceiling. Piotr watched her from the couch, stunned. Silent. His cheekbone was already purpling from the blow Cribbins had landed on him. After what could have been two minutes or two hours, Sophie sat up and said to him, 'Let's see what's in the container.'

Piotr went to fetch it, then handed it over. 'Here, I think you should be the one to open it.'

It was an old chocolate tin. Sophie took it and held it in her lap, tracing her fingers round the contour of its lid. The branding on the tin was still recognisable, but had faded significantly after its long stint beneath earth and paving stones. Gripping with her fingernails under the rim of the lid, she opened it up. Inside there were some yellowed newspaper clippings. Six in total. The first one showed a picture of a young girl with a shy smile and thoughtful eyes, beneath her was a caption that read: Lorraine Box, aged 12, goes missing at local fair.

A shiver coursed through Sophie. 'There she is,' she said, showing Piotr the clipping. 'Lolly Box.'

The next five clippings all showed photos of girls who were of a similar age to Lolly Box, but from different places around the UK. From first to last, the cases spanned a date range of fourteen years. The details were: Sandra Benson, aged 10, fails to return home after school. Gail Atkins, aged 8, goes missing on last night of carnival. Tracey Featherstone, aged 10, feared dead at seaside. Sonia Massey, aged 11, last seen in local shop. Jeanette Todd, aged 10, missing from football ground.

Beneath the newspaper clippings were Cribbins' trophies: a red hair slide, a pink ribbon, a gold signet ring, a blue enamel bangle, a silver crucifix pendant and an elastic bracelet with multi-coloured plastic hearts attached. And alongside them was the golden carriage clock. The clock that sent him over the edge. Beneath the clock, at the very bottom of the tin, there was a one-way train ticket to Harrogate. Phyllis had been right, after all, when she'd told Sophie's mother that if Ronnie Cribbins was to find out that she was going to leave him, he'd never let her go.

Piotr put an arm around Sophie's shoulders and it was

only then that she realised she was crying. 'Such a waste,' she said, looking at the contents of the tin. 'Such an awful, tragic waste.'

'Yes.' Piotr nodded, his face sullen. 'But now at least the girls' families, they will finally learn the truth.'

'How are we going to explain it all to the police though?'

Piotr shrugged. 'We will tell them that I have been doing some renovations in the yard. That is all they have to know. We do not need to mention any of the supernatural stuff.'

'What about Addy Adkins? Will you tell them about him?'

'I am not sure.'

'You should.'

'There is no proof that it was him.'

'By the sounds of it, I don't think he'll be troubling you or me again anyway.'

Piotr raised his eyebrows in question.

'Let's just say, my younger self saw him off.' Piotr took the tin from her and moved to put the lid back on. 'Wait,' she said, taking hold of the carriage clock. 'I want this.'

'Why?'

'Cribbins, he was scared of it. I'd like to keep it.'

'But he is gone now.'

'Still, I'd like to hold onto it. Just in case.'

'Okay, if it makes you feel better.'

'Yes. It does.'

'So, how about a cup of tea?' Piotr pressed the lid down on the tin and headed towards the kitchen.

'Shouldn't we call the police?'

'I think it would be odd if I were to say that I have been doing work in my yard at this time in the morning. Yes?' He turned; the dryness of his comment was supported with a cocked eyebrow and wry smirk. 'I think we should have a cup of tea, compose ourselves, *then* call the police. These girls, they have waited almost forty years for the truth to be revealed, I am sure they will not mind another couple of hours.'

'Yes, you're right.'

While Piotr disappeared into the kitchen, Sophie stayed on the couch. Wearied and shell-shocked. After only a few minutes had passed, her phone started to ring. It was Gareth.

'Hey. Is everything okay?'

'Sophie, I'm just calling to let you know that we're good to go. The snow eased off overnight and the roads are now passable. I've booked new flights, so we'll be heading back shortly.'

'That's great!' Sophie closed her eyes, welcoming the sense of relief that rushed through her body, making her muscles completely lax. 'Thanks for letting me know.'

'Is Caitlyn coming home?' Piotr said, having heard Sophie on the phone and coming to re-join her.

'Yes. Finally.'

'This is good news.' He smiled. 'Do you need to go and let Nora and Lenny know?'

Sophie nodded but made no attempt to move. When Piotr sat down, she lifted her feet up onto the couch and leaned into him. He wrapped an arm around her shoulders.

'I just need a while like this first,' she said. 'If that's okay?'

'Of course.'

Sophie knew then, in that moment, what medical treatment she would opt for: the one-off disease modifying treatment. She was determined to take control of her life again. To become stronger than she ever had been. No more fear. No regrets. 'Would you do me a favour?' she asked.

'If I can. But first tell me about the rhyme your

younger self sang. What did it mean?'

Sophie allowed a small, wearied laugh to escape. 'It was just a game I used to play as a kid. The ball would always drop whenever I got to poor man. So that's who I thought I'd marry. A poor man.'

'And your younger self thought that *I* am your poor man?' Piotr laughed, despite his attempt to sound offended.

'You know, I think maybe she did. Whether you're poor or not, she definitely seemed to like you.' Sophie flashed him a wink.

'And what about you? Do you like me?'

'You're alright, I suppose.'

'Ha!' Piotr nudged her away playfully, but she grabbed his arm and cosied up to him again. 'So, what was the favour you wanted to ask?' he said. 'What would like me to do?'

Nuzzling her head against his shoulder, Sophie closed her eyes and smiled. 'Talk to me in Polish for a while. Tell me anything you like. And don't stop until I say.'

# 39

# Back

Gareth Holmesworth put the last of the suitcases into the boot of the car then turned and looked back towards the wooden lodge. It was a large two storey building nestled like a dream at the end of a long drive. Folding his arms over his chest, he grinned. 'Stunning, isn't it?'

Andrea draped an arm round his waist and slipped her thumb into the back pocket of his jeans. 'It certainly is.'

For the first time in days, the sky was startling blue and all around them Morzine was a white winter wonderland.

'Next time we're here, we won't have return flights,' Gareth said, tilting his face to the sky and breathing in deeply. 'We'll be here for good. Our new home.'

Andrea looked up at him and smiled.

A silver car cruised past on the main road, its tyres shushing through wet snow as it took the tight bend cautiously. Gareth and Andrea both turned to watch.

'We'd better get going soon,' Andrea said. 'In case we hit any bad spots.'

'Yeah. Are the kids about ready?'

'Almost. Niamh decided she wanted some toast after all. And Caitlyn volunteered to do the washing up.'

Gareth laughed. 'She's a good kid, our Caitlyn.'

'Yeah, she is.'

'It would be great if she was to come out here with us too.'

Andrea's pale blue eyes widened and she swiped her tongue over her bottom lip. 'But, you know that couldn't happen, right?'

'Why not?'

'Sophie.'

Gareth bristled and moved away. Andrea's arm dropped to her side. She stood and watched as he began to pace about on the drive. A bird chirruped in the trees across the road and somewhere an engine rumbled. Andrea could feel Gareth's anger churning.

'Caitlyn loves it here,' he said, irritably. 'She loves being with Olly and Niamh. She'd have the support of a proper family if she was to live here with us. We could give her more than Sophie ever could.'

'But Sophie's her mother,' Andrea said, her voice suddenly timid above the lorry engine that thundered closer and the bird that twittered more shrilly as though competing.

Gareth's eyes flashed with dogged annoyance. 'And *I'm* her dad.'

'I know you are.' Andrea began to chew on a fingernail. 'But…'

'But nothing. Why shouldn't she be here?'

'Look, I'm gonna go and check on the kids, see if they're ready. We'll talk about it later.' She turned towards the lodge. Didn't want to get into an argument. Didn't want the journey back to the UK to be a stretch of uncomfortable, sulky silence. 'We really should get going soon.'

Andrea had only walked a few paces when the lorry reached the bend in the road. Its horn blared, making her spin back round. She then watched as it swerved from the main road, ploughing onto their drive. It all happened so fast. One moment Gareth was standing behind their car, the next he was pinned between the bumper and the front of the lorry. Andrea would never forget the redness of the snow. The way it had spread.

Later, when the police asked what had happened, all she could tell them was that the lorry driver had swerved to miss a girl who was standing in the middle of the road; a dark-haired girl who hadn't been dressed for winter and who'd held three tennis balls in her hands. And from the side of the road, the girl's friend had watched on: a taller redheaded girl, with a birthmark that covered the left side of her face.

# Acknowledgements

I'd like to thank my readers, who support this thing I do. Dr Cleland, Barbara Wingrove and Dr Petheram for having my back. Hannah Thompson for the time and effort put in to editing Cribbins, I certainly feel like I've learnt a lot over the years from your red pen of wisdom. My good friend Benn Clarkson for championing me through the various stages of Cribbins and being my CMYK saviour again. My mam and dad for their unending belief and support. Heather Kelly for sharing daily trials and tribulations with me (ha!) and for plugging my work anywhere and everywhere. Prednisone for inducing the feverish bout of insomnia that was the catalyst for this story. The real villain, who was true gold and too good not to write about. Elizabeth Bage for being a beta reader and great source of encouragement. Kathryn Roebuck, Caroline Howard and Mark Illingworth for being part of my street team since the very beginning. Denise Sparrowhawk at Hartlepool Central Library for being so supportive of local authors. Marvin and Delilah, just because. And Derek, as ever, for continuing to be my number one fan.

# About The Author

R. H. Dixon is a horror enthusiast who, when not escaping into the fantastical realms of fiction, lives in the northeast of England with her husband and two whippets.

Visit her website for horror features, short stories, promotions and news of her upcoming books: **www.rhdixon.com**

**IF YOU ENJOYED READING THIS BOOK,
PLEASE LEAVE A REVIEW ON AMAZON.
THANK YOU!**

Printed in Great
Britain
by Amazon

31717709R00156